Looking bloody good, old boy

GILES CURTIS

Chapter One

"Looking bloody good, old boy," Arthur Cholmondley-Godstone shouted. He wasn't sure if Brayman had heard. It was very windy, and the rope bridge they were perched on was swaying violently. Arthur had always had a head for heights, but he could see that Brayman was having second thoughts.

"Don't you feel alive?" Arthur yelled, yanking the bungie rope which, as luck would have it, was attached at one end to Brayman.

Brayman was feeling alive. He was feeling very alive, so alive that the prospect of hurling himself off the bridge began to seem a lot less appealing than it had when Arthur had suggested it over lunch. At the time, and for a few hours afterwards, it had made perfect sense. It had been quite some lunch. He had never eaten such exotic food. The tastes had danced around his mouth and much of it still lay in his stomach, barely digested. Then there was the alcohol. A whisky to start, or was it a gin? He couldn't remember, but there was a hell of a lot to follow. But the alcohol had dissipated and there was a stark reality emerging. There were rocks down there.

"There's nothing like the adrenaline rush. It's a natural high you get when you push the boundaries."

Brayman, ordinarily a mild mannered man, turned to Arthur and said, "Then you can fucking well jump!"

Arthur was something of an expert at pushing boundaries, although they were invariably someone else's.

"Of course. Do you want me to go first?" Arthur said, so agreeably as so disarm Brayman, who now felt guilty for his apparent rudeness and aggression. Arthur moved closer to him. "Isn't that a fantastic view?"

Brayman hadn't really noticed. He was more concerned with an accident he may have had in his trousers.

"Come back here and just savour it for a moment," Arthur encouraged. Brayman jumped at the chance, hoping it would be the only jump he'd make that day. He wasn't sure whether he would continue the bucket list of high risk sports Arthur had suggested, but he was certain he wasn't going to jump off that damn bridge. The wind died, which wasn't the death that Arthur was hoping for, but it made conversation much easier.

"That's it, now take a look."

Until three weeks ago, Brayman had never left England, but Arthur had persuaded him to fly to Victoria falls, sandwiched between Zambia and Zimbabwe. It was quite an experience. Brayman took a look, comforted by the knowledge that he was now safe. It was a fine view. The bridge was carelessly strung across a sharp valley, at the bottom of which a river flowed over polished white rocks forming white swirls that veered off, creating random patterns. He cast his eyes over the trees, rust-coloured with autumnal decline, but somehow colour coded.

"Beautiful, isn't it?"

The view, Brayman had to admit, was beautiful. Normally rust-coloured trees made him anxious – at least they had in his garden centre, as it rendered them unsaleable. But he no longer needed to worry about that. Good fortune had hardly ever blown his way, until a property developer decided to build on the land behind him. It didn't take a genius to realise that there was only one way in, and that would involve the purchase of his garden centre. And now that the money was happily invested with Arthur. He was secure for life, and had nothing to worry about.

"Let's just stay here for a moment and then I'll lash myself up," Arthur said cheerily. He hunted around his pockets until he found a hip flask. He was confident he had packed at least two.

He twisted open the top and took a nip. He looked down for the first time and noted that it was, not to put too fine a point on it, a fuck of a long way. He took another nip and then offered it to Brayman. Brayman didn't take a nip. He took a swig, and then followed that with something approaching a gulp. He had grown to rather like brandy, through Arthur's influence. He was still learning and keen to learn more.

"Lovely brandy," he muttered.

Arthur raised his eyes. It was actually a fine, blended scotch whisky. It was over thirty years old and sublimely smooth, which rendered a gulp possible, when a nip would have been wiser. Much wiser, as the quality and smoothness was such that it successfully masked the fact that eighty per cent of it was alcohol. It was, of course, fabulously expensive.

"Very lovely," Brayman said again, by way of a request for more. Arthur was delighted to oblige.

Brayman was beginning to see the point. The wind, the clarity of the view, the smell of the air. He had never been to Africa before. He hadn't been anywhere. Even a school trip years ago had only taken him to Blackpool. He'd never had either the time or the money. Now he had both.

"You're right," he said, suddenly feeling quite talkative. "There is a quality to the air and the view is to die for."

Arthur's eyes lit up at the thought.

"But it's more than that. It's being in touch with nature, with, as you say Arthur, the boundaries. There is a beauty I hadn't noticed before. Sometimes," Brayman continued, now grasping the philosophy, "there is beauty in everything. A piece of wood, a blue sky, a kind act."

Arthur wasn't so sure about the kind act, but he knew Brayman was progressing nicely. He passed him the scotch without being asked. Brayman took another mouthful, very much more than a nip and too generous for a mere gulp.

"Up this high, this close to the sky, you can almost feel God. You can sense an order, a reason, a purpose, a function. Just feel that air. Can you feel the air, Arthur?"

Arthur could, he really could.

"You see the great thing about the nursery business is you nurture and see things develop and grow, but do you know what the problem is?"

Arthur didn't.

"Scale. No, focus. No, it's not that, it's perspective. You sit on your three and three quarter acres and that's all the world you see. But here, here you can see so much more. God, you can feel it. Can you feel it Arthur?"

Arthur could feel something. He could feel relief that the likelihood that the bungee rope would be attached to his ankle was diminishing. He looked down again, and discovered that it was still a fuck of a long way. It would have been handy to know, to gauge the length of the rope. He sensed that Brayman was in need of direction, and had a suspicion that if he steered him away from jumping, he would be more inclined to take the leap, as it were. Something moving in the water prompted a thought.

"And we have yet to see the crocodiles and hippos, or lions and cheetahs."

There were so many hazards that Arthur had yet to introduce him to. He intended to go on and mention the monkeys and giraffes, but Brayman interrupted him.

"But we haven't finished here."

Arthur raised his eyes.

Brayman breathed in more of the high quality air he had so recently become very fond of. He suddenly felt very masculine. A man in control of the world's destiny.

"I'm ready to go."

Arthur knew what he meant, but pretended he didn't.

"I'm sorry?"

Brayman pointed down.

"Are you sure?"

"I," Brayman said grandly, "Have never been so sure."

Arthur looked over the side, reminded himself that it was indeed a fuck of a long way, and then with wide arm movements measured the bungee rope. When he finished it looked convincingly like a fuck of a long way minus about ten feet, allowing for the stretch with the eleven or fourteen stone that Brayman might weigh. After a few minutes he was almost ready. He checked the rope, but found it was spiralling around him alarmingly. Brayman had already jumped.

"Bugger," Arthur muttered to no one in particular.

In the ensuing few seconds Brayman was lucky enough to have a lot of thoughts running through his mind, assisted as it was by the most adrenaline it had ever pumped into his body. His body was fit to burst with the stuff. His very first thought was to do with being master of the world's destiny. The only destiny he was master of was his own, and it had coincided with a powerful gust of wind that had seemingly come from nowhere. It was unusual in that it blew across the valley rather than along it, as it might normally do. It brought him in sight of the polished white rocks, reminding him of similar stone he had sold in the garden centre. There was a lot of profit in stone. Other thoughts involved his mother. She had always let him know that she had found him a disappointment. He then saw his first crocodile, bearing an uncanny resemblance to his mother. Still, there was nothing disappointing about flying through the air. She should see him now.

The rocks were growing larger and they were not, Brayman noted, accompanied by a yank from his ankle and some comforting deceleration. It was then that it struck him that he might be seeing his mother rather earlier than he'd planned. The thought struck him just before the rock did.

Chapter Two

"Please, have another brandy," urged Arthur Cholmondley-Godstone.

Arthur then delivered the speech. He could deliver it in almost any condition and in any position. Even on a precarious bridge. He was not averse to repeating the speech. Today it was lunch with another client.

"There is an art to life. Life is not about going to work and paying bills. It is not about loyalty to a cause or a people. It is not about what others think or do. It is about living, and living is seeing, doing, feeling, tasting and not denying, and passion. Seeing everything the world has to offer, enjoying everything there is to taste and savour, and exploiting every sense you've been blessed with. Living is about the best, the best of everything. And now you are not just my client, but my friend, and together we must explore these things."

Clivert looked at. Arthur. He had admired the man from the first moment he'd laid eyes on him. Clivert tried to suppress a small burp, but it rolled around his stomach, which was pressing on as many major organs as it was capable of, and graduated into a noisy belch. It would have echoed embarrassingly round the stark, minimalist restaurant, but they were the only remaining lunchers. The other stragglers had left over an hour ago.

"You're doing so very well," Arthur reassured him. The restaurant was enormously expensive, but made up for it with the obscene decadence and richness of the food that Arthur always favoured.

"Cigar?" Arthur suggested, reaching for two of the fattest cigars Clivert had ever seen. Maybe his feeling for Arthur was stronger than mere admiration. It was difficult to tell, but he was never the same in his presence. There was something about

Arthur. Derek nodded to Arthur who proceeded to light the cigars apparently immune to legislation.

"Eh?" Clivert said. He understood the question, but small pains in his chest were making it hard to respond. That, as well as being quite sublimely drunk. He'd always enjoyed drinking and getting pissed, but was beginning to wonder if he'd ever truly grasped intoxication. He was currently inhabiting a different level. At first he'd protested when Arthur had suggested that the fatty part of the foie gras was the best bit. And this was no ordinary foie gras. As if overfeeding the geese wasn't enough, the chef had wrapped it in goose fat. Indeed, it appeared to be mostly composed of fat, which accounted for the 'gras' part of the title. Then he'd humoured him, but now he was moving into a submissive phase. He took the cigar and sipped the brandy. Arthur inspired a strange level of devotion in him

"These are the finest cigars known to man," Arthur began. He looked more closely at Clivert. He tried to remember what his grandfather, Henry Cholmondley-Godstone, had told him.

"Rolled on the thighs of exotic Cuban girls," he said, although his grandfather had said nothing of the sort, but it was in the spirit of family thinking.

"Thank you," Clivert muttered, although he wasn't sure what for. Picturing exotic Cuban girls was a bit of a leap for him and, although he hadn't admitted to Arthur, it wasn't his thing at all.

Arthur beamed his approval.

"You're doing so very well."

And, indeed he was. Clivert had always had a facility for figures, and he had worked hard shifting money and paper in the city with a relentless drive, the sole purpose of which was to take early retirement. And he'd made it. Now fifty-one, he'd enjoyed a life of spectacular leisure for an entire year. At the beginning he had considered various worthy causes as a focus for his energies. But Arthur had deterred him, insisting he should explore the world of the gourmand. Arthur was relieved to discover that Clivert, a product of the city after all, could find no reason not to indulge himself. There had been a few close moments, but Arthur had successfully steered him away from the gym and back to the world of fatty foods, high alcohol consumption and smoking. Clivert was doing very well.

"You're doing so very well," Arthur reminded him again.

Clivert smiled the smile of the praised protégé. He was having a good time, but he always felt like that in Arthur's company. And there were other great aspects to his life. Not rising at five in the morning was one, although after a few months he had forgotten the pain, and therefore no longer understood the pleasure. But there was joy in knowing that every month Cholmondley-Godstone would deposit enough money into his account for him not to care what anyone thought. And he didn't.

"Finished already? You should try this little liqueur."

Arthur stopped for a second, wondering if he was overdoing it. He sat back and looked at his client. Clivert had always been overweight. It was one of the reasons they had offered him such a generous deal, and a year of doing very little had delivered him a mountainous stomach, as if something were gestating in there. Arthur was also pleased to note that an already florid complexion had blossomed into a pizza-like explosion. It was quite magnificent.

"Toilet," Clivert suddenly said. The word was filtered through the undigested remains of the chocolate and brandy pudding, garnished with a further brandy and the semi-inhaled fumes of the Cuban cigar. Arthur had insisted that it should be fully inhaled and had demonstrated it himself. Clivert weaved uncertainly towards the toilet, as yet unsure as to the purpose of his visit. Something was going to go.

Arthur used the time to phone the office.

"He's in very fine form. Not really a cigar man, can't tell a good brandy from cooking, but likes his wine and really likes his chocolate."

Arthur let his father, Charles Cholmondley-Godstone, digest the information. But the path ahead was obvious.

"We'll send him more bonus cases of wine, tell him it's all part of the five star retirement package. The cheap stuff with the fancy label will do. And a very large box of chocolates, every month. Strike that, every week. Tell him it's for research, we need his feedback to make sure he's eating it all. Oh, and chuck four hundred cigarettes in."

"My thoughts exactly."

"How long?"

That, Arthur thought, was always the question. Clivert was fifty-one. The average life expectancy for a man was seventy-eight; adjusted for as yet unknown medical advances, perhaps eighty-one. And Clivert had paid in generously, expecting an indexed-linked income starting at around £100,000 per year. Over the next thirty-one years it would add up to well over three million pounds unless, God forbid, he lived even longer. Arthur had studied his family history and it made very encouraging reading. Only one relative had made it to sixty.

"Two years. Five maximum."

Arthur, now forty-seven himself, had been groomed from a young age in the business and had developed an uncanny knack to predict these things. The Clivert worse-case scenario represented a one and a half million profit for them. But in this particular case, Arthur was wrong. He hadn't noticed the gurgling noises from the gents' toilet.

It was hard for Clivert to assess what was happening to him. In fact, it was hard for Clivert to assess anything at all. Something was happening, and it didn't feel entirely unpleasant. Arthur had helped him to effectively anaesthetise the pains he should have been feeling. Instead he felt a lightheadedness, which was quite pleasing. It felt like an out of body experience, perhaps because that was what it was. His major organs were shutting down, as Clivert grasped the toilet seat whilst being gripped by a massive seizure. Put another way, he was fairly certain he was dying.

Chapter Three

"Delightful to meet you, Eddie," Arthur said, pumping his hand enthusiastically.

Eddie B was a rock star, and it upset him. Through the seventies he was a big seller, during the eighties he hit the big stadiums, and in the early nineties he penned *I'm Wasted*. It was the biggest selling record of the year and was played all round the world. As if Eddie wasn't wasted enough, he then got drugs, and then religion, and then drugs again. All without ever giving up alcohol. His manager brokered a deal which gave him a fabulous one-off sum in payment for the royalties on all his songs, even *Wasted*. And Eddie did it all. He wrecked as many Ferraris as marriages, he sniffed, smoked, injected, hallucinated, sucked, licked and ejaculated it all away. But Eddie was upset not because he was a rock star, but because he used to be a rock God.

"Hey, you too, Arthur, man," Eddie said after a pause. He did everything after a pause, like an old fashioned long distance phone call. He led Arthur into his loft apartment. It didn't take long, as it was essentially one large room, with twenty foot ceilings, a mezzanine with a bed and a bank of windows overlooking a North London canal. He'd bought it to bring his mistresses to when he was first married, and then kept it on for the second, third and fourth marriages. The houses had been far more impressive, but they'd all gone. Just the loft apartment remained.

"Nice flat," Arthur observed. The huge white walls were adorned with a vast collection of guitars, which his manager had insisted on him buying.

"A lot of guitars," Arthur said.

"Yeah, my Cunt said I should buy them."

"I beg your pardon?" Arthur said. Even though he wasn't averse to female genitalia making demands, he wasn't entirely sure he'd heard him right.

"My manager. That's what I've always called him, my Cunt. He said buy 'em, 'cos I'd never want to sell them and there's money in 'em. Like, valuable."

Arthur raised his eyes and wondered, should they agree a deal, what he might be referred to as. He'd seen plenty of pictures of Eddie B and wasn't surprised to find that in real life he was much smaller. Most of his left ear was peppered with piercings, and tattoos wound round him like an unwelcome boa constrictor. His hair was still thick, at least it appeared to be, as it was bathed in so much product that everything stood upright, adding four inches to his height. Eddie B tried very hard to look like a rock star.

"And are they?"

After a pause, Eddie said: "Are they what?" He had already forgotten his previous sentence.

"Valuable?"

Arthur watched as Eddie visibly digested the question and then, after a further pause, he pointed.

"Clapton, Hendrix, Page, and you see that? Presley."

Arthur noticed with glee that Eddie's hands shook. He was sixty-one, nearly out of cash, and very unhealthy-looking. Excellent.

"Why don't you sell them?"

"My Cunt put them in a trust, with the flat," he said, raising his arms. "Can't touch 'em until my seventy-fifth birthday."

If ever Arthur had seen a man least likely to make it to his seventy-fifth birthday, Eddie B was it. But if there was no money, then Arthur had wasted an afternoon.

"So?" Arthur asked.

"My Cunt's done a deal."

"I thought…" Arthur ventured.

Eddie sighed. The former Rock God, who had been forced to mere Rock Star status had, somewhere along the line, it might have been a very long line of cocaine, told the Cunt to fuck off. It took him a long time to realise that his Cunt had been the best friend he'd ever had. If his manager hadn't placed everything that Eddie still owned in trust, then Eddie would have drank, inhaled or injected it. He had been grovelling to him for two years. He had even been forced to call him Howard, but that was too much for him to sustain.

"I've done an album, like."

His manger had pointed out that they had already done *The Best of Eddie* and then *The Very Best of Eddie*, followed by *The Ultimate Eddie* and then *The Cream of Eddie* and then the *Best of the Cream of Eddie*. After that came *The Ultimate Best of the Cream of Eddie*. His manager had suggested *Flogging a Dead Horse Eddie*. But then along came the fashion for unplugged albums. His Cunt did one last good thing for him. He got him into the studio with good musicians who could cover up his shaky hands, and Eddie had growled into the microphone. It wasn't bad. The record company liked it enough to offer him a decent lump of money, if he accompanied it with a tour.

"Three million quid, like. But my Cunt won't give to me, direct, like."

But, Arthur discovered, the Cunt was prepared to give it to Arthur, which made him very happy indeed. What happened next was more like music to Arthur's ears than anything Eddie B had ever achieved in his musical career.

"Brandy, Arthur?"

"Excellent," Arthur beamed.

It was eight o'clock in the morning.

Chapter Four

Arthur was feeling good. He generally felt good when his clients were not feeling good. Somewhere between the extreme sports and an extreme diet, he'd hope to get them all. And today was the AGM.

The annual general meeting was always a lavish affair. A Cholmondley-Godstone ancestor, three hundred years earlier, had won a fine building near Marble Arch in a poker game. It was off the Bayswater road, an area of great grandeur at the time, but it was followed by a period of decline, and then a further period which brought in immigrants. They were mostly wealthy immigrants, but they weren't the sort the family approved of, but now it was going through a further phase. London appeared to be awash with money and the residents were changing. They even had a former prime minister as a neighbour. But none of this concerned the Cholmondley-Godstones, who were immune to fashion.

The Cholmondley-Godstone ancestor lost the house in another poker game, but he was able to buy it back when four of his richest clients suffered heart attacks within weeks of each other. CPR had yet to be invented and they all went out like a light. Their opulent lives had been the primary factor, and it gave the founding Cholmondley-Godstone an idea. First, brimming with confidence and good cheer, he would extract an obscene sum of money in the name of investment, and would then offer an assurance of a fine retirement fund stretching into old age. It was, more specifically, a non-refundable lump sum in exchange for a lifetime's guaranteed bountiful income. After which, he would do his damnedest to ensure there would be no old age.

As the current active member of the family, Arthur would make his enquiries. He favoured early retirees, those who had immersed themselves in work and never found time for leisure activities, which invariably meant they didn't have the stamina for them. A bad family medical history was essential. He particularly relished heart problems. And, if he'd chosen wisely, his clients would be wrapped up in a nicely obese package to which he just had to add further excess. He encouraged them to smoke, eat rich food and take unnecessary risks. It was simple and most of the retirees, with money and plenty of time on their hands, were willing victims. He famously unburdened a wealthy industrialist of most of his fortune on a Monday, to have the pleasure of identifying him in the morgue on the Wednesday. It had been a hell of a lunch.

It was allied to the discovery that the Cholmondley-Godstones were blessed with a quite astonishing constitution. They had spent the previous weekend celebrating Arthur's grandfather, Henry Cholmondley-Godstone's one hundred and third birthday, and he was by no means the oldest in the family. Even the Queen knew of them, as the family name had appeared so many times on her telegrams. Enormous quantities of alcohol, vats of cholesterol, rich food and a sedentary lifestyle, as was the family habit, did not bring them down.

Their work was historic. If excess didn't get their clients, then the family would assist them in other ways. Cholmondely-Godstone advice included suggesting that Horatio Nelson pursue a career in naval warfare, that Guy Fawkes act on his political misgivings and, more recently, encouraging a novelist to express his anti-Islamic views.

The building was lined with six foot high oil paintings of ancestors who all bore a remarkable resemblance to each other, and to Arthur. An altercation some years ago had prompted them to fit a half inch thick steel front door, but their work had become more subtle and there had been little trouble since.

It was Arthur's office and his home. He lived in a large apartment on the top floor and inhabited the building on his own, as most of the family had moved out to the country. The AGM was to be held in the lavish ballroom on the first floor. There was a magnificent fireplace at one end, with three floor-to-ceiling windows and a twenty foot high ceiling garnished with ornate plasterwork.

It was going to be quite some lunch. A celebrity chef had been brought in to prepare the food and the enormous Cholmondley-Godstone cellar had been raided. It was the same every year. It gave all eleven of the surviving Cholmondley-Godstones an opportunity to catch up, as well as savour, an overview of the company's profits in which they all held an interest. Although they specialised in early retirees, normally around fifty, they themselves found eighty a more comfortable age. Arthur was the youngest and the only remaining Cholmondley-Godstones working in the field. This was a problem.

There was one major flaw in the family gene, which concerned some of the uncles, still only in their early eighties, and looking forward to another thirty years of fine living. And that was a very small sperm count. Therefore the first announcement heralded good news.

"Ten pounds and three ounces, a baby boy."

There were cheers, but they were slightly muted. Jack Cholmondley-Godstone was to be eighty the following year and the mother of the child was not yet thirty, but Jack was very tall and slender and did not remotely resemble a Cholmondley-Godstones. Arthur, like the others, was around six foot, and possessed an unusually wide pair of square shoulders, and a set of internal organs that were far larger than average. His square head sat on his square body from which a pair of tree trunk legs sprouted. Jack, although a Cholmondley-Godstone by name, very probably did not have the gene and nor, they all suspected, did the baby boy. Also his sperm count was just too high to be a proper Cholmondley-Godstone. The pressure on Arthur was mounting.

"Any news, Arthur?"

They all turned to Arthur, who was beginning to find the burden of being the last in line a bit of a struggle. It wasn't for the lack of trying. Although his hedonistic ways had made it difficult to keep down a steady relationship, it had provided him with plenty of opportunities to spread his insipid seed.

"Not yet," he said.

There was muttering around him. It wasn't friendly and, if Arthur were honest with himself, he knew there was a growing tide of suspicion that he was batting for the other side. The Cholmondley-Godstones were a family of great tradition and even greater prejudice.

"I told you," his great grandfather whispered in a way that wasn't a whisper and suggested issues with his hearing aids. "Raving queer."

Arthur chose to ignore it, but it hang in the air like a cheap prostitute's perfume, which would have more accurately defined some of Arthur's sexual experiences. He knew it was a project he would have to find time for. He was fairly certain, with the years of physical abuse he'd subjected his body to, and that aberrant gene, that adding up his sperm count would not require a calculator.

"Well?" Arthur's father, Charles, said. It was a pointed 'well.' The family saw it as his duty, as if it were part of his terms of employment to deliver a son.

"I'm working on it."

His father nodded, but didn't believe him.

"See? Raving queer." Henry, his grandfather, still hadn't resolved the issues with his hearing aids.

Arthur knew that the way forward was to look backwards. Backwards that is, at his back catalogue of sexual adventures. There were a couple of women he'd spent some time with, one in particular. Although they were close at the time, there had been so much brandy and scotch under the bridge that he couldn't recall her name. Cheese was involved, he was sure about that. But either way, he was fairly certain that somewhere in his past, there was a sturdy, thriving and hopefully almost indestructible Cholmondley-Godstone. Of course there were his African adventures, in particular there was Gloria, but the family were unlikely to approve of her. He wouldn't ordinarily have cared, but there was pressure on him. It would have to be a boy, and he would have to have the gene. The female Cholmondley-Godstones didn't tend to live long, although there was the possibility that their men merely grew tired of them. And the Cholmondley-Godstones who weren't blessed with the gene didn't tend to make it through a family lunch. Although lunch invariably ran into dinner, and occasionally even breakfast.

"And now the annual report."

Arthur perked up and tried to pay attention. He had always been competitive and remembered, with a smile, the tears welling up in his father's eyes when Arthur had managed to push his expenses past the million mark. There had been applause. So much pride. This year he had really excelled himself. He could feel a tingle of excitement as the speaker approached the moment when this year's expenses were to be read out.

"And the expenses for this year are…"

For some reason the speaker felt the need to inject a dramatic pause, which suggested he was inclined to watch too much television. In the past it had been a competition, but with the declining family numbers there was only Arthur left, which meant the winner was no surprise.

"Arthur Cholmondley-Godstone, with five million, three hundred and twenty-seven thousand pounds."

Arthur, with a beaming smile, turned to accept the applause. He had quite excelled himself. It had been a year of fine wines, luxurious travel and generally living very well.

"Thank you," he muttered modestly. It took a moment for him to realise that the announcement had not been accompanied with applause. Arthur was not a sensitive man – empathy would not have been an asset in his business – but he sensed something was wrong. There was a shuffling of feet and mutters of outrage. Arthur was not involved in the investment side of the business, it was patently clear that it was not his métier, but he'd heard talk. Markets were tough, returns were poor and there was a suggestion, and this needled Arthur, that he wasn't doing his job. Finally a jeer came from the rear of the crowd. It was an expensively educated voice, but that was another characteristic of the family.

"How many have you lost?"

Arthur floundered. It really rankled with Arthur that the traditional family values of excess were now being frowned on. With thinking like that, what chance did he have? But unfortunately it was true. It had been a terrible year. He had been so careful with the family histories and cultivating a suicide diet for his clients. And nothing. No one had died. Too many had become wrapped up in healthy lifestyles, and their doctors had the incredibly irritating habit of prescribing blood pressure and cholesterol pills. It was most irritating. He'd tried so hard, with the high risk sports and the rich lunches. And then there was the rock star.

Arthur stood tall and tried to reassure them.

"Don't worry, I have a few on the brink."

Chapter Five

Arthur left the annual meeting as soon as it was politely possible. Although he had consumed two or three bottles of wine, several brandies and half a bottle of Cointreau, he was feeling very sober. It had been a very sobering evening. For the first time they were short of money. He would have to, God forbid, spend less money. The very thought sent shivers down his spine and aggravated the pain in his leg.

And then there was the child business. His father, Charles, was applying pressure. Family tradition was everything. He was a man with strong opinions and many of them veered towards the bigoted.

"Queers and blacks," his father had said. "Can't stand them. They should be…" What should happened to them varied, but it was never nice. This time it wasn't just his grandfather making insinuations, his father had joined in. It was true he'd not been the kind of son who'd brought back girlfriends and, now that he lived on his own, his father had no way of knowing who came home with him.

"Number one on your to-do list," his father had told him once again, "is father a son. It's too late for me."

When his father had said it was too late, it hadn't been due to his concerns regarding good parenting. He'd never really believed in any kind of parenting, that was what boarding school was for. The problem was that his sperm count had ground to a halt, from the modest level that was the family trait.

"You've got to find out," his father had instructed him.

And he had. That morning Arthur had been to his absurdly cheerful Harley Street doctor, whose office looked like the inspiration for a Rolls Royce interior with all high-tech mod cons. It didn't make it any easier to provide a sperm sample. That still had to be done the old fashioned way. But Arthur had succeeded, and left the building looking forward to an extravagant lunch. And that hadn't gone to plan. Normally the lunch would have carried on through dinner and late into the evening, but Arthur found himself at the end of too many jibes. It was hard to tell if it was the five million expenses, or the rude health of his clients, or it might have been his failure to father a child laced, as it was, with the inference that he was gay. Arthur had always been the golden boy. The longest lunches and the most extravagant habits, and the shortest-lived clients. It was quite a fall from grace. It irritated him so much he called a client and left early.

Arthur limped into the hotel. He was a regular guest and it was the kind of hotel that provided a butler for each of its guests. It was a situation which Arthur found most agreeable, but he feared would be brought to an end soon. He had been instructed to shave off four million pounds from his expenses. The prospect of taking ordinary scheduled flights sent a further shiver down his spine. He had argued that it simply wasn't possible for him to suggest that his clients drink ordinary plonk. Next he'd be forced to eat in a Harvester. The thought made him nauseous. It sounded ghastly, even though he didn't know exactly what a Harvester was.

As his butler helped him to a chair and pressed a glass of champagne into his hand, he decided that the savings could wait until tomorrow. Arthur thanked him and asked for a brandy. The butler apologised and reached to remove the champagne, but Arthur had already knocked it back. The champagne was for his thirst, the brandy was for his leg, which hurt like hell. Brayman must have weighed more than he'd guessed, although he hadn't bothered to guess, but when the rope wrapped itself round his leg, Brayman may have been travelling at a hundred and sixty miles per hour, or whatever terminal velocity might be. It was bloody lucky he hadn't taken his leg off. He didn't want to starve the oxygen to his groin area. There were enough problems there already.

They'd been forced to return early after a stay in hospital. A stay that had been necessary for Arthur, not his client, He watched Brayman approach. He looked in appallingly rude health.

"Arthur, what a fantastic trip," Brayman said cheerfully. For a second, Arthur couldn't remember whether he'd invited him or not. For a while, he'd been delirious with the pain.

"I'm glad you enjoyed it," Arthur said. He motioned for the butler to fetch him a drink, and the butler willingly obliged. They had acquired an understanding. It hadn't occurred to Arthur, but his closest relationship may be with the butler. Although it was rivalled by Rogerman, his chauffeur.

It was cocktail time. A moment later two multicoloured fizzing drinks arrived. Brayman sat next to him.

"It's a shame about the hospital."

Arthur had sent too many of his clients to that African hospital to spend more than a minute there. It wasn't supposed to be him in need of the facilities. Normally if the fall, the tiger attack or heart failure hadn't got them, the hygiene of the hospital would. They got the first flight out of there.

"Beautiful country," Brayman enthused.

Arthur tried to hide his irritation. The man stood tall, enervated, his eyes alive with new-found energy. This was not what he was hoping to achieve.

"Gosh, what's this?" Brayman asked, draining half the glass, and then stirring it enthusiastically. The man was unbearable.

"It is a particularly pleasing cocktail," Arthur muttered.

"It's sort of milky," Brayman observed.

Indeed it was, replete with the fullest-fat milk available and scented with the most unhealthy foods Arthur could find, and then laced with eau de vie. Pure alcohol. It was his own creation.

"A delicious mixture of all that is good for you," Arthur said.

Brayman breathed the fumes in. He'd made a decision. Today would be the first day of his new life. It was actually the moment he'd landed on South African soil with Arthur, but it was easier to think of it as today. He had never travelled before and his life had been small. That was to change. A wider outlook was on the horizon for Brayman. Hell, he thought, the horizon was the horizon. He had been bullied and corralled all his life. By his parents, his schoolmates, his employers and even his employees. And then there were women. Or rather there were very few, and those that he had known had abused his kind, unassuming nature. He drew air into his lungs. The room was scented with something he'd had little contact with before. Money.

"A very rich taste," he observed.

Arthur eyed Brayman carefully. If he wasn't mistaken, the man appeared to be slimmer. Much slimmer.

"And," Brayman continued with the enthusiasm of a puppy, "I've given up smoking."

Brayman looked at him again. He really was a nauseating man.

"I'm sorry, what was that?" Brayman asked.

Arthur realised that the groan he felt on the inside had managed to escape his lips.

"Great news," Arthur said through clenched teeth.

But Brayman didn't notice. Not just had he now seen a crocodile, he'd actually had contact with one. The rope that had encircled Arthur's leg had shortened the bungee to exactly a fuck of a long way, less ten feet, and allowing for the stretch from

Brayman's twelve stone, to ensure that his fingers had brushed the polished white rock, and he had sprung back up into the air. Landing on a crocodile was quite an adrenaline rush. The animal had turned its head and snapped close enough for the crocodile to smell Brayman's whisky-fuelled breath. On the third bounce the bungee rope snapped, and Brayman landed on a bank of soft sand. It was a hell of a trip. One hell of a trip.

"What's next?" Brayman asked with more enthusiasm.

Arthur breathed in, smiled and nodded to his butler, who delivered more of the fiery, fat and cholesterol-laden, high-alcohol drink.

"Do you know, I feel I'm really learning so much from you. I've never thought about life for living. It's like you've shown me a telescope."

"Really?" Arthur asked, desperately trying not to make his boredom too obvious.

"Yes, but looking the other end. Before I only saw a small picture, but turn it round and I see the bigger picture, and do you know what the bigger picture says?"

Arthur was very nearly caught out with the break in Brayman's diatribe.

"What?" Arthur landed upon, which set Brayman off again.

"The Taj Mahal, the Hanging Gardens of Babylon, New York. Hell, anything – diving, flying, skiing. Everything. All the things that can be done and which I haven't done."

"Quite so, old man. Have another drink."

Arthur breathed in. It had been a hell of a bad day. He told himself to stiffen the sinews and conjure up the blood. He was not going to let this man defeat him.

Chapter Six

Eddie B had made it through the first gig of the tour. It hadn't been the 'total crock of shit' that one music paper had predicted. He'd missed so many notes to begin with that he'd given up trying and that, with the whisky he drank while on stage, had given his voice a gravel it hadn't previously possessed. He made Leonard Cohen and Tom Waites sound like choir boys. The young had responded well, although he took exception to one who kept shouting "Way to go, you old fucker." It had been intended as praise, but the sixty-one year old in Eddie objected. But it was a wrap and he'd got through it, and his Cunt had rewarded him with a little pile of cash. Five grand.

"Fantastic gig, Eddie," Arthur said, deploying the word 'gig' for the first time in his life and thankful he'd had earplugs with him. He shuddered to think what it would have been like had they plugged the instruments in.

"Hey, thanks, Arthur," Eddie said, noticing for the first time that the adrenaline had carried him along. He wondered for a second if he could get someone to inject it directly into his blood stream, so that his body wouldn't have to go through the tiresome ritual of actually manufacturing it. The guitars and instruments had been packed up and they were sitting on some scarred old loudspeakers.

"Hold on, Arthur."

Eddie removed a panel from a loudspeaker and fished out a bottle of Scotch.

"Shit," he muttered. It was empty. He fished out another.

"Shit," he muttered again. It was also empty.

"I've got some in the back of the Rolls," Arthur offered.

The Rolls struck an nostalgic chord with Eddie. He had floated through twenty years on a comfortable bed of Rolls Royce and he missed it. He didn't have a car any more, after the third ban when he parked his ageing, smoking, yellow Mercedes convertible in the canal. It had been astonishingly expensive to fish it out.

"Cool, man."

Arthur led him out to the car, but he was going to have to take it easy.

"Hey, mega cool," Eddie said in a way which wasn't cool at all.

They sunk into the back. Arthur motioned for Rogerman, the chauffeur, to take them on a tour and reached for the decanter. He poured two large whiskies.

"And your next gig is in a week?" Arthur said, using the 'gig' word for the second time in his life.

"Yeah, right. Bigger gig this time, but same thing. Nothing like the eighties mind, but not bad either."

Eddie wolfed down the whisky and presented his glass. Arthur filled it up.

"How many gigs are there, in total?" Arthur asked, now having said the word 'gig' enough times not to feel the need to record it.

"Twenty," Eddie said, topping himself up.

He watched as Eddie gulped the liquid back and was introduced to a new problem. If Eddie pegged it now, he would make a small loss on him.

But if he met his maker after he'd delivered the full tour, then Arthur would get the full whack, and then he'd be quids in. A very tidy profit indeed.

"Like, nineteen more to go," Eddie said, having grappled with the troublesome calculation of subtracting one from twenty. He topped himself up again.

Arthur thought it extremely unlikely that the rock star, who used to be a rock god, in front of him was going to make it through the week, let alone nineteen more gigs. After the gigs it would be fine, but he was going to have to enter very new territory, and try and keep him alive. The thought made him feel queasy.

Chapter Seven

"Jean!" Arthur yelled. He often yelled at his secretary, but found it made little difference. He had selected her because her CV suggested she would be utterly unemployable elsewhere. There was a conspicuous and rather lengthy gap, which suggested a period of incarceration, which Arthur was surprised to discover involved a sex crime. He'd rather hoped it would be fraud or even murder, anything that didn't burden her with a strong moral sense. That would be no good at all.

"Jean!" He yelled again. Sex crimes, he thought. It was incredible. Arthur had quite a talent for investigation and particularly enjoyed the salacious details of the court case. It appeared she had tied down and raped a man. Perhaps it was no surprise, as she was quite easily the most unattractive woman he'd ever come across.

"Jean!" He shouted again, but with less enthusiasm as he was resigning himself to the likelihood that he would have to make his own coffee. He pressed his hands on the desk and raised himself up. His leg was still hurting. Jean appeared. In Jean's defence, Arthur was very specific about the kind of coffee and the process required to assemble it. It took some time. She dumped the coffee on his desk, and followed it with a pile of files. Jean had heard him calling, but occasionally she liked to let him wait. Even better if she could get him on his feet. Jean had grasped fairly early on why she'd got the job, and she worked efficiently. But she wasn't going to be bullied.

"Yes, Arthur?" Arthur had invited her to call him Arthur, as his surname was something of a mouthful, which reminded him of something that had been said at her trial. She used his name rather a lot.

Arthur looked at the coffee and said, "Thank you." And then, "What are these?"

"They are files, Arthur."

"Yes, I can see that, Jean. What are they for?"

"Clients, Arthur. New clients."

"New clients? But I haven't, er, dealt with my existing clients."

"Indeed, Arthur."

Arthur sat down and opened the first file. He read through it quickly and was pleased to find all the perfect elements: an obese man with a terrible family history. He relaxed a little. Jean nodded and left the room.

"Arthur," Jean yelled a moment later.

"Yes, Jean?"

"Phone, Arthur."

"And who's on the bloody phone?" Arthur shouted, and then added: "And why are you bloody shouting when we have an intercom for such things?"

Jean had now had met her daily quota for winding up Arthur. She didn't want to lose her job, but there was only so much she could take.

"It's Brayman."

"Oh fuck it," Arthur said, until he realised that he was addressing Brayman.

"What's that, Arthur?" Brayman said, with nauseating enthusiasm.

"Oh nothing, old boy. How are you?"

"Feeling great, thanks. How are you? Is your leg okay?"

His leg was not okay. It was very much not okay. It was the shit-end of not okay. It hurt like fuck and he hobbled like an old man. The whole thing filled him with fury.

"It's fine, old boy, absolutely fine."

"Good to hear it," Brayman said. He meant it too. It was not within his nature to wish anyone ill. He had no capacity for it. It was all strangely liberating for Brayman, who felt that he was taking the first few steps in life, as if he were a teenager. The old Brayman had grown cynical and bored with his life, but now it was different. Everything fascinated him. Everything and everybody. He had even met some women, the sort that he would previously have thought were hopelessly out of his class. And they'd been interested. They hadn't even known about his wealth, which prompted unusual thoughts in Brayman. Something had changed in him, his bearing, or something. Whatever it was, it was irritating the hell out of Arthur.

"I was thinking we could take another trip," Arthur volunteered, a little sheepishly.

"Excellent, I'd love to," Brayman said, with no hint of sheep-like behaviour.

Arthur would normally give his clients a few more months before moving to the next stage. But needs must.

"It's a cheese tasting event. You'll love it."

He'd noticed that Brayman had held back a little with the cheese and that, Arthur felt, was no way to keep up the cholesterol levels. Also he thought they could kill two birds with one stone and track down the cheese girl.

"Fantastic, when is it?"

"Next Friday, old boy."

"Excellent."

They agreed to meet and Brayman hung up. Arthur gave it some thought for a moment, but the frantic buzzing of the intercom made him jump. He still had the phone clasped to his ear.

"It's the phone, Arthur."

"And who the bloody hell is on it?"

"Your grandfather."

"Oh, fuck it," Arthur said.

"I'll have none of that, old boy," his grandfather drawled.

"No, no, it's not you," Arthur said hastily, but he was talking to the same breed.

"Indeed," his grandfather murmured, "Now I've got you, I'll be over in a moment."

It was unusual for Henry to ask for Arthur. It was even rarer for him to come up to his office.

None of which boded well for Arthur. He tapped the desk. It didn't help. He knew roughly what was coming. Although over a hundred, Arthur's grandfather hopped up the stairs and slid into the chair opposite Arthur. It wasn't what he expected.

"It's your father."

"What's up?"

"He's in hospital."

Arthur could think of no sturdier seventy year old.

"My God, ill?" Arthur asked.

"Don't be silly old boy, he got hit by a bus. It made quite a mess."

"A mess? Of what?"

"Of the bus, of course."

"Well, what about him?"

"He's broken a few things, but I think he'll mend. But we need more of us with the gene, Arthur. We're not going to live forever."

"Yes, I get that," Arthur said hastily.

"No you don't. You need an heir and you need him soon."

Arthur's grandfather got up, the message delivered and went off to think about lunch.

Arthur's door swung conveniently closed and left him in silence with just his thoughts. They were a little cluttered, but there were a few things that were clear. The first was that Arthur had spent the last thirty years in hedonistic pursuit and he had done many things. Quite a few of them had been with women, and he'd never much cared for contraceptives. Beyond the cheese girl there were other possibilities. The only problem Arthur found was that it was difficult to remember names. There was a Claire and a Vanessa, a Mia, a Florence and an Elizabeth, of that he was certain. There was also a Jane, a Shirley, a Zoe and a Ann, and there were a number of Sarahs, but that wasn't the problem.

He was going to need to know surnames, and as he was barely able to remember first names, this didn't bode well. He would have to start with location. If he could remember that, and he generally could, then he might be able to find out more.

Maybe he was getting ahead of himself. He thought about the cheese girl. They'd had sex a lot, although he hadn't taken notes on the matter, so the actual number was difficult to discern. It was a summer, he remembered that. It was a warm summer, and there hadn't been many of those in England. Of course, he couldn't rule out the possibility that he had warmed the experience with the heat of nostalgia. For a second Arthur concentrated on trying to piece together the number. It suddenly seemed important, like an election poll, or it could have been an erection poll. Either way, it made sense that the more frequent, the greater the chance of conception. He thought back, it must have been at least one or twice a day for the whole summer. Arthur was fairly certain it was twelve summers ago. He'd had quite a time with her. It was unusual for Arthur. It even verged on a normal, conventional relationship.

Arthur felt he'd made progress. Moments were flooding back to him, and now he could even recall the curve of her breasts. They were large with cherry red nipples. Now what the hell was her name?

Chapter Eight

Brayman breathed in. It had been quite a surprise.

"Are you okay, honey?"

Brayman looked down at the most fantastic looking girl he had ever seen, and tried to mumble an appropriate response. But while she found it easy to talk with her mouth clamped around his genitals, it defeated him. She appeared to smile, which under the circumstances was another skill, and didn't wait for a reply. They had met in a pub. Brayman had slid out of his car and smiled at her, but he wasn't in the new BMW he'd bought. He was in his battered pickup. He couldn't get comfortable in the BMW. The seats moved in every direction, as did the steering wheel, but he just didn't feel right. The pickup worked just fine and, as its name suggests, he had picked up. Big time.

"Very okay," he finally managed.

His life had changed so fast, it was as if he'd been injected into another body, enjoying another very different existence. He had lost weight, and changed his clothes and, with Arthur in South Africa, had even acquired a tan. But it wasn't any of those things. He hadn't realised how stressed he constantly felt with his garden centre. And all that weight had been lifted. He even looked taller.

"Me too," she murmured. How she managed it was a mystery to Brayman, but she was clearly very talented. He was slightly distracted as he was becoming increasingly aware that he was going to be late for Arthur. He was tempted to look at his watch, but knew that would be very bad form. He was astonished he'd managed it twice already, and initially had doubts he'd score a third. But those doubts were evaporating rather quickly. He wasn't even aware he was groaning. A moment later the blonde emerged victorious. He couldn't recall her name or whether she had mentioned one. She grabbed his wrist, twisted his arm and looked at his watch.

"I'm late, must go," she said and moments later they were heading in different directions. Brayman was new to this brief liaison business and wasn't quite sure of the form. They exchanged cards with a promise of meeting again, although he was a little uncertain whether she really meant it. He'd certainly had a very good time. He dumped the pickup in the car park at the train station, and was heading for London moments later. He had considered taking a cab – he could certainly afford it – but he hadn't quite got used to the idea, and the train was quicker. When he reached Paddington, he did take a cab, marvelling at the comfort and ample space they provided, and arrived at Arthur's office only forty minutes late.

"I'm sorry I'm late," he offered deferentially.

"No problem, old boy," Arthur murmured, and shook his hand. In another life, and different circumstances, he would have liked to crush this hand, but he contained himself. Brayman was in two minds as to whether to tell Arthur about the circumstances of his lateness. It certainly involved the kind of self-indulgent, living-well kind of hedonistic behaviour that Arthur had been preaching.

"This way," Arthur motioned and in a short walk, with just a hint of a limp, they turned into an austere-looking building.

"Cheese?" Brayman asked.

"No, this is the whisky society. I'm a member. Just a little snifter before the cheese."

"Excellent," Brayman said with a ring of irritatingly good health.

Arthur ordered something from the whisky menu, sixty percent of which was alcohol, which was not too excessive in his view. He threw the first one down. The heat tippled down his throat, spread its way through his intestines and finally arrived somewhere in his blood stream. And not a moment too soon. He needed it for the pain in his leg and to restrain him from throttling Brayman. Brayman broke the silence.

"Gosh, this is nice," he said with what was becoming his trademark enthusiasm. It was nice too, not like the whisky he'd tasted before. But then everything tasted different now.

"So, what's the plan?"

"My car is ready to take us."

"Excellent, will it take long?"

"Oh, three hours or so."

"Three hours?" Brayman didn't like to complain, but he was beginning to think he could manage a fourth time with the girl, whose name turned out to be Mandy.

He was really getting into excess, as Arthur had encouraged, but he was also thinking that Mandy was such a nice name. They knocked back a couple more whiskies in quick succession, all of which prompted Brayman to marvel still more at what a lovely name Mandy was.

Arthur had decided that they were going straight to the cheese place. It was a bit of a trek, it was in the west country and would probably take four hours. But it might kill two birds with one Brie. He knew a nice hotel there, which would give him time to track her down. He just had to remember her bloody name.

Chapter Nine

The cut glass tumblers chinked in the back of the Rolls. The car had been in the family for over forty years and Arthur was of the opinion that they were ready for a replacement. But that wasn't going to happen now. Rogerman had been the chauffeur for as long as he could remember, and hadn't appeared to change either. "Rogerman, old boy," Arthur said, but didn't need to finish the sentence. His communications with Rogerman always favoured the minimal. Rogerman knew where they were going. The traffic and the gentle cruising speed of the car stretched the journey to nearly four and a half hours.

   Arthur looked out the window. They had continued drinking the whisky in the car, and Brayman had drifted into a fitful sleep over an hour ago. Arthur was grateful of the peace. Despite his hearty constitution, the alcohol was beginning to tell him stories, not least that there was a sturdy young son of his at the end of the journey. He couldn't remember how it had ended with the mother. He was fairly certain that 'not well' would cover it. It was before his life was burdened with a mobile phone, so the boy would be at least ten or twelve or maybe even fifteen. These were details that Arthur was not good at. It prompted another thought. It was just after and there was a girl he'd given his number to, was it Molly? He couldn't remember. Anyway, she had pestered him until he'd done something. What was it? Then he remembered. It was another occasion on that wobbly bridge in Zambia, a few years ago. His client had just thrown himself over the edge and by some strange miscalculation Arthur had measured exactly the right amount of bungee rope, which was irritating. And then she called. It was the twenty-seventh time and Arthur had hurled the phone over the edge. It was a brick-like phone of some weight, and it caught his client rather nastily on the head. He didn't make it.

Savouring the memory made him feel happier. But none of this was helping him remember the bloody girl's name.

Brayman's dreams were becoming alarmingly vivid and, it had to be said, quite disturbingly sexual. He was on a sexual assault course, which involved a variety of activities that would ordinarily have been outside his imagination. His old imagination. The new Brayman was different and, he couldn't help remembering, Mandy was very skilled. He'd never thought of sex as being something that required skill. It was more instinctive, he'd thought, as was life. But this was, he was learning, very much not true. He was grateful for the tuition that both Mandy and Arthur had provided. The thought settled him for a while.

Arthur had a thought. He wasn't one for technology. His life involved old leather high-backed chairs and everything steeped in multi-generational history. There were few things modern that interested him, although he'd make an exception with a new car. He fumbled around for a laptop that was held in one of the leather-lined, walnut-topped cubby holes in the back of the Rolls. He discovered that it was also equipped with what he understood was referred to as a dongle. It was simple. The cheese house was bound to have a website, and it was likely there would be names there. Brayman next to him was becoming increasingly animated in his sleep. He seemed to be grunting in a manner Arthur thought rather unseemly.

Brayman, in his dreams, had attained a level of sexual invincibility that would challenge Superman. There were no limits and that suited Mandy fine. He really liked that name. It seemed to work on so many levels. It was clearly particularly effective on a very base level, a level he had really enjoyed in both reality and currently his dreams. And then there was something classy about it. And warm and kind. Brayman's mind, working as it was, entirely separately from him, had recreated the conversation that led up to the sex. This time it was laced with wit and warmth. She was quite something, Mandy.

The computer, like all computers, Arthur was discovering, was a bastard. It appeared to be deliberately missing the point and operating with painful sloth. Arthur had told it this a number of times, quite loudly. But it hadn't woken up Brayman. Eventually it decided it had wound up Arthur enough, and directed him to the website. It was most interesting. There was a big family story. It involved lots of names, but none of them were female. And then there was a picture. It was a large group shot, but eventually he found her. She'd worn well. But what the bloody hell was her name?

For a second, Brayman's mind steered him away from the business of pleasuring and being pleasured, back to his former self, in the garden centre. It was very inconvenient. One year he'd ordered some Christmas trees too early. There weren't enough and all the pines fell out. The following year he ordered too many, too late. It nearly bankrupted him. Even his brain was becoming bored of dreams of Christmas trees-past, and very kindly brought him back to Mandy. Or rather Mandy was now on top of him. My God, that girl had fantastic breasts. He was now running his hands over them, much as he had that morning, but making a much better job of it. She asked him to do it more softly.

"Softly."

Arthur's eyes rose to the highest point they could occupy on his head. Did he say Sophie? Had he heard right? How would Brayman know? Was it Sophie? It really rang a bell.

Brayman was ringing more than just bells. It was as if his his hands were equipped with an infinite number of receptors. He could feel everything. And then, just as she had earlier that day, she asked him to move to the sofa. It had struck him as odd at the time. Why the sofa? When he got there he found out. She really did know what she was doing.

"Sofa," he muttered.

Arthur couldn't believe it. Sophie. How did the bloody man know? The thought corresponded with a huge pothole, which the old Rolls was incapable of disguising. It was the kind of hole that could be found at the end of a long tree-lined drive, leading up to the kind of country house that had been inherited by a generation who could not afford its upkeep. There was less money than there used to be in cheese.

"Are we here?" Brayman asked happily.

"We are indeed, old boy."

The car came to a halt and Arthur was rather surprised to see an entourage of people welcoming them. He had to admit that Jean had become quite skilled at organising his life, and predicting his indulgences. They were right on time. Arthur bounded out of the car before Rogerman had the opportunity to open the door for him. He was feeling really rather enthusiastic.

"Arthur, old boy, delighted to see you," a florid-faced man greeted him.

"Quentin, lovely to be here. Sorry we're so late."

Quentin pumped his hand, and then a moment later he pumped the hand of what he thought of as Arthur's pigeon. Their products were known to bring on aneurysms and, whilst this was something of a marketing challenge, he had grasped that it was clearly a boon for Arthur. He also hoped that this trip alone would pay for the kitchen roof.

"Arthur, how nice to see you."

Arthur had been looking out for Sophie, but hadn't been able to see her. It was as if she'd sprung out from nowhere. And because they had anticipated Arthur spending an obscene amount of money, she was on her best behaviour. But it was a challenge.

"Sophie, you look wonderful," Arthur managed to say with some charm.

"You remember my name?"

"Of course, I think about you all the time," he said, just a shade less convincingly. He was also aware that Brayman was looking at him strangely. He didn't want him to witness this. He was going to have to try and steer Sophie away. And then what? He hoped that would come to him at the right time.

The house was white-faced and obsessively symmetrical, with an arrangement of bushes and flowerbeds in the same manner. Despite that, there was something a little faded about the place. They were directed into the house through the grand double doors and into a reception room, whose sole purpose was to boast about their products.

Brayman looked at it all wide-eyed. It was now around eight and he was fairly sure, although he couldn't be certain, that they hadn't eaten anything at lunch, just the Scotch. He was hungry.

"Lovely, lovely," Arthur cooed, holding himself in maximum charm mode. But he was going to have to spend some money to keep them there, and the office wasn't keen on that.

"Have you eaten?" Quentin asked.

"Well no, we haven't, but we can't take up too much of your time." Quentin and Sophie, and the rest of the entourage, assured him that the pleasure was all theirs.

"Well, as luck would have it, we have quite a large charity function on tonight. It would be delightful if you could join us."

"That would be splendid," Arthur said, smiling maniacally at Sophie.

They took a tour of the factory, and Arthur obliged by buying enough cheese for both the kitchen roof and the small toilet block at the rear of the building.

He'd get in trouble with the office, but he thought of it as a double investment. It could deliver Brayman into bad habits and produce an heir. The banquet was larger and grander than Arthur had imagined. There were at least a hundred guests. He had to be seated near Sophie. He turned to Quentin.

"I don't suppose, old boy, you could seat me near Sophie. It would be great to catch up."

Quentin, a tall angular man with glasses that magnified his eyes, turned and looked at Arthur, his florid complexion turned a little more florid. They had drawn lots as to who was going to have Arthur on their table. Quentin had lost and knew that Sophie would not be happy. But Arthur had yet to pay his bill.

"Of course, old boy."

Chapter Ten

Sophie had not had a good day. It had started with all the small things. First the washing machine, and then the computer. Why, she asked herself, did all the domestic appliances have to break down at the same time? And why at the most inconvenient time? As far as she could remember almost everything she possessed that could break down, had chosen to do so on a weekend, and always when there was little cash available. And then her only child put a foot through the glass in the patio door. And then Sophie had been called in to help with the banquet. And, as if that wasn't bad enough, along came Arthur Cholmondley-Godstone. "Sophie, how delightful to see you. I believe I'm on your table."

Sophie choked. They hadn't told her at first. And then they had to. The very last man on the planet she wanted to see. She had spent many nights wondering if she were capable of stabbing him in his sleep. And then she had got over him, or she thought she had. Except he was here and on her bloody table.

"Arthur, how are you?"

Arthur explained that he was in fine health, which came as quite a disappointment to her. She had hoped for cancer, but she imagined that the cancer wouldn't be able to stomach him either.

"Married yet?" Arthur asked with a level of sensitivity she had come to expect from him. But Arthur had an agenda, and he intended to pursue it.

"Yes," Sophie blushed slightly. She couldn't believe the cheek of the man. How dare he ask such a personal question. It had taken her by surprise, as had her answer, which was not quite the truth. Or rather had been, but then it had been followed by divorce. She wasn't going to give him the pleasure.

"Excellent, I knew you'd make a fabulous wife and, I'm sure mother." Arthur had hoped for a response. He had, by his standards, phrased it with some subtlety. Sophie wasn't giving away anything.

"And you Arthur, are you married?"

"No, sadly not," Arthur demurred.

"Sadly for whom?" Sophie asked, tiring of tact. It went over Arthur's head.

"And do you have any children?" Arthur returned to the agenda.

Sophie thought about the big bouncy child that filled her life. The glass in the patio door had nearly taken a leg off, and then there was the issue of security. There was a gale blowing through the back door. The child may be accident prone but, she had to admit, was the most important thing in her life.

"Me? What about you?"

Arthur did find the circuitous way that women spoke very irritating at times. Why couldn't she just answer the bloody question?

"No, I haven't been so lucky," Arthur said with something approaching sincerity. Sophie tried to remember what it was that she had liked about him in the first place. It certainly wasn't his sincerity. She didn't like to think it was the money, she wasn't that kind of a girl. Or was she? For a second she panicked, thinking that maybe she was exactly that kind of girl. Now, she reasoned, was not the time for talking herself down. She'd deal with that later.

"I just wish I had fathered a son. Someone to cherish," Arthur said, almost with tears in his eyes. He could be quite the performer. He hoped that if she had a son of his hidden away, the prospect of some inherited wealth might fleece him out.

Cherish wasn't a word she had expected to tumble out of Arthur's lips. Perhaps he'd changed. Sophie was pretty sure that he couldn't even remember what had gone wrong between them.

"What went wrong between us?" Arthur asked, reminding her that he hadn't changed at all. The old irritation brought her back, and unfortunately it coincided with a lull in conversation on the rest of the table.

"Herpes," she said angrily. It turned out that conversation was not that fevered in the neighbouring tables either.

That was it, Arthur thought. He'd acquired most sexual diseases, but they never seemed to affect him. However, he was more than capable of passing them on. It might have coincided with a mention of love. Her, not him. Was there talk of marriage? Oh damn, he thought, there might have been. Herpes was not a very conventional wedding present.

"…is very widespread," Sophie said very loudly, trying to cover things up. It prompted people in the tables beyond the neighbouring ones to ask what she had said. They weren't sure, but it was clearly something about herpes. It was Arthur's parting gift and, if that wasn't enough, it came back to haunt her every now and again. Mostly when she'd managed to forget about him.

"Quite so," Arthur muttered, although he wasn't sure to what he or she was referring to. For a moment he thought about running with the widespreadness of herpes, but had a feeling he'd just dig a deeper hole.

Brayman watched Arthur from the other end of the table. It hadn't been too difficult for him to put two and two together and reach herpes. He had a feeling he knew what Arthur was after and chatted politely to the young girl next to him, who gave him a potted history of the family all the way down to the children.

Sophie had decided she'd had enough. She got up, ignored the daggered looks from her father and uncle, and walked out. She did so with her shoulders back and her head held high. She'd worn the black dress, the tight one she knew she looked good in. She wondered why she'd chosen it. As she walked, she hoped that the world was seeing a women with dignity and not, as she feared, a woman with herpes.

Arthur looked at her recede with something very close to sadness. His upbringing had not been especially warm, and had not placed much emphasis on friendship, let alone love. There was some part of him, buried very deep, that might have had some facility for it, and just for a second it tore at him. Unfortunately the meal and fine cheeses were followed by a series of speeches which were spectacular in their dullness. Arthur, warmed by a new sensitivity, tolerated it, but did so by ensuring that his and Brayman's glasses were instantly and constantly refilled. He was therefore very drunk indeed when they tumbled into the rear of the Rolls. He was also very uncharacteristically emotional and saw no reason to spend another moment in the west of England. He knew a club in London that never closed.

"Rogerman, old boy," he began, but realised that this was a sentence he would have to finish, as Rogerman was heading to the hotel.

"Change of plan, Rogerman old boy, back to the city."

Rogerman raised his eyes, but said nothing. He had been abused by the Cholmondley-Godstones all his life, but rather than despise them, he was furiously loyal. He actually felt they had a divine right. Rogerman steered the car on to the motorway and headed for London.

"A great night," Brayman slurred.

"Really? I thought it was fucking awful." Arthur's brush with the possibility of instant fatherhood had brought out a new candour in him. That and the alcohol.

"Well, the speeches went on a little," Brayman replied reasonably, "but the food was very fine, and the cheese was something else."

It was, Arthur remembered, the quality of the cheese that had taken him there in the first place. And he was fairly sure that Sophie had kept him coming back. They could have married. Obviously he'd have kept the flat on in London, and spent some time away from the family home – that was his business, after all. But they could have had a nice Georgian rectory, probably with a tennis court, maybe even a swimming pool. And dogs, definitely there would be dogs. Arthur didn't actually like dogs, but he could imagine them outside the house. There would be a gravel drive with one of those sort of roundabouts with a statue in the middle. In a fleeting moment Arthur had created a picture of the kind of life he'd always hated. But this time it looked great. It put him in further confessional mood.

"I take it you had something going with Sophie," Brayman said. Had Arthur been in normal Arthur mode, he would have despised the impertinence of the question, but today he didn't notice.

"We were going to get married," he said solemnly.

Brayman wasn't sure whether it was a good idea to mention the herpes. He decided against it.

"She seemed a little angry," he ventured instead.

"Indeed, she was. Very angry. Really very angry."

"Perhaps another time, you can try again. People don't remain angry forever," Brayman said.

"Do you think so?"

"Answer this," Brayman said with increasing boldness, "How do you feel about her?"

"How do I," Arthur paused, "feel," he paused again, "about her?"

"Yes."

Arthur's capacity for feeling had never extended much beyond the visceral, but he thought he got what he was saying.

"There could have been a Georgian rectory, with a gravel drive and a pair of dogs," Arthur explained.

Brayman's experience of feeling was spectacularly recent, but even he recognised that Arthur had probably not quite grasped the point.

"No, not the idea of a *life* with her, but her. How do you feel about *her*?"

"I like her. A lot," Arthur said, forgetting that he had only recently remembered her name.

"Would that be love?" Brayman said, but knew that he'd have to keep going. "If you stood in front of her, exposed, and said that you love her, what would she say?" Brayman didn't let Arthur answer, "The thing is you don't know. You don't know until you try it. You must try."

Brayman was the most impassioned he had ever been, and he didn't know about Arthur's Sophie, but he was determined to tell Mandy. And Mandy was the kind of girl who could reply with her mouth full.

Arthur was thinking. Brayman was right. There could even be a child there, and if there wasn't, he was fairly sure that Sophie was young enough to bear one. They'd had a good time together, he remembered.

"Rogerman," Arthur said impetuously, "Turn the car round, old boy, we're going to the hotel."

Rogerman's eyes raised again and he turned the car obediently. It wasn't a car that liked to change direction rapidly. Unlike, it appeared, Arthur.

Brayman loved a good rom-com, particularly the run to the airport or, in this case cheese factory, to declare an undying love. His eyes watered at the thought.

Arthur wondered if she still lived in the same house, he thought it likely. Now all he had to do was use the next thirty minutes to hone his speech. And Brayman was all ears.

"So what are you going to say?" he asked, returning to the enthusiasm that would have infuriated a more normally non-love-struck Arthur.

"I really quite like you," Arthur said grandly.

"No, seriously."

But Arthur was serious. 'I really quite like you' was the biggest emotional leap he'd ever taken. It was stretching his boundaries as far as they were capable of going.

"I mean, I think, she'll want something a little more than that. A bit more personal." Arthur didn't seem to react.

"A tad more intimate," Brayman added.

And Arthur saw it for what it was. A fruitless disaster. A cringe-making error of disastrous proportions. He wasn't thinking right. What he really meant, in a vocabulary he was more comfortable with, was that it a horrendous fuck up.

"Rogerman, old boy." Rogerman's eyes lifted to a new level, but his arms turned as they approached a junction and the Rolls veered off the road and onto the roundabout and back to London.

Brayman couldn't hide his disappointment. He had been looking forward to the rawness of the speech and the emotion, or it might have the other way round. Brayman was pretty pissed. They travelled in silence for a while. The car hummed along with just the occasional chink of cut glass clashing. It was interrupted by an electronic beep.

Arthur looked around with irritation. As far as he was aware the damn car practically predated electricity. It took a moment for Brayman to realise that it had come from his phone. Like many things in his life, it was new, expensive and fantastically complicated. And he had not the slightest sense of how it should be operated. Eventually he got it. It was a text. He'd heard about these sort of unsolicited texts. It was quite pornographic in its nature. It took him a moment longer to connect the number with that of the card in his pocket. It was Mandy.

"Sounds like Mandy," Brayman slurred absentmindedly.

"I beg your pardon?" Arthur said, now verging on sober and no longer lovelorn.

Brayman didn't want to tell him about Mandy.

"She seemed such a lovely girl."

"Well yes, she is. Of course,"

And then a further thought struck Brayman.

"Of course, she has a child. It's a lot to ask to…"

But Arthur didn't let him finish the sentence.

"How do you know?"

"I asked the young girl who sat next to me. She was her cousin."

"A girl, I imagine," Arthur said, returning to more languid form.

"A girl? I don't think so, I think she said it was a boy."

Brayman tried to remember, but he was fairly sure she was brushing her thigh against his, and that had made it harder to concentrate.

"A boy?"

The Georgian house came back, and the dogs. Were they Labradors? He couldn't remember. Then he tried to picture the boy. He'd be ruddy faced and on the fat side of stocky. He'd constantly kick balls through the conservatory windows. Did they have a conservatory? He couldn't remember. But it didn't matter, the boy would be too young and not his. Arthur asked the question anyway.

"I don't suppose she mentioned the age of this boy?"

"Actually she did," Brayman said, and was rewarded with quite the most violent gaze anyone had cast on him.

"Sorry, he's eleven." Brayman had been distracted by the text. It looked like a fourth time was a real possibility. Just the thought prompted a warmness in his trousers, which confirmed that he was certainly up for it.

"Eleven! Are you sure?"

Brayman was trying to send a text. He was new to the business, but it wasn't just the mechanics, all those little buttons. What was he going to say? Well, he knew what he wanted to say, but that wasn't the problem. It was how to say it. It really would be better with just a hint of humour. He thought about asking Arthur, but he had gone quite red-faced.

"Rogerman," Arthur roared. Rogerman's eyes were perched as high as they could manage. He steered the car back to the hotel.

Brayman watched in desperation as the car turned and the prospect of the fourth time, that would be his first fourth time ever in one day, evaporated. He knew he couldn't halt the will of Arthur.

But it coincided with a further thought. Arthur tried to recall his brief conversation with Sophie. Hadn't he ask whether she was married? He had, definitely. What the bloody hell had she said? He hadn't really been listening. She had looked fabulous in that black dress. It had distracted him. And then he remembered. Rogerman was guiding the car carefully round a very large roundabout. He was wise to keep his eyes on Arthur.

"Rogerman," Arthur said sheepishly, but Rogerman was one step ahead of him.

Brayman began texting furiously. He was getting some sort of Pavlovian erection every time they headed for London.

"It's no bloody good, old boy," Arthur said, almost with affection. "She's bloody married."

Brayman continued to tap on his phone and said, without looking up. "No, she's divorced."

"Rogerman," Arthur yelled, but they were already turning. It was going to be a very long night.

Chapter Eleven

Sophie almost ripped off her cocktail dress. It was her little black number. It was simple, elegant and fitted her well. And she looked pretty damned good in it. But right now she hated that dress, and now it had a tear in it. It was the sort of tear she'd liked to have acquired from a passion-fuelled liaison with a gypsy-locked maverick industrialist. God, she hated that bloody dress. She put on the vilest clothes she possessed: a track suit. Unlike the dress, it made her bum look big and her tits look flat, both of which were fine with her.

She opened the fridge and shifted things around. It was not an organised fridge, but she knew it was there somewhere. She was growing quite fevered, she hoped the kids hadn't eaten it. But there it was, tucked behind a lettuce. An Indulgence. Chocolate, single cream, double cream, triple cream and then more cream and chocolate. She loved those things. She slumped in the chair, but then noticed that the remote control was the other side of the room. She was next to the CD player, and so could listen to music without moving, but she couldn't take the risk she might end up listening to Joni Mitchell. She got up, crossed the room, grabbed the remote and slumped back into the sofa. She'd left the Indulgence on the table. It was out of reach. That Indulgence really was a metaphor for her life.

"Hey?"

Sophie turned to the boy. Despite his stocky, almost manlike appearance, he was a little boy and he wanted her to put him to bed. This time she rose from the sofa without effort and led him back to his bedroom. He slid into his bed and she delivered the kiss he hankered for. The other bed was occupied by her child, who was snoring quietly, exhausted. She sighed and went back to her Indulgence.

Chapter Twelve

Arthur was beginning to feel very sober. With sobriety there was an acute awareness of time, and three in the morning was late by anyone's standards. It would have been much earlier had they not spent most of the evening driving to and from London. Even Arthur could see that knocking on Sophie's door now would not be a good idea. Brayman had even become quite short with him, which was not something he wished to encourage. And then they got to the hotel.

The hotel was small, quiet, classy, expensive and very closed. There appeared to be no means of entry at this time. Arthur was not going to give up easily.

"Right, this way," he said, using his phone to light a path to the rear of the house. Brayman followed him, while Rogerman stayed with the car. They were all grappling with different issues. Rogerman's was simple: he was exhausted. Brayman had to contend with a runaway libido that was driving him crazy. In his mind he had raised the prospect of another time with Mandy to biblical proportions. If he thought too much about her, he couldn't walk straight. But Arthur was on a mission. It was a military manoeuvre. And like all major conflicts, it was rife with bungling, incompetence and, worst of all, indecision. And Brayman wasn't helping.

"When it comes to declaring your love, you shouldn't waste a moment longer. What did he say in Harry met Sally?" Brayman's rom-com instincts were back on form.

"Harry met who?"

"Sally. He says when you decide you want to spend the rest of your life with someone, you want the rest of your life to start as soon as possible."

"He said that?" Arthur had no idea who Harry or Sally were, and assumed they were friends of Brayman. But he was keen to get into the spirit of things.

"Yes," Brayman assured him.

But the part of the sentence that struck most of a chord with Arthur was 'the rest of your life.' That was quite a long time by most standards, but a bloody long time if you happen to be a Cholmondley-Godstone. He was a young man, not yet fifty, which meant that could be another fifty years, probably more.

Brayman could see Arthur digesting the implications. He had a vested interest, not in the outcome with Arthur and Sophie, but an increasing desire to get back home and see Mandy. If this would secure it, that was fine with him. Maybe there was a possibility of an early morning romp. It wouldn't qualify as four in a day, but it was a detail he was happy to overlook.

Arthur's feeling of dread was building. He was beginning to hyperventilate. It was making him quite ill, and that never happened to Arthur.

"Have a drink," Brayman said, passing a large Scotch.

Arthur looked at him uncertainly, but took it anyway. It was certainly the moment for a drink. It filtered through and calmed him. And then he began to think. There were two issues here. One was the 'rest of his life' with someone, most specifically Sophie, and the other was an offspring, a boy, an heir. He took the second glass Brayman offered him, and decided to concentrate on the second part. They couldn't get into the bloody hotel anyway, so why not pop by Sophie's house? He seemed to remember she'd been very fond of that house, telling him she hoped to live there all her life. It wasn't the Georgian rectory he had in his mind, but a modern bungalow. But at least that would give him the opportunity of looking in all the bedroom windows. It was a warm evening, all he had to do was lay his eyes on the boy. How difficult could that be?

"Rogerman."

There was no response.

"Rogerman!" Arthur yelled.

After a long pause, Rogerman sprung back into life. He turned the key in the ignition and after an equally long time, as if it was operating in sympathy, the car sprang into life.

"Dear God," Arthur muttered, and fired out instructions.

Rogerman was like a sat nav reluctant to find satellites, and another enormous pause followed as he attempted to digest his orders. He set off with a jerk. Arthur recalled the village and remembered that Sophie's house was the last on the left. Rogerman knew where to go, and ten minutes later they came to a halt outside the house.

"Move round the corner," Arthur instructed.

"We'll have to go on foot."

Rogerman steered the car to a halt, but the car was too exposed.

"A bit further, Rogerman."

He drove a bit further, but this time they were even more exposed.

"A bit more."

Rogerman raised his eyes, but obeyed.

Arthur had decided that he didn't want to get caught and to achieve that he'd have to be out of sight.

"A bit further."

They came to a halt, but a bit further on Arthur could see a dark country lane.

"There," he pointed.

It wasn't until he got out of the car that Arthur realised how far away they were. He grabbed a full bottle of whisky.

"Okay, we're on foot now."

Rogerman sat rigid with just one thought in his head. 'We?' It was the same question Brayman was asking himself.

"Come on, Brayman."

Brayman mentally abandoned his plans with Mandy, and pulled himself out of the car. He realised then that he was really very drunk, but took a swig from the bottle anyway. It was a very dark night, moonless and cloudy, and the trees around them created dark shadows. Arthur began to whisper loudly.

"You see, I understand that the rest of my life should start as soon as possible, but before that it would be nice, just to get another look."

Brayman wasn't sure what he wished to get a look at, but passed back the bottle. Arthur needed to fortify himself and took a huge swig. He wasn't well equipped for journeys of the emotional kind. He took another swig. All he had to do was get a look at the kid. He couldn't remember if he'd mentioned this to Brayman. He turned to ask him, but found Brayman wasn't there.

"Brayman!" he hissed.

What was wrong with everyone, he thought. Brayman had discovered a ditch that ran to one side of the small track they were following. As he had stumbled into it, he was also discovering that it was lined with a bed of stinging nettles. Whatever he reached for to drag himself out, bit back.

"Arthur," he wailed.

"Quiet!" Arthur spat. Brayman clearly hadn't grasped the covert nature of the operation. He was making a lot of noise. Eventually Arthur leaned over and grabbed some stinging nettles.

"Bugger."

For just a moment Arthur wondered whether he was drowning in the ditch, and whether he should leave him there. Unfortunately, a moment later, Brayman managed to pull himself out.

"Shit," Brayman muttered. His arms, legs and face were covered in welts, although the pain in one part of his body was offset by the pain in another. It was most unsettling. But mostly it was the healing power of the whisky that was seeing him through.

"Actually, "Brayman said, "I do have an allergy problem with nettles. You might have to get me to hospital if I have an anaphylactic shock."

Arthur stopped in his tracks. He couldn't understand what was wrong with him. This whole son and heir business had made him take his eye off the real business at hand. He turned and took a good look at Brayman. But it was dark.

"Are you all right, old boy?" He asked with something that sounded just like concern in his voice. It was not unlike Shere Khan, the tiger in Jungle Book, most specifically as voiced by George Sanders. But Brayman had too many problems of his own to notice. His breathing had become encouragingly erratic. Arthur hunted through his pockets until he found a lighter. He flicked it close to Brayman's face. For a second the orange flame flared and lit him up. It gave Arthur quite a fright.

"Shit," he muttered. Brayman looked like a Victorian side show. It was, Arthur thought, quite perfect.

"I think I'm okay," Brayman suddenly croaked. Air seemed to be entering his body again.

"Are you sure?" Arthur said without hiding his disappointment.

"As long as I'm not exposed to it again, I should be fine."

Arthur's eyes flared bright at the thought. It raised the ethical issue that was at the core of his business. The

Cholmondely-Godstones did not kill their clients, they merely encouraged them to take decisions that would facilitate a short life. Or, put another way, they don't actually push them in the ditch that's going to kill them, but getting them to teeter on the edge of their own accord? Well, that was another matter.

"Which way," Brayman suddenly asked.

Arthur sighed and took another nip of the whisky.

"This way." It was back to plan A. Arthur looked ahead and realised that it was quite a long way.

Chapter Thirteen

Rogerman's wife had been pestering him as to how he wished to spend his seventieth birthday. She pestered him so much, that eventually he'd said, "Alone." He hadn't actually said it loud enough for her to hear, but he had found the whole thing very stressful. Rogerman liked the undemanding and peaceful nature of his job. Arthur didn't engage him in unnecessary and distracting conversation, and he was grateful for it. But the toing and froing had given him pains in his chest. He didn't like to complain. In fifty years he had never complained. But for most of those fifty years his wife had complained. She'd raised the art of complaining to Olympic levels. And now that the kids had left home, he'd lost his allies. That left an awful lot of complaining to stomach on his own.

The solution had been staring him in the face. He was amazed it had taken him so long to see it and grasp it. He had watched Arthur wine and dine his clients into an early grave and, six months before his seventieth birthday, he had launched a plan of attack on his wife. The richest food and the strongest alcohol. He was pleased to say that Mrs Rogerman now wore a very florid complexion.

Rogerman let out a little burp. There was something pounding in his chest. He hadn't managed to eat that much, and only had chocolate in the car. He ate it anyway, and a moment later he had quite a sugar rush. It made him dizzy and added to the pounding in his chest. And then there was the fatigue. Rogerman's new enforced diet – he'd had to keep up with his wife – prompted his wife to sleep all the time, while he seemed incapable of it. He couldn't remember the last time he'd had a good night's sleep and he'd been driving for hours. The desire to give into it was overwhelming. Rogerman went with it and closed his eyes.

Chapter Fourteen

Despite the dark night, Arthur could see the house coming into view. Just the sight of it prompted fantasies of the marrying kind. They might have been nightmares. Arthur focused. He held Brayman's arm, who was wheezing slightly, and directed him into the shadows. Arthur remembered walking round the house, and was pleased to see that it was exactly as he remembered. It wasn't to his taste, it was far too modern, but he could see that it was practical and set in a nice garden. He peered through a window and reminded himself of the layout. The far bedroom was the one that he remembered most, but his interest was in the spare rooms. The first was empty. He waved to Brayman to check the other side, although he was less than clear as to what he should check it for. Brayman was mostly there to keep him company.

Arthur had a closer look at the house, it couldn't have been further from a Georgian rectory. He struggled to picture a pair of dogs. They flashed through his mind. First spaniels, but they weren't right; then poodles. Wrong again. Then dachshunds. He was beginning to think something was wrong with him. He redirected his mind to a time in the bedroom. Sophie had a small mole under her left breast. He felt back on track, and a pair of golden retrievers appeared in his mind. Much better, he thought. He looked again at the house and his memory faltered again, and the image faded. This was becoming so difficult.

Arthur breathed in and out slowly and tried to refocus his mind, but it kept wandering towards thoughts of a domestic nature. He struggled again to picture the dogs, but a moment later he didn't have to. They weren't the pair of golden labradors he'd envisaged. They were as black as the night, except for their white teeth, which were bared and ready for action. Arthur tumbled back.

Brayman had seen them coming and dropped into the shadows. He'd always had a way with animals and wondered whether he could calm them. It was either that or leave Arthur to them, but Brayman couldn't do that. He moved out of the shadows and strained his eyes to look for Arthur, but couldn't find him. It was if he'd disappeared. A moment later he didn't have to strain his eyes, as the entire area was lit by powerful floodlights. It wasn't, as he might expect, followed by the wailing of police cars, but the repeated clicking of loading guns.

"Shit," Brayman muttered to himself and wondered, for a second, whether Arthur had taken him on another high risk sport.

Arthur had problems of his own and scrambled on the floor, realising that he had fallen into the garden shed. It was well-stocked with weapons. The only problem was which to choose, and the timing of his exit. He hated Dobermans, they were definitely not in his picture of domestic bliss. And by the slathering, growling sound they were making the other side of the shed door, Dobermans weren't fond of him either.

He looked at the tools and grabbed a scythe. He twirled it around and nearly took his foot off. The shovel seemed a safer bet. He took it in his hands and experimented with it, as if he were wielding a cricket bat. Arthur prepared himself to bash the door open and make mincemeat of the Dobermans.

"Freeze."

Brayman raised his arms, discovering an adrenaline rush that rivalled landing on crocodiles. He'd never had a gun trained on him before. The man in front of him, however, was dressed in military uniform and was wearing sunglasses, even though it was the middle of the night. He looked like he had a lot of experience training guns on people.

"Back," he said. The Dobermans retreated. The man cleared his throat.

"What are you doing, motherfucker?"

The man, Brayman deduced, appeared to be American.

"What am I doing here?"

"You got me, asshole."

Brayman couldn't, for the life of him, which appeared to be entirely the issue at stake, answer that. He was fairly sure Arthur hadn't mentioned the purpose, or perhaps he had. He had been so distracted by Mandy and her smooth skin, although now he thought about it was more her firm breasts, that he couldn't recall the purpose of their visit.

"You're gonna give me a good reason why I shouldn't blow your fucking head off?"

"Er…"

"Do you know, motherfucker, what a 7.62 bullet does to a man's head?"

Brayman really didn't.

"It might as well be a melon, asshole."

The gunman shifted his stance, which Brayman took to be a bad sign. Then he remembered.

"Sophie," Brayman said suddenly. That was why they were there, or was it Sophie's child?

The man held the gun high and raised his sunglasses high on his head. His blue eyes fixed on Brayman and pierced in a way that suggested that they had pierced many times before. Brayman had no interest in such things, but couldn't help thinking that the face looked a little familiar. It took a while for him to place.

"What the hell happened to your face?" The man with the gun asked, more out of curiosity than concern.

"Er…"

"Sophie, you say?" the gunman said, suddenly finding himself no longer curious. Now who the hell had he hired the house off? He hadn't organised it, one of his staff had, but he had signed the papers. Maybe it was a Sophie. He was just pleased it wasn't Bella Rae, that girl had really caused him some hassles. The lines he'd been learning had been astonishingly apposite and the gun prop very handy. Either way, this guy was no paparazzi.

And then Brayman got it. He'd seen *The African Adventure*, or was it *African Romance*? Either way, the man in front of him with the chiselled good looks, and the eyes that knew how to pierce, bore an astonishing resemblance to an actor. What was his name? Brayman found it just as a door swung open, Arthur flew out, and a shovel came slicing through the air. Chiselled as the actor's features were, they didn't require further chiselling, and were no match for a shovel. He went down like a sack of potatoes.

"Shit." They looked down at him.

"Bugger," Arthur muttered.

"Do you know who that is?" Brayman asked.

"Know? Why would I fucking know? How do you fucking know? I know who it fucking isn't. How could you possibly fucking know? Well who the fucking hell is it?" Arthur was getting quite manic.

"Rocky Deep."

"Who the fucking hell is Rocky fucking Deep?"

"An actor."

It had been a very convincing performance. They looked down at him. He was face down. There was a large brown patch in his trousers.

"Is that?" Brayman began to ask.

"I think it might be."

"I think you may have killed him."

Arthur looked down at the crumpled heap in front of him. It was quite a mess. It was a shame he wasn't a client.

"We better get out of here," Arthur said, regaining some composure.

"Shouldn't we call an ambulance or something?" Brayman suggested.

"This way," Arthur commanded. Brayman followed, despite having the distinct impression they were travelling in the wrong direction. Thirty minutes later they passed the house again.

Arthur's head was in turmoil. This was really turning into a crappy night. He had been so thorough in his instructions to hide the car, it took nearly two hours to find it. Arthur's leg was aching, and he was relieved to flop into the rear seat of the Rolls.

"Rogerman."

There was no response.

"Rogerman."

Brayman leaned over and prodded Rogerman.

"He's asleep, I think."

Arthur found it most inconvenient. This time he filled his lungs.

"Rogerman!!"

Brayman shook him again.

"Arthur," he said slowly, "you don't think…"

"I don't think what?"

"I don't think he's breathing, Arthur."

"Well, who's going to drive the bloody car?"

Arthur got out of the car and addressed Rogerman directly.

"Wake up, you lazy bastard."

"Arthur, I really think there's a problem."

"Of course there is! Who's going to drive the bloody car?"

He shook Rogerman, but it was evident that there was not going to be any waking up. The chauffeur had sat in the same seat for over forty years and it had sagged with him, as if it were a part of him. It held him in the same position he adopted for guiding the car. Brayman opened the front passenger door and slid next to Rogerman. He looked at the slumped form and wondered what to do. He had a feeling it would be up to him.

"Didn't we pass a hospital about half an hour ago?"

"Did we? I didn't notice, but who's going to drive us there?"

"You'll have to drive us, Arthur."

"Oh bugger, but we'll have to move him first."

Brayman tried to yank Rogerman to one side, but he didn't shift.

"Come on then," Arthur encouraged from the rear of the car.

"I can't move him. He won't move. You're going to have to help."

"Oh bugger." Arthur got out of the car and opened the driver's door.

"I'll push him, you pull."

They heaved, but the hammock-like grip of the chair and Rogerman's white-knuckled clench of the wheel refused to release him.

"The inconsiderate bastard's got rigor mortis."

"Come on, damn you," Arthur encouraged. Rogerman's face remained immobile. It wasn't a typical reward for fifty years of unfailing service.

"Push!"

"Push!"

"Push!"

But Rogerman refused to move.

"One more time," Arthur ordered.

Brayman changed his grip, ready for the big tug.

"Push!"

Brayman's hands slipped off the uniform that had wrapped Rogerman's bony body for many years. It prompted Brayman to stumble back.

"Come on. Pull!"

Arthur walked round the car in irritation.

"Stop mucking about."

It took Arthur a moment to realise that Brayman had tumbled into the ditch. The rasping noises coming from the ditch were drowned by the wailing of sirens. Arthur ducked out of sight. For a moment Arthur considered leaving him there, but it was one thing to explain one corpse, another to explain two, and another again to explain three. He was going to need Brayman to help get him out of there. And quick.

"Where are you?"

"Agh, agh, aah," Brayman explained.

"Oh bugger, come here." Arthur waded into the nettles and rather than lift Brayman out, he took the more expedient route of dragging him through the nettles.

"Are you okay?"

The sirens were reminding Arthur that they needed to get the bloody hell out of there.

"Agh, agh, agh," Brayman repeated.

Brayman was having difficulty standing. He was also having difficulty breathing. It seemed less important that his thinking was also impaired.

"Pull yourself together, man," Arthur ordered.

It seemed to work as momentarily Brayman stopped making any noise at all. He fell over instead. It was accompanied by more sirens.

"Get up, man. For God's sake."

Even Brayman was sufficiently lucid to realise that it was more for Cholmondley-Godstone's sake. He got up.

"Excellent. Now shift up next to Rogerman."

Brayman obeyed, and Arthur closed the doors around them and got in the back seat behind Rogerman. He leaned over the dead body that had once been Rogerman, and grabbed the steering wheel.

"Right. Start the car."

Brayman's bloated face turned and looked at Arthur. He turned back and found the key. The old engine obligingly burst into life.

"Okay, handbrake next."

Brayman released the handbrake, still failing to grasp what was to come next

"Now press the accelerator pedal."

Brayman began to twitch alarmingly. Arthur didn't notice. It was a good time to go.

"Get on with it, man."

Brayman's allergy to the nettles was reaching a new level. His whole body straightened, a consequence of which was that Brayman did press the accelerator. To the floor. Arthur hadn't actually driven a car for some years, and he was now realising many things, at least one of which was that they should have put on the headlights.

"Steady," Arthur yelled, but Brayman's body had decided that it would be best for his brain to attend to repair work rather than a cognitive response. The Rolls was old and heavy but, Arthur was discovering, it was capable of quite a turn of speed. It would have been useful for him to have been able to see where they were going. Were it not for Rogerman's deathly grip on the wheel they would have landed in the ditch the other side of the road. Rogerman's eyes were wide open, but unseeing, while Brayman's were screwed shut, which left only Arthur. The dark night and the absence of lighting meant that Arthur had only a marginal advantage over the other two. But there was something about the shadowy line of trees that suggested that they were approaching a corner very quickly.

Brayman's battle with the nettles was, from his point of view, not going well, but his next convulsion involved his body contracting. It only lasted a few seconds, but it prompted him to release the accelerator pedal. It was close. The verge was deep and bumpy, but between Arthur and Rogerman they were able to steer the car through the corner with a wing mirror and a scrape the only casualty. As they rejoined the road with a thump, Rogerman's right hand fell off the steering wheel and brushed the lighting switch, bathing the road in light.

"Brayman! Brayman!"

Brayman could hear his name being called, but it was distant. He couldn't be sure whether it was Arthur calling him, or a voice from a white light. There was certainly a lot of white light all of a sudden. He was not a religious man, but he'd always imagined that his final time would be like this. The thought coincided with another convulsion, which prompted him to floor the accelerator.

"Brayman! For fuck's sake!"

Now that Arthur had a clear view of the road, it was even more frightening. The steering wheel seemed to buck in his hands, but he couldn't be sure whether it was the car or Rogerman doing the bucking.

The swelling around Brayman's eyes meant that he was unable to see, but he could hear Arthur screaming. He'd assumed the sensation of speed was related to his calling towards the light, and not that fact that he had the accelerator pressed to the floor.

"Bray-fucking-man!"

The road was long, straight and narrow, which was all good. But it lead to a T junction the other side of which was a row of very unforgiving trees, which Arthur could see was very bad indeed. It was beginning to look like he was going to die.

"Arthur, I can't see," Brayman said.

"Take your foot off the pedal."

"What?"

"Take your foot off the pedal!"

"Eh?"

Although Brayman could now hear, he wasn't quite capable of processing the instruction. But Arthur had made his own plans. He was bailing. But the next convulsion sent Brayman's foot flying off the accelerator pedal and hard onto the brake. The car screamed to a halt. Arthur was saved by Rogerman, Were it not for the rigidity of his body, he might have flown through the windscreen, which is where Brayman went. He, in turn, was saved by the extensive swelling, as if he were a human airbag.

It was suddenly very silent. Arthur was lucky to find all his teeth in tact, as most of the impact had been absorbed by his left eye. Rogerman had not moved, but the seat formally occupied by Brayman had been vacated.

"Brayman?" Arthur shouted a little cheerfully, before he realised that it might be a slightly difficult death to explain.

"Yes, Arthur?"

Arthur jumped. Brayman was standing by his side, looking rather cheerful. It was as if, Arthur thought, the impact had punched the poison out of him. The man was extraordinarily punchable.

"You okay?"

"Yes, strange, isn't it?"

The bloody man, Arthur thought, was quite nauseating.

"That's quite a black eye you've got there, Arthur."

It was a thought that was interrupted by the distant hum of sirens, and the reminder that this was supposed to be their getaway.

"You steer, I'll do the pedals," Brayman said, back in enthusiastic puppy mode. Arthur sighed and leaned over Rogerman.

Chapter Fifteen

Courtney Mbabwe knew he was different from the others. His mother and her friends had raised a collection of children, of which he was one of the oldest. The fathers came and went, but they were more like tourists, just catching the sights. There was never an intention to actually take up residence. It was a situation that didn't seem to bother either his mother, or her friends. It wouldn't have bothered him either, had he not found Google. His earliest acquaintance with it involved downloading pornography. He had a secret thing for slim-built white women. It was a bit of a specialist interest, but his mother had always told him to go with the flow. The computer was the newest addition to the local library, and quickly had more viruses than the local whore house.

Courtney had developed a talent for repairing the computer, which was made much easier when the library had a second computer donated. That way he could search what was wrong with one, from the other. There were very few computers, or even phone lines, where he lived but, he was discovering, there was another world out there. It was a world where every household had a computer, where there was information. There were other things like family units and endless advice about good and bad parenting, and finding partners. It was confusing. It seemed like a much easier life, meat came in packets from shops, and hot water flowed form taps, but everyone seemed so troubled. They were worried if they did have a partner, and worried if they didn't. It was all upside down. But there were plenty of slim white women.

Then there was the music. Courtney wasn't very musical, while the rest of his family liked to sing and beat drums and make melodies. Courtney couldn't see it. It was accidental, but on one internet exploration he came across a group of girls singing. Fortunately his lack of musicality took the edge off pitch and tone, but there was something about their energy. There was a dark-skinned one like him, an emaciated one, a ginger one, and one who looked too young to be cavorting nearly naked. But somehow he liked the noise.

When it came to dancing, Courtney wasn't a hit either. He was enthusiastic, certainly, but always off the beat. The whole concept of the beat was slightly alien to him. But that was not to say that Courtney was without talents. He had gathered an incredible facility for the English language. He was passable at the other dialects they spoke, but he bordered on pedantic when it came to English. It wasn't just spelling and grammar, but accent. He'd used the Internet as a guide and aside from an alarming moment listening to a footballer, who he understood was married to the emaciated one, he liked what he heard. He even favoured a more old fashioned way of speaking. If it had been in his family's vocabulary, they might have called him eccentric. But they weren't a family who called each other names, or judged people. Different was just different.

Courtney knew he was not going to become a fisherman or weave roofs, like his older brother. He was going to leave, few of the men seemed to hang around for long anyway. He wasn't sure where he was going to go, except it would have lots and lots of electricity and computers. But it was a very long way to go. There weren't short-haul aeroplane operators who would promise to take him somewhere else for the price of a sack of potatoes. There weren't even passports. It made the leap from where he was seem a very big one.

The problem was that he was different from the others. He was cheerful and easy going and kind hearted, like his mother and siblings. He was strong, square built, and when they had to drag the trees down from the hills he could work longer than the others. He fitted in, in most ways, he just wasn't the same. For one thing he'd always had a talent for exploitation. They were blessed with few possessions and, as a consequence, did not have much of a hankering for them. But if one of his siblings had two things they cherished, Courtney could talk them out of both of them.

He was going to make a journey, he just hadn't decided where to, or how.

Chapter Sixteen

"Have another coffee. Just knock it back."

Arthur hadn't even made back to the office when he received a phone call from Eddie's manager. He topped the cup up with more coffee.

"Another mouthful or two."

It was a new tack for Arthur. The first half of Eddie B's second gig had not gone well. When Eddie began to sing his platinum selling record *I'm Wasted*, it was clear that he was the eponymous writer of the song, and very much wasted. So wasted that the audience hadn't responded well, although they liked their rock stars to be dissolute, they were less keen after they'd forked out fifty quid for a ticket.

"A whisky would be better, Arthur."

"Of course, of course, but after the gig. Just another mouthful of water. Perhaps if you get up and walk around a bit."

Much as the word 'gig' was new to Arthur's vocabulary, so was the experience of sobering people up. He had a feeling he was going to be doing much of both.

"Where's my Cunt," Eddie asked.

"I think he left when you said fuck off cunt," Arthur observed.

"Did he? Did he do that? He did?"

"Yes, I believe so."

"What a cunt."

Arthur was not cut out for nursing and, five minutes into his first attempt, he was contemplating killing Eddie. But there was money involved. This was business.

"But," Arthur said, "Your Cunt did say you wouldn't get the money unless you finished the tour. Give me that."

Somehow, from nowhere, Eddie had found a rather fine cut glass tumbler filled with whisky. He knew he'd left it somewhere.

Arthur grabbed the glass, and then looked for somewhere to put it. Nowhere was out of Eddie's reach, so he knocked it back himself. He was going to have to change tack.

"I'll tell you what, Eddie, shall we go on a proper old fashioned bender?"

"Brilliant Arthur, that's what I've been saying. Where's that glass?"

"But how about if we start in forty-five minutes."

"Forty-five minutes?" Eddie asked, confused.

"Yes. That's, like, after your next set," Arthur said, injecting the word 'like' in a sentence for the first time. He hoped that wouldn't become a habit as well, but that it would convey the correct nuance to communicate the message.

Eddie's face fell, but he could just about see himself getting through forty-five minutes. The audience had begun to chant.

"I'm wasted! I'm wasted! I'm wasted!"

Arthur sincerely hoped they were, as Eddie got uncertainly to his feet and weaved a very precarious route to the stage. The other musicians filed in behind him. Eddie's music wasn't very demanding, and Eddie wasn't big on communication. The musicians had to wait to hear the first gravelly word of the song that Eddie had randomly chosen to sing, and then they fell in behind him. Eddie had a habit of repeating songs he'd already sung, having forgotten the experience almost immediately.

"I'm wasted," he began. It helped that the lyrics were, at best, limited, and that all the audience knew them.

"I'm wasted," they screamed. They screamed so loudly that Eddie, who was inhabiting a different space from the rest of the world, could actually hear it. It became quite a rousing, if not quite sobering, performance. Eddie got up and wandered around the stage looking for the bottles he'd hidden, but the band had removed them. Eddie wasn't big on dancing but, now he found himself upright on the stage, he thought he'd give it a go, until it was replaced by another thought.

"I'm wasted," he growled again. It didn't seem to matter when in the song. It reminded him of an eighties gig, or it could have been the nineties Dates were, like, so uncool. But it had been a big gig, and he had been on something, or more accurately he had been off his head on something. He looked at the crowd in front of him. It was the first time he'd bothered. They all looked a bit older, but sturdy enough. That was what had prompted the thought. Eddie was ready to crowd surf. He waited for the chorus this time.

"I'm wasted," Eddie screamed. He opened his arms like a bird, the kind that can actually fly. The audience began to detect the possibility that he was proposing to deviate from normal behaviour. Eddie wasn't on talking terms with normal behaviour, and was surfing a memory of glorious eighties excess, or it could have been nineties. Which ever, it was excessive. He was a rock god again.

Eddie hurled himself onto his audience.

Arthur looked uncertainly. Even with earplugs, the noise was deafening. It was a mystery to him why people would want to pay good money to be subjected to this unpleasantness. No one anticipated the sixty-one year old deliberately throwing himself off the stage and, as the audience weren't in the first flush of youth themselves, they weren't quick to react. But they didn't need to, as Eddie had thrown himself at the only hole in the crowd. He hit the floor with quite a smack.

"Oh shit, man," a chartered accountant from Cheam said, but only Arthur had heard him.

The crowd made a bigger circle round Eddie, who lay in a crumpled and unmoving heap. The band had been instructed to continue regardless of Eddie – their money was dependent on in it

– but they could tell something was wrong. The guitarist moved to the edge of the stage and looked down. No movement, nothing. He turned to the rest of the band and shrugged. They were all rather tired, as they'd had a gig at a Bar mitzvah that afternoon. Several minutes passed, by which time Arthur had made his way through the crowd to Eddie. He wasn't moving. He didn't seem to be breathing. He looked up at the guitarist, and made a cutting gesture with his hand and neck. He was going to have to get an ambulance. An absolute silence fell. The audience looked on dumbstruck. And then from no where, a growl emerged from under the crumpled heap that was Eddie. But within a beat it was loud and clear.

"I'm wasted," Eddie screamed and the gig continued.

Chapter Seventeen

Arthur's leg had started hurting again, acting in concert with the pain in his face, and the sinking feeling in his stomach, that was telling him that everything was going shit-shaped in his life. It had taken quite some time to steer the car to the hospital, and much longer to explain Rogerman. But that was something Arthur had some practice at. The immediate prognosis had been death by natural causes, which was aided by Rogerman's age. By the time they had arrived at the hospital, Arthur's former chauffeur had begun to release his grip on the wheel. He'd fitted rather neatly into a wheel chair, until a doctor had stated the obvious and declared him dead. Fortunately the hospital was understaffed, and Rogerman's unusual entry into the building went unnoticed.

Arthur was back in the office and feeling determined. He'd bought every newspaper and scoured them all for news of the murder of a top Hollywood star. He looked through them twice. Then he checked the internet. Nothing. Either Arthur hadn't killed him – it was hard to tell what contact the shovel had made – or they had yet to discover him. But that was strange, given the wail of police sirens at the time. At least the Rolls hadn't been parked close. Arthur concluded that there was little to connect him to the murder except Brayman. And he was doing his best to do something about that.

"Jean!"

Jean had been reading *Fifty Shades of Grey*. Given her recent incarceration for strapping down and raping a very unwilling victim, this was not a good thing. Her period away had been shocking, and with it she had packed away her lustful feelings. Getting them out again was a very bad idea.

"Jean!"

She decided that this time round she would pay for it. But she had no illusions about herself, and had doubts as to whether she could find someone who would be prepared to, and if they were, whether she could afford it. It wouldn't be cheap.

"Jean!"

But because she didn't conform to the world's perception of beauty, didn't mean that she should be denied the sensual pleasures that were available to others. This bloody book was going to drive her crazy.

"Fucking hell, Jean. What's the matter with you?"

Arthur had been forced to get himself to his feet and walk to the neighbouring office. It was bloody inconvenient.

"Sorry, Arthur," Jean said.

Arthur had never heard her apologise, and was a little taken back.

"Right, whatever. Lunch. Who?"

"Clivert."

"Clivert? I thought he was in a coma."

Jean sighed. She was fairly sure she'd mentioned it to Arthur, but perhaps she hadn't.

"No, he's out now. Apparently a full recovery. That's why I thought a good lunch might be good for him."

Arthur raised his eyes. Whatever else he thought about Jean, he had to admit that she was a bloody good secretary.

"Where?"

"The Pig Farm."

"Jean, my dear, you are a genius."

Jean blushed, which, along with the fifty shades of lust she was experiencing, brought her back into dangerous territory. Arthur didn't notice. He had a new spring in his step. It was a feeling in his bones, at least those that didn't ache, that his luck was set to change. The Pig Farm was inspired. A restaurant that eschewed vegetables and embraced the fattiest and most unhealthy parts of the pig. Genius.

"Arthur?"

"Yes, my dear?"

My dear, Jean thought, nobody had called her that before.

"You have a new chauffeur. He's collecting the Rolls this morning. I've arranged for him to take you to the restaurant."

Jean was rather proud of herself. She'd phoned agencies and thought about placing an advertisement in the local paper, and then she remembered a conversation she'd had with Rogerman. She'd not talked that much to Rogerman. He had not been a talkative man, but every now and again she'd make him a coffee. It transpired that Rogerman had not been fond of his wife and nor, she remembered, his son. But his son held a driving licence and there was something fitting about him entering the organisation. It was the kind of business that favoured tradition.

"Wonderful," Arthur said with real warmth. The day was definitely getting better, if only Clivert could crown it was a monstrous and final coronary. He glowed at the thought. There was a buzzing noise.

"It appears," Jean said with a scatter-toothed smile, "he's here."

"Excellent."

"Oh, and by the way, the chauffeur's name is Rogerman."

"I beg your pardon?"

"Rogerman had a son in need of work. He can drive and he is the same suit size as his father."

Jean had barely met the new Rogerman. He seemed young, but he showed her some respect, and that was a step in the right direction.

"How very convenient." Arthur was grateful he wouldn't have to go through the process of learning a new name.

"Tell him I'm on my way down."

Arthur moved as if on top form, galvanised by a feeling of well being. This was going to be a good lunch. He took long strides out of the office. His day was almost spoiled by the sight of Rogerman on the landing.

"Dear God," Arthur shouted, and then, "My God."

Rogerman junior was the spitting image of his father, but with spots. A lot of spots.

"Mr Cholmondely-Godstone thank you for giving me the opportunity to…"

Rogerman had spent all morning rehearsing a speech. Words were not really his thing, so it had been quite an effort. Fortunately Arthur cut him off, as the words were fading from his memory already.

"Not at all. The pleasure's all mine, old boy. Delighted to have another Rogerman on the team."

Rogerman beamed a gummy smile. It was indeed very kind of the firm to take him on but, to be fair, he had been clean for nearly three weeks. Apart from one small incident. They strolled amicably down the stairs and met Clivert, who was looking up hesitantly at Arthur.

"Clivert, how delightful to see you."

Arthur pumped Clivert's hand. He was a little disappointed to see that he had lost weight, but his complexion was reassuringly pallid, pockmarked and florid. Rogerman led them to the Rolls, and moments later they were ensconced in the rear, and Arthur reached for the decanter, not bothering to check the time. It was never too early. But his hand didn't quite make it. Rogerman junior's experience with cars had been mostly of the stolen variety, so it was quite a pleasure to be legally steering a car. He wasted no time. They set off at great speed, throwing Arthur back.

"Rogerman."

The car snaked along the road, the engine making itself heard for the first time in over thirty years. Rogerman also had some skill at stolen car video games. But the concentration required was total and he didn't quite register Arthur's voice. The second time he did.

"Rogerman!!"

Rogerman was not used to being addressed as Rogerman. Indeed it was fair to say that he had hardly ever been addressed at all. But it was quite demanding for him, as the Rolls was a big car with a large engine, and elderly steering. Eventually he released the throttle and slowed the car down. Rogerman had broken out in a sweat. But he knew where the restaurant was, since he'd been a regular guest at the nearby magistrate court.

After a while he decided to augment the driving experience with some music. He knew it wouldn't be to Arthur's taste, but he had headphones for that.

Despite the reduced pace they arrived at the restaurant earlier than Arthur had anticipated. He waited for Rogerman to open the door.

"Rogerman."

"Rogerman!"

The Def Leppard blasting through Rogerman's headphones had soothed him, but made communication difficult. Arthur was determined not to let it upset him, and opened the door himself. He'd speak to the boy later.

"This way, old boy."

Arthur hadn't noticed a woman standing outside the restaurant and collision was inevitable.

"I'm so sorry," he muttered, with actual charm.

"Arthur?"

"Sophie?"

Chapter Eighteen

It had been another bad morning for Sophie, although nowhere near as bad as the previous evening. It was an evening which had started inauspiciously.

"Sophie, you need to get out," her friend Rachel had told her.

"I'm fine."

"No, you're not."

And when she thought about it, it was true. She wasn't fine. Ever since she'd let her house to that actor and moved into the family home, she was definitely not fine. She loved her house, and never felt comfortable in the large, rambling and very tatty house. And living in it had curtailed her social life. Or, put another way, nuns have a greater chance of getting laid. Every step out of the house provoked an inquisition. Despite the size of the house, it proved almost impossible to slip out unnoticed. And even though she was a grown adult, with a child of her own, the family treated her like a child. All in all, it was agony.

"Let's just nip down to the pub."

Her friend Rachel was not really a nip-down-to-the-pub kind of girl. She was more a wild who-knows-where-the-evening-might-go kind of girl. But the alternative was another night in.

"Hell, why not."

The house sat on the edge of the village, whose name it bore, and the land around it stretched almost to the neighbouring town. Luckily the pub wasn't too far away, but the pub Rachel wanted to go to was the other side of the village, closer to where Sophie used to live.

"Which pub?"

"The Anchor?"

Sophie knew that Rachel would suggest it, but at least she wasn't likely to come across any of her family.

"It's a bit of a trek," Sophie pointed out nonetheless.

"We might see Rocky Deep."

Even though she'd let her house to Rocky, the agent had carried out all the negotiations, and she'd yet to meet him. She wasn't a Rocky Deep kind of girl, either. The night was cool, but warm enough to make the walk not unpleasant.

"You need to move out of this old wreck," Rachel said.

"God, don't I know it, but it's saving me a fortune."

"The cheese business still not good?"

"Not great," Sophie said.

"Even after Arthur Chum-Wotsit made a visit?"

"Well, it all helps, but I don't think there's a fortune in cheese any more."

"No, but there's a fortune in Arthur," Rachel pointed out, returning to the point she was hell-bent on making. They walked through to the other end of the village, and eventually through the pub doors. The pub was old and traditional, and she knew quite a few people there, mostly on nodding terms, which was as far as she wished to know them.

"Okay," Rachel said, and cast her eyes around the pub. It had nooks and crannies, so a thorough view would have taken some time, but it wasn't necessary. There was a new star shimmering in the corner, surrounded by a coterie of admirers. They ordered their drinks and stood back and looked. But Rachel wasn't a standing back and looking kind of girl.

"Let's say hello to him," Rachel said, as Sophie knew she would.

Rocky was enjoying himself. It wasn't because it might be the kind of evening that would end with some horizontal action. Rocky wasn't a horizontal-action kind of guy. But he was gifted with an enormous ego, and there was nothing better than an evening having the hungry beast fed. He'd managed to turn a PR disaster round into a moment of vigilante-style heroism.

"Sometimes," he said, "you gotta stand up and be counted."

He chose not to mention that when the blade of the shovel had come slicing through the air, he had fainted. It was, he had reasoned to himself, very frightening. He hadn't mentioned shitting himself either. It wasn't quite standing up and being counted in the conventional sense.

"How many were there?" an adoring face asked.

Rocky turned and cast his fully-watted smile at the adoring face, who blushed as if in response to the heat. She couldn't wait to tell them all at the office.

"Three, maybe four."

His small, but carefully selected gender-specific audience made an unconscious 'arrh'.

"And they were armed?"

Rocky shrugged in casual acknowledgement, but he knew the power of details.

"Pump action shot gun."

He couldn't stop himself demonstrating the action with a few clicking noises.

"And you with just a shovel?"

Rocky shrugged with the casualness of an ordinary citizen just doing his best. Rachel and Sophie had moved close enough to overhear.

"Oh for God's sake," Sophie muttered. If she were to write a list, a very long list, of all the things she didn't need, it would feature an egotistical male. She'd had more than her fair share. A positive deluge of the bastards.

"Yeah, but look at those shoulders." Rachel observed.

The shoulders that Rocky had just shrugged were admirable for their width, but she wasn't sure about the rest. Rachel, however, was clear on the matter.

"I'm going to have him."

Rachel was tall and striking and generally got what she wanted.

"Oh for God's sake," Sophie muttered, but this time at Rachel.

"Come on."

"Oh for God's sake," Sophie muttered again, but she wasn't sure at who or what.

Rocky saw them coming and threw them a welcoming smile. He was rather pleased by the way he'd turned the story round simply by playing the opposite character.

"He just shit himself." He shrugged those shoulders again.

The coterie were in awe at this highly be-shouldered man, who could wield a shovel against a man with a pump-action shotgun, and induce the latter to shit himself. It was story that couldn't take too much scrutiny.

"Oh for God's sake," Sophie muttered.

This time Rocky heard it, but pretended not to. He could turn any woman. He just needed to fire one of his charm missiles.

"Hi, gorgeous," Rocky said to them. Gorgeousness was something of a criteria for entry into his coterie.

"Oh for God's sake," Rachel muttered. He was much shorter than he looked on the screen, and sort of smarmy. She'd met a number of actors, who had elicited the same response in her. She shouldn't have been surprised. She looked him over, and had to admit that in an obvious film-starry way, he was good looking. And while no rugby player, the physique had been clearly honed. He just seemed slightly phoney. But all the same, he'd be quite a scalp, a notch on her bedpost.

"Hi," Sophie said calmly. While Rachel saw one thing, Sophie, whose judgement with men was never anything less than very poor, saw something else. There was, she thought, something human about him.

"Get you a drink?"

Rocky liked to drop a few words from sentences while still preserving the essence. Rachel cacked a little, while Sophie held up her drink.

"S'not a drink."

The white wine and soda was fizzing gently in her glass, when Rocky grabbed it and hurled it to the floor. It was the kind of big gesture that his scriptwriters favoured. He nodded at the barman, who produced something with Jack Daniels in it.

"S'drink."

Rachel watched in stunned amazement as Sophie smiled. There were many things that were beginning to make sense to her about Sophie and men. Sophie hated pretty much all hard liquor, but she took a sip. It was better than she'd expected. Arthur used to drink the stuff all the time, she remembered with something closer to disdain than nostalgia.

"S'what you doing?"

"Oh for God's sake," Rachel muttered. She couldn't think of a more asinine question. Rocky and Sophie didn't seem to notice. Rachel was deciding whether she should guide the ship, as it was surely heading for the rocks, or abandon it altogether. Rocky was rich and successful and he had those shoulders but, she thought, yuk. He definitely looked better from the other side of the pub, Rachel thought, or better still from the comfortable distance of a television screen. Close-up was different, and Rachel realised that her much-hacked bedpost was in no danger of further notches.

"It's, like, a role that, like, demands, you know, great concentration."

It was a line Rocky had delivered many times, so it would have been reasonable to assume he might have mastered it by now. Sophie didn't seem to notice that Rocky's facility for words wasn't quite the same without a team of scriptwriters to supply them. She even quite liked the sunglasses. He seemed to radiate something. It was probably just familiarity, but Sophie didn't seem to notice.

"Wow," Sophie said, equally bereft of words. Rachel wasn't there to witness them, as she'd taken the abandon ship option. She knew if she stayed she'd upset Sophie, and that wasn't the object of the evening. If Sophie wanted the film star, she could have him.

"Yeah," Rocky said, to fill the dead air that frequently came from saying almost nothing of value. But Rocky was changing his game plan. The ego beast had been fed, fed to bursting. Now it was the turn of the little beast. He didn't deploy it very often, blessed as he was with a minimal libido, but this girl, he thought, was, like, different. He removed his sunglasses.

"Hey, wow," Sophie said, entirely forgetting the years she had spent at the country's finest university. His eyes did their piercing thing. They pierced so deeply, Sophie entirely forgot to mention that he was staying in her house. Rocky moved aside and put his other admirers in the shade, politely dispensing with them, and turning back to Sophie on whom he was now going to direct the full floodlight.

"Shall we, like, make tracks?"

It wasn't clear whether this was an invitation. If it was, he could make a possible rejection seem like a misunderstanding. But Sophie wasn't attuned to nuance, and followed him straight out of the pub into the cold night air. At least it was closer to her house than the rambling manor house.

"Hey, great," Rocky said by way of acknowledgement that they were headed in the same direction, in every sense. Rocky grabbed her hand, and when she turned, he realised that a kiss would be easier to deploy than a smart one-liner. It would have been a good time for Sophie to mention that he was staying in her house. But she didn't.

"Hey, great," Rocky said, once the kiss was adequately concluded, and it seemed appropriate to say something. They pottered in each other's arms down the quiet lane to the house. This would have been a good time for Sophie to have mentioned her house. But she didn't. She could have said something when they tumbled through the front door that could be described as both his and hers. But their tongues were entwined, which made it difficult.

"You're gorgeous," he said, just as he had in *African Adventure*. It was kind of a signature line. Sophie felt as gorgeous as the actress he had delivered the line to. He fired out the halogen smile and piercing gaze all at once. It was almost too much for to bear. But the line had put him off a little, as it reminded him of the actress he'd delivered the line to. He tried not to think of Bella Rae, as it seemed to wither his manhood. And his manhood was on very good form. It wasn't something he could ordinarily rely on, but today it was stretched to almost average.

Rocky threw open the door in the way that is much easier if you're renting. She would have commented, but he was shedding clothes with an urgency that would have befitted one of his finest romantic comedies. It was more luck than skill on his part, but he was feeling good about the evening.

"Actually," Sophie said, "this is my house." She said it as if they were to share it for the rest of their passion-filled lives. Sophie's timing wasn't good

"I beg your pardon?" Rocky said, dropping into a speech pattern from earlier in his life.

"My house," she said simply, and adopting the abbreviated sentence-thing that Rocky had been so enamoured of.

"You're the Sophie who lives here?"

Rocky pictured a large man wielding a shovel with some skill. It made his knees go weak and his penis retreat. What kind of trouble was this girl in? There was an uncertain feeling in his bowels.

"Yeah, I let it out."

Sophie could sense something wasn't right. The eyes that had pierced, now looked popped and manic, and a button mushroom had appeared in place of his almost average tumescence. Please, she thought, not another humiliation. Rocky was thinking the same thought. The strength of his imagination was the key to his talents as an actor, and he didn't want to get mixed up with the kind of person who had enemies who burst out of sheds. There was no question about it. He was going to shit himself.

"Go! Out!" he wailed.

He gave her a gentle push and she staggered out of the house and into the night almost completely naked, and wailing the wail of someone who had been humiliated too many times in her life. It was pitch black and she'd already lost her knickers. Getting the rest of her clothes on wasn't easy. The walk back to the family house was a long one and featured a stumble, when the heel of her shoe broke. And then a tumble into a ditch, face-first. Her fall was broken by a thick bed of stinging nettles. She was still itching the following morning. And that was the morning she had to get on the train and visit The Pig Farm to sell some cheese. She'd hoped that Derek, the owner, was going to ask her out, she was sure he was interested. But her face looked like a pepperoni pizza.

Chapter Nineteen

"Arthur?"

Sophie couldn't believe it. On the train ride her face had returned to its former shape, and a few judicious dabs of concealer had done most of what the label implied. She had pressed all recent experiences with a Hollywood actor into the most distant recesses of her brain, and she had attempted to reassure herself that she was an attractive, passionate woman. It was the self-esteem rebuilding process that Rachel normally helped her with, but today she was doing a very creditable job all on her own. She tried not to mutter out loud, and disturb the other passengers. Instead she internalised her self-worth. By the time the train had arrived in London, she was almost back on form. She was feeling good. Well, perhaps not good, but certainly okay, which was quite an achievement. And then she bumped into Arthur.

"Sophie?"

Arthur was feeling on good form, albeit a little dizzy from the erratic drive, but good. Clivert was wheezing already. And he had decided, while Clivert was telling him something, that he was going to start afresh and find himself a fertile woman. Once he'd arrived at that thought, it prompted a brief examination into the other qualities he would like his fertile woman to possess. The interruption had halted his thoughts and he'd only arrived at servile.

"Mr Cholmondley-Godstone, how delightful to see you." Derek the owner had suddenly appeared from nowhere. And he wasn't lying. It really was delightful to see Arthur, who held the record for the highest spend in his fine restaurant. He was also a man who appreciated fine, fatty meat while eschewing the effete vegetarian. He hadn't noticed Sophie.

"Thank you." Arthur pumped his hand enthusiastically, thankful that it had given him a brief excuse not to confront the Sophie problem. He turned and found that Sophie had turned and was marching in the opposite direction. She was muttering something maniacally. And Arthur had heard it.

"This way," Derek said with a smile he couldn't make any bigger.

Arthur and Clivert snaked their way into the restaurant, and towards Arthur's favourite table, but Arthur stopped.

"This table would be nice."

It was a sizeable restaurant, perched on a corner and with large windows on either flank. This table gave Arthur the best view along the road. He really did want to talk to Sophie. If they got back together it would resolve so many issues, and there would be plenty of opportunities for him to live as he liked to when he was away.

"Are you sure, Mr Cholmondley-Godstone?" Derek's smile faded as panic spread across his face. They were running a sweepstake on this lunch. This was a perfectly reasonable table, in most regards it was the same as the other. It certainly had the same number of legs, and was the same shape and size, but it wasn't the best. And Mr Cholmondley-Godstone only every wanted the best.

"Absolutely, a little change won't do any harm," Arthur reassured him. But Derek wasn't reassured, he didn't want Arthur to change any of his habits. A diversion away from the best was a worrying one.

"Aperitif?" Derek asked, his face now mainly featuring anxiety.

"Excellent." Derek's relief was palpable. But Arthur's mind was elsewhere. He'd heard Sophie mutter something about herpes. There were a number of swear words that preceded it, but then she'd said something else. It was a name. It sounded like an actor's name, but how could she know?

Derek was hovering, one shoulder tilted at its most obsequious. He was hoping that Arthur would plump for the usual. It was fantastically expensive and Derek had composed it himself. It involved the fat from the pig, fermented with various herbs and spices and then, for good measure, mixed with pure alcohol. And topped off with a humorous name. But Arthur didn't seem quite there, as if he might need prompting.

"Porky Deep?"

Derek was surprised to find Arthur wheezing. Arthur couldn't believe it. Surely the only person that knew that he had murdered that Rocky Deep actor was Brayman? Now everyone seemed to know. It wasn't entirely his fault. He only meant to kill the bloody Dobermans.

"The aperitif?" Derek reminded him.

"Of course, of course."

Arthur's mind switched back, and he remembered the house special aperitif. He kicked himself for being so easily distracted. Arthur looked anxiously along the street, and then turned to the matter at hand.

"You are looking in most magnificent health. You really are looking bloody good, old chap."

Clivert blushed, but the florid nature of his complexion made it difficult to tell. It was the best it was ever going to look.

"Thank you, Arthur. It's so very kind of you to say so."

Arthur smiled approvingly at his lunch partner, and settled into more usual form. He was fairly certain he'd delivered the speech to Clivert before, but saw no harm in setting the lunch off in the right direction and repeating it.

"There is an art to life. Life is not about going to work and paying bills. It is not about loyalty to a cause or a people. It is not about what others think or do. It is about living, and living is seeing, doing, feeling, tasting and not denying. And passion. Seeing everything the world has to offer, enjoying everything there is to taste and savour, and exploiting every sense you've been blessed with. Living is about the best, the best of everything. And now you are not just my client, but my friend, and together we must explore these things."

Clivert knew the speech word for word, but loved watching it dance off Arthur's lips, particularly the bit about being his friend. Arthur had begun to fill his day. He thought about him when he woke up, and when he went to bed. And most of the time in between.

Chapter Twenty

"You have got to be kidding me," Rachel said, but Sophie wasn't sure which revelation she was referring to.

"Arthur Choldmondely-Whatever," Rachel confirmed.

Sophie sat in a pub. It gave her a view of the restaurant. She'd come all the way to London, and she wasn't going to go back without flogging some cheese. God, she hated cheese. But she couldn't enter the restaurant with Arthur there. The only question was, how long would lunch take? And why did Arthur have to be there? It seemed like one coincidence too many, as Sophie had never considered that they were united by the unhealthiness of their products. She looked anxiously at her watch: it was barely twelve thirty. There was a nagging thought in the back of her mind to do with lunch and Arthur, but she left it there. She'd phoned Rachel instead. Rachel had already driven to town. There were some essentials that needed to be shopped for, and Rachel intended to hunt them down like wildlife in the bush.

"I'll be there in about an hour."

That left Sophie alone with just a gin and tonic, and her thoughts. They were very angry thoughts that weren't made any less angry by the second gin and tonic, which was also larger than the first. And no sign of movement from the restaurant. There were a few people wandering in, and a few staggered out, but none were Arthur shaped. She couldn't face Arthur with his client and with Derek. Arthur would blow her chances with Derek, and vice versa. Why was everything so difficult?

She was fairly sure Derek hadn't noticed her, and she had phoned to say she would be late, very late. For a while she wondered if she would be late enough to prompt a dinner invitation. That forced her to think of herself and Derek. She tried to imagine her friends saying 'Sophie and Derek.' It was a struggle. She wished he was called something else. Anything would do. 'Sophie and Luigi,' 'Sophie and Sebastian,' 'Sophie and Sam.' Somehow 'Sophie and Derek' wasn't doing it for her. Fortunately a car rolled up in front of the pub. The long legs of Rachel threaded their way out of the car and into the pub.

"Gin and tonic?" Sophie volunteered, with more than a hint of a slur.

"I'll get them," Rachel said quickly.

Rachel was not one to let normal conventions like drinking and driving stand in her way, but she had a sense that the situation required at least one of them to be sober. She'd had a hasty look in the restaurant and was surprised to see the solid form of Arthur dominating the place, so at least it wasn't a wild goose chase. She decided to start by mentioning it to Sophie.

"He's in there. I saw him. So at least it isn't a wild goose chase."

"Is that what it is?" Sophie asked.

Rachel couldn't tell at this stage what it was, and made the mistake of saying exactly what was in her head.

"It's more about fleecing the golden goose."

"What?" Sophie asked with obvious irritation, but Rachel didn't notice and carried on with the analogy.

"He's laid his golden egg. Well, more his seed, really."

"What?" Sophie said, with a level of distaste that was sufficient to register with Rachel, who opted for a U-turn.

"I mean, you're the golden egg. The prize."

This didn't help, and was clearly still going in the same direction. Rachel tried again.

"Maybe you and Arthur are just destined."

It was a hopeless line, Rachel thought, completely unconvincing, but Sophie bought it nonetheless.

Sophie smiled. The annoying part was that she believed in destiny, in a bigger picture. As if it were no coincidence that she should bump into Arthur. There was someone upstairs moving the pieces, and they'd shifted them so that Sophie would collide with Arthur. Rachel sat down.

"'Sophie and Arthur' sounds all right, doesn't it?"

Rachel knew there would be few shopping scalps taken that day. She clearly had a lot of work to do.

Chapter Twenty-One

Arthur was feeling better again. Although it was stretching the definition of an aperitif when you have five of them, he felt very much better. For a moment Clivert had stopped talking. It had been quite a long impassioned speech, which hadn't quite captured all of Arthur's attention.

"Splendid, old boy."

Arthur didn't notice Clivert's face fall, as he had just told the tragic story of the death of his mother and confessed to the only person in the world that he was, as his father had always suspected, a homosexual.

"I'm getting quite an appetite, how about you?"

Clivert nodded enthusiastically. Everything about Arthur made him enthusiastic. He wandered if the word 'appetite' was code for something. He was so new to this business, that he might have missed an undertone. Or it could be an overtone. Whatever it was, Clivert hoped that it might lead somewhere. Somewhere exciting. His doctor had told him to do a number of things, and here he was ignoring them all. He was so enthusiastic he chose to ignore those pains in his chest that sounded like vagina, which made him laugh as that was the very last thing he was interested in.

"The boar's fat sounds delicious."

Clivert couldn't agree more. Now that he was on his own, so to speak, as in no longer requiring the approval of his parents, he had stepped out a little. That morning he'd bought a pink shirt and left his top lip unshaven. It wasn't much, but it was a start.

"And for the wine…"

Arthur scoured the wine list and then, unusually, he looked at the column with the prices and said, "The Chateau Buzet." He couldn't remember ever drinking a cheap wine, he must have done so at sometime in his life, but he couldn't remember when. But four million pounds was a lot to shave off his expenses. He was going to have to start making compromises

"The Chateau Buzet." he repeated, as the order had appeared to have gone unnoticed.

Derek looked at him as if he had been slapped in the face. The Buzay? What was the man thinking?

"I'm sorry, I don't think I heard that quite right."

"The Chateau Buzet."

Inside Derek was saying, "Chateau-fucking-Buzet?" But it came out as "Right away." Albeit with a choke. He felt as if he would never be able to smile so widely again. He plodded to the back of the restaurant.

"May I say," Arthur ventured, "you're looking splendid."

Clivert blushed all the way to his pink shirt and a bit beyond. He was hoping that this time he would have the courage to tell Arthur how much he loved him. Another drink might help.

Arthur beamed widely at Clivert, oblivious to where Clivert's mind was going, and not hearing a single word the florid little man was uttering. It was more of a monologue. And there were things on Arthur's mind. Unusually for Arthur, he chose to air them. Ordinarily he was more than capable of sustaining a four hour lunch without saying anything of any depth, meaning or purpose. But there were things chewing at him.

"You don't have children, do you, old boy?"

Clivert face dropped. He was horrified at the distinctly heterosexual turn the conversation was taking. Children? What was he thinking? Was this a new undertone? Was Arthur testing him? Clivert was capable of convincing himself that it was a good sign. But Arthur didn't bother to wait for a response, he wasn't that interested anyway.

"You see, sometimes you have to look at life and wonder what it's all about, don't you think?"

Clivert had digested every syllable of Arthur's speech regarding life, and now he was offering a different view, which if he wasn't mistaken, involved having children. But Clivert's mind took a further leap. Perhaps it was a further test, perhaps Arthur wanted to adopt, like Elton John. But Arthur never found out what Clivert thought, and proceeded with what was on his mind.

"You see there is this woman, Sophie."

The words were like a hammer blow to Clivert's heart. He was getting chest pains, and they hadn't even got to the boar's fat. How could this be a test? Was Arthur actually trying to tell him something? Clivert had rehearsed his speech all morning. It was about the best in life. And Arthur was the best.

"A woman?" Clivert managed to say.

"Yes. Sophie."

Who, Clivert thought, is bloody Sophie? And why does she have to intrude on a conversation that was going so well?

"Anyway, Sophie," Arthur repeated, having almost noticed that something wasn't quite right with Clivert. Arthur was back in dangerous territory, and he had no idea how he got there. But what had Sophie been doing at the restaurant?

"I mean, what was Sophie doing here?"

As far as Clivert could tell, Sophie was getting in the way of one of the most important moments in his life. He had never declared love before.

"Do you think the child is mine?"

Clivert spluttered. He couldn't recall the mention of a child. Arthur looked at him for a moment, and then realised he had tumbled off the rails. It coincided with Derek's arrival with the wine. Arthur looked at the label and looked horrified.

"Chateau-fucking-Buzet? What were you thinking, man?"

Derek didn't want to say what he was thinking, but now he was smiling on the inside. A moment later he returned with the seventeen percent treacle-thick wine that was almost impossible to shift to anyone else, and carried an enormous price tag. Arthur wasn't going to get through this moment without some help.

Chapter Twenty-Two

Rachel was trying to think of the best way to express it.
"I mean, what the fuck were you thinking?" probably wasn't it.

"You saw his shoulders." It wasn't the most spirited defence of her night with Rocky Deep, although Sophie got to see a lot more of him than just his shoulders. Not that there was much more.

Rachel was going to go further, but sensed that Sophie was looking too fragile for another assault. She needed to get a good look at this Derek to make sure that Sophie wasn't going to make any further foolish mistakes.

"But Arthur Chum-Wotsit, what were you thinking?"

Sophie wasn't sure what she was thinking. It was the lack of thought with Arthur and Rocky that had got her where she was, which wasn't a very good place.

"That's why I'm waiting here."

Her mind was full of so many conflicting thoughts. When she saw Arthur there were two, the one she expressed, which involved herpes, and the other one she'd had difficulty admitting to herself.

"Yes, but why are you waiting here?"

Rachel was beginning to find her a little exasperating. Rachel didn't struggle much with conflicting issues, which made it harder to understand other people.

"I'm waiting for Arthur to leave."

It was all prompted by that strange little moment when Arthur seemed to express joy at the possibility of parenthood. She'd felt guilty too. Perhaps she should have told him at the time. But she was still sore emotionally and otherwise from the herpes, and he'd disappeared. He had a habit of disappearing.

"Why are you waiting for Arthur to leave?"

Rachel was not patient by nature, and if she wanted a man she'd walk straight through the door and grab him, probably by the balls.

"Why?"

Sophie had much to explain, and not just to Arthur, but decided to fall back on the get-her-out-of-a spot phrase.

"It's complicated."

Nothing was complicated to Rachel. And now was the moment to express it.

"If you want Arthur, don't skulk in here. Go inside the restaurant and grab him."

Sophie eyes dilated in panic. That was way too complicated, not least with the restaurant owner.

"But what about Derek?"

"What about Derek? Do you want him more than Arthur?"

Sophie fidgeted with the beer mat, which suddenly seemed like her best friend. It certainly wasn't telling her to march in and make a fool of herself. The Rocky Deep scars were still raw, literally, as she'd lost her knickers and she'd had to use a mirror to inspect some of her more sensitive areas. The nettles had been merciless.

Rachel looked down at the graveyard of empty glasses.

"And how long have you been here?"

It had been some time, but Sophie's answer was interrupted by the wail of an ambulance which came to a halt outside the restaurant. They looked at the flurry of activity with interest. Two paramedics jumped out and then ran back for a stretcher. There was a lot of shouting, most of it from Derek, as the bill had yet to be paid.

"That's Derek?" Rachel asked with horror.

"Yes, that's Derek."

In Derek's defence, he was not looking at his best. He had brought out some of his most coveted cognac. He kept it locked in a safe for good reason.

"Oh dear," Rachel muttered.

Sophie sensed it was more a response to Derek's appearance, rather than any possible tragedy that they were witnessing. A moment later two paramedics emerged struggling with the weight of a large body. They could hear crying. Loud fits of sobbing were coming from a man in a pink shirt.

"Isn't that – "Rachel asked.

The immobile body of Arthur was heaved into the back of the ambulance. Clivert explained that he was very much close family and was let in with him.

"Arthur. It's Arthur."

Sometimes it takes a knock on the head to see the light, and Sophie was shocked enough to find she was feeling something that wasn't jubilation. It was the very opposite of jubilation, much like Derek, despite having shifted the most expensive bottles of alcohol-based beverage he possessed.

"The thing is," Sophie said, unaware of the tears that were flowing freely down her face.

"The thing is…" She was so wrapped up in emotion she couldn't bring herself to say what the thing was.

"The thing is," she tried again, now moving towards sobs. They were sobs of what could have been, as if she'd entirely forgotten about the herpes.

"What is the thing?" Rachel asked with undisguised irritation.

"The thing is, it's Arthur."

"Yes, I can see that. Remember Arthur and the herpes?" Rachel was realising that she was going to have to stop being so kind, for Sophie's sake.

"No, you don't understand. It's Arthur."

"Yes, Arthur, the bastard," Rachel reminded her loudly, silencing the pub.

The word bastard made Sophie sob all the more.

"No, you don't understand."

But Rachel did and told her.

"You are only attracted to pathological bastards."

And then Sophie said it. It was the thing she had always refused to say. The secret she'd always kept.

"Arthur is the father."

Chapter Twenty-Three

Arthur's dreams were serene and pleasant, or they would have been were they not continuously punctuated by some noisy sobbing. It had started in the ambulance and showed no signs of abating now that they were in the hospital. He was picturing a warm place, and for some reason there was a pair of Labradors at his feet. But this wasn't the kind of dream that required too much close examination, which is why he didn't worry about the rough stubble that was brushing his cheek. He didn't remember Sophie's kiss that way.

"Arthur."

Nor did he recall her uttering his name with such passion but, he reminded himself, this was a dream. The urgent touching was strange too. He was drifting on the edge of consciousness, and a distant part of his mind was trying to do some piecing together. It was asking questions like what the hell happened. It was very strange.

"Arthur."

As was the broken voice. Arthur knew many things about Sophie and, right at the moment, he could recall the line of her neck, the length of her fingers, the way her waist pinched in, emphasising her womanly figure. The fall of her breasts, and even the general size and shape of her nipples. But he couldn't for the life of him remember a broken voice.

"Arthur."

There it was again. It was annoying, as his brain had put so much effort into conjuring up such a clear image of Sophie, and this clearly wasn't her. He wondered why she'd been at the restaurant and why she'd left. A stubbly face brushed against him again. This time Arthur opened his eyes.

"Whoa!"

Clivert was straddling him. It was quite a shock as their eyes met. Neither Arthur nor Clivert knew what to do. It brought about another seizure.

"Aggghhh."

The stabbing pain ran through most of his upper body, freezing everything. Luckily for Arthur, this time it was Clivert. The nurse wasn't entirely surprised to find them locked in an embrace, as Clivert had mentioned his undying love. But it took a moment for her to realise the extent of the problem. Arthur was about to scream 'Get this bastard off me,' when Clivert collapsed and tumbled onto the floor. It was quite a hard landing. She pressed a red button and a series of bells went off summoning further help.

A moment later two pissed women entered the building. One seemed to be weaving slightly.

"Are you next of kin?" The nurse asked flatly.

"Well, not exactly," Sophie tried to explain. Rachel was still looking at her open-mouthed, as she had been for nearly forty minutes. Arthur Chum-God-Fuck the father, who'd have thought?

"I'm afraid you'll have to wait," the nurse said with something closer to sympathy and then added, "But don't worry, his boyfriend is with him."

"His what?"

The nurse had been in a same sex relationship for some while, and was very active in the union. She hated prejudice.

"His boyfriend," the nurse said slowly and clearly, and then turned to help someone else.

Sophie's mouthed moved, but no discernible speech came out. Rachel had used up her full quota of surprise, and steered Sophie out of the hospital and towards a pub, as getting truly trashed seemed the only logical solution to the problem.

"Why didn't I see? Surely I would have seen? He seemed keen to do, you know. I mean I would have known. Homosexual? No surely not. I don't believe it."

Rachel shook Sophie's shoulders.

"You have to forget him. Move on. Don't throw good money after bad."

It wasn't quite the metaphor that Rachel was after, but it seemed to do the trick.

Chapter Twenty-Four

"You have the face of a librarian, but the tits of a porn star."

It was a song Eddie was working on. And by Eddie's standards, saying it out loud was not particularly reckless behaviour. But he may have directed it at the wrong target. It was also a sentence that had arrived accidentally on his lips. Almost everything that tumbles into Eddie's mind makes it out of his mouth, and this was no exception.

"I beg your pardon?"

Eddie had taken the day off, or at least that's what he had told himself. It would imply that he had days 'on', which hadn't been the case for about thirty years. But he had decided he wanted to write songs again, and on those days his input of stimulants would be lower. Not too low that it might stifle the creative process, but even Eddie recognised that there was a stage of inebriation after which he couldn't remember the last line he uttered or snorted. It made song writing a lengthy business and, as one thought often didn't relate to another, it was also unfashionably surreal. But he'd taken the day off.

"The face of like and the tits of a thingy."

Eddie had woken early at just after eleven, and finished a bottle of brandy with his breakfast. The brandy had provided the greater calorific intake. He'd picked up a pad of paper on which he'd scrawled some lyrics. He liked to write about being a rock star. He was one, and most people weren't. He'd written down words that rhyme with star. They included 'far' and 'tar' and 'mar' and 'par', but they weren't helping. With that almost settled, there was nothing that contrasted more with a rock star, than a librarian. If he could get a chorus to work, then he might be able to hang a few notes around it, and the rest would follow. But 'par' tended to suggest golfing analogies, and that didn't work for Eddie. It had been very distracting.

"What did you say?"

Dorothy Bosumford was grappling with many issues. She was hoping to make changes in her life, but the grappling was getting in the way. Her time at university should have been the moment for this, but it left her even more confused. She had specialised in gender studies, and it had told her many things but, she was finding in the larger world, very few of them were useful. It had made her angry. Then there was the general issue of orientation. Orientation of the sexual kind. She'd watched the other students homing in on each other like horny pigeons. There were lots of cross gender and same gender liaisons, but it just served to remind Dorothy that she had orientation issues. It was most disorientating. It made her angry. And what was wrong with working in a library? It was a job she enjoyed.

"How dare you, you squalid, vulgar little old man."

Eddie had consumed enough alcohol to hospitalise most people, but he caught that line. He had wandered into the library to use the computer to help him with his song, before he continued his day off in the pub. Eddie didn't like to travel too far for his inspiration, and the library was conveniently located opposite the pub that sold cheap beer. His decision to enter the library was also influenced by the fact that the pub had yet to open. And it would help with the juxtaposition of librarian and rock star, but if he was having difficulty rhyming 'star,' 'librarian' was presenting an altogether tougher challenge. And then there was the librarian in front of him. Eddie didn't mind being called 'squalid' or 'vulgar,' but he objected to 'little' and very much objected to 'old.'

"Hey man, who are you, like, calling old?"

Dorothy Bosumford may have had the face of a librarian and the breasts of a porn star, but she was only thirty-four, despite the messages that the floral-patterned Laura Ashley dress gave off.

"You, old man. You must be a septuagenarian."

Eddie, it was true, had not worn well. It was to be expected, as most machines would have worn out if they'd been subjected to the same mileage as Eddie. But that wasn't the thought going through his head.

"Hey man, that like, rhymes with librarian."

Dorothy was filled with anger, but a non sequitur like that drew her to a halt.

"What?"

"It rhymes, like."

Dorothy would have left it there, but Eddie suddenly noticed, for the first time, that the librarian did indeed have tits like a porn star. It was quite a coincidence. They were trapped and strapped and generally being held hostage by sexual disorientation issues, but they were there. Which was more or less what Eddie chose to say.

"Hey man, those little babies are, like, bursting to get out."

Dorothy drew a very sharp breath. She was aware that her breasts appeared to have a life of their own. They certainly didn't look like they belonged to her, but she'd done her best to conceal them.

"They're, like, fighting to get out," Eddie continued, warming to the theme.

"Get out, now!" Dorothy yelled. She sang in a choir and had a surprisingly powerful voice. All the ears in the already silent library, and a few in the street, were ringing.

But Eddie's strong imagination was at work, and he began to envisage those breasts making a break for it. They were a pair of twins united in their struggle to break out and be clothed in silk and lace, and paraded for the world to see. Eddie was unable to voice this thought as Dorothy, who really had anger issues, rolled up her shirtsleeves, clenched her fist, and punched him.

Eddie went down like a sack of potatoes. It was quite a surreal experience for him, and it prompted all sorts of creative thoughts. It was as if the song was writing itself.

You've got the face of a librarian,

Hey, but I ain't no septuagenarian,

My friends say I'm so cool I could be a Rastafarian,

But girl, you've got the tits of a porn star.

But, Eddie thought, there was something not quite right with it, it wasn't quite there. By the time he made it to his feet, the police had arrived. Everything would have been fine had he not said what he always said when in trouble. He said it very loudly too.

"I'll just phone my Cunt. He'll sort it out."

The local police force had recently sent their junior officers on a course to help them deal with abusive language. And this was not acceptable. Eddie was hurled into the back of a police van and taken to the station.

Chapter Twenty-Five

"The good news, Mr Cholmondely-Godstone, is there is nothing wrong with you, or rather we can find nothing wrong with you. Heart, lungs, blood, even liver and kidneys, all in good shape."

"Great," Arthur said, ready to leave.

"But the thing is, Mr Cholmondely-Godstone, you did collapse."

"Well, never mind," Arthur said, not remotely curious as to the cause, but rather irritated by the inconvenience. He looked up at the two white-coated doctors and got up to leave.

"Just one moment," the doctor said. "We have a couple of questions." He nodded to the other doctor, who had remained silent. It was his turn to speak.

"Is there anything troubling you?"

"No," Arthur said firmly.

"You're not under any stress?"

"No."

"You're not struggling with any moral issues?"

"Eh?" Arthur said.

"The thing is, that this kind of collapse is sometimes prompted by certain things in your life you do not want to face. It can be psychosomatic."

"What?" This time Arthur didn't let the doctors stand in his way. He was getting out of there. Arthur reassured himself that he'd just had a little flutter, minor and inconsequential, and that was all that had prompted his collapse. If bloody Clivert hadn't panicked, he'd have been up and about a second later.

"Thank you for that, but I really must go," Arthur said, and gathered his things. He had nearly left the building when he met the triage nurse.

"Where are you going?" she asked him with an agenda that was clear to her, but a mystery to Arthur.

"I'm leaving."

Arthur headed for the remaining doors that separated him from freedom.

"You bastard."

It took a moment for Arthur to realise that it was directed at him, but he wasn't hanging around any longer. Clivert could stew in his own boar's fat. The nurse, however, hated those who would not admit to their true selves.

"He stood by you," she continued, hoping that her supervisor had not overheard her referring to a patient as a bastard. But this man clearly was. She had seen how heartbroken Clivert had been, and this man was walking straight out on him.

"He was there for you," she shouted.

Clivert had wailed and professed a love with such passion that it had prompted her to look at her own life, and conclude that no one would ever love her like that. He'd shown the kind of devotion she'd been looking for all her life.

"Eh?"

Arthur's body had done a fantastic job of repairing itself. His body had never failed him before, but it had taken a small stumble and now it was back up. His brain was still a beat or so behind.

"He was there for you."

Arthur's capacity for moving on was such, that he scarcely remembered Clivert mumbled words, and so the message the nurse was attempting to convey was still not clear to him.

"In your time of need."

If Arthur had thought about it, he would have been confused. He wasn't sure what had come over him. It might have been just a touch of indigestion. If they'd just left him there, he would have been fine. But Clivert had become quite hysterical. Whatever it was, he'd collapsed into the pudding, knocking the Louis XIII bottle of Cognac flying. He hadn't heard Derek screaming something about eleven grand.

"You can't walk out on your boyfriend." The nurse stood in front of him with her arms crossed over her chest. It was a protest, not just for Clivert, but for everyone. Love like that should never be ignored. Finally it clicked into place for Arthur.

"Oh," he said. He thought about pushing past her, but she made quite a formidable presence.

"No, of course," he said. "I'll be back in a minute."

The nurse relented, and Arthur was out of there. The good news was that Clivert very much wasn't. There had been some discussion that Arthur had overheard, but he hadn't listened to all of it, about Clivert not making it through the night.

Chapter Twenty-Six

Brayman had enjoyed quite an eventful day. Mandy had left that morning and, after they'd had sex for the second time, she'd suggested that they shouldn't be exclusive. The line was sandwiched between vigorous sex and noisy flurries of kisses and goodbyes. She had quite innocuously slipped it in there, so that it would be hard for him to notice, and difficult to protest too much about. And then she was out the door. She was far more vocal during sex than any other time. Brayman was beginning to question the extent of their rapport.

"Another coffee, sir?"

"Yes, please."

There was no question, Brayman was knackered. He no longer needed to go to work, which left huge gaps in the day. Arthur's suggestion had been to eat three very hearty meals, and if he was extravagant enough they'd overlap. Brayman couldn't bring himself to live like that, but had followed another suggestion of Arthur's. He'd taken up horse riding. Arthur had recommended the stables. They were very relaxed, and within a week they had him galloping through woods and rocky ravines.

Brayman had discovered quite a talent for it. He'd left Mandy's and gone straight to the stables. Fi, who ran the stable, had an appetite for life and, he discovered, for him too. He'd not had time to shower between Mandy and Fi, but Fi didn't seem to notice. They were out in the woods. It was urgent and frantic, and very exciting. When they got back to the house it was still urgent, but for Brayman slightly less exciting, as it was his fourth time in as many hours. But he surprised himself, and managed to be just a little bit frantic.

"Are you ready to order sir?"

"No, not yet. I'm waiting for someone."

Brayman had arrived at the restaurant early. He was waiting for Arthur, and not feeling in the fullest form. After he left the stables, Fi had some children to teach and her husband was due back. Brayman stopped by at the home. He hadn't told Arthur, he didn't feel it was within the spirit of Arthur's advise, but he was volunteering at an Alzheimer's home. It had been surprisingly satisfying. He and his fellow volunteers took a group, ranging in age from sixty to ninety, to lunch. He really felt he was making progress, and he found their lives fascinating. After lunch he'd given Penny, another volunteer, a lift home. She'd invited him in for a coffee, which he accepted as he was tired from the morning's activities, and a coffee was what he needed. It wasn't, he discovered, what she had in mind.

"A penny for your thoughts?"

Brayman had managed a fifth time. More than managed, he'd enjoyed it. Penny was much older than him, and he might have been in two minds about it, but she reappeared in a negligee, which was making almost no effort to disguise an astonishing body. But, bloody hell, he felt tired.

"Ahh, Arthur. How nice to see you."

It was nice for Arthur to see Brayman too. He was looking really quite delightfully knackered.

"How are you finding the freedom to live?"

Arthur was poised to give his stage two speech. He generally only gave it if his clients weren't killing themselves from the advice held in the stage one speech. Even today, Brayman looked way too healthy.

"There's nothing quite so satisfying as putting something back and making your mark. Now that you're freed from the tedious realities of everyday life, you must find your passions."

Brayman had no idea what Arthur was on about, but was grateful for the drink that was suddenly pressed into his hand. He had no recollection of anything being ordered. Arthur was a magician.

"Yes," Brayman said.

Arthur's eyes narrowed. This was not the impassioned response he'd hoped for. There were two directions he liked to take his clients. One involved supporting the troops in Afghanistan, or Syria, or wherever dangerous conflict happened to be. The closer they could get to the troops the better. The second was to find an extreme religious or philosophical belief that would enrage a psychotic group. He'd had doubts whether Brayman would embrace either. His thoughts were interrupted by his mobile phone. He looked at it curiously, and saw that it was the office. Jean wouldn't interrupt him in the course of his most critical moments at work. It must be important.

"Hello."

"Arthur, it's Jean."

"Yes," Arthur said with irritation that Jean wasn't sensitive enough to pick up on.

"It's Eddie. He needs someone to bail him out."

Eddie's manager had carried out his last big favour, after an endless succession of favours, in 1976. His secretary passed him onto Arthur. Arthur got up and moved away from Brayman.

"What did he do?"

"He attacked a librarian."

"Are they charging him?"

"Not sure. You'll have to find out."

Arthur wasn't keen on the sound of that. It wasn't his remit. Then a thought occurred to him. On the dissolute activity front, Eddie was excelling. In fact he was excelling to such a degree that he likely to kill himself before the end of the twenty gig tour, and the delivery of the money. Brayman, on the other hand, was not embracing a dissolute life in the way Arthur would have liked

"Okay, I'll go and get him."

"Oh and another thing, Arthur. He's been let out of hospital."

"What?" Arthur screamed apoplectic with rage. Why don't these people die?

"No, it's your father."

"Oh," Arthur said casually. "Was he in hospital?"

"You remember, he got hit by a bus."

Arthur didn't.

"And Clivert died," Jean added. Jean had a most interesting conversation with a rather aggressive nurse. Jean knew little of Arthur's private life, but she thought she had a sense of the man. It was rather surprising to learn that Arthur's partner had died, but more surprising to discover that that partner was a man. If those two details had raised her eyebrows, the fact that the deceased was Barry Clivert pushed them into her hairline. She wondered why he been so delighted to have lunch with Clivert.

"Oh dear," Arthur said, although he really meant excellent, but he'd become quite practised at expressing sadness at the good news of a client's demise. He had quite a spring in his step as he returned to the table. Arthur sat down and asked Brayman a question.

"Do you know Eddie B?"

"The rock star?"

"The very same."

"Of course I do. I'm a great fan."

"Excellent," Arthur beamed. Introducing the dissolute Eddie to Brayman sounded like something that could happen to two birds looking to collide with one stone.

Chapter Twenty-Seven

Eddie was beginning to enjoy himself. While the two young coppers that had brought him in had never heard of him, the desk sergeant had.

"Hey man, no problem," Eddie said as he signed autographs.

He had explained at some length what he had meant by 'my Cunt.' The use of 'my' was relevant and no insult was intended or implied, except to his manager, who, Eddie also explained at some length, was a cunt. Such a cunt that he didn't even come and pick him up, which was a shame, as it had reminded Eddie of the old days. He didn't get into trouble as often as he used to.

"Hey you guys," the desk sergeant said to the junior coppers, "you must have heard of *I'm Wasted*?"

The two looked at each other.

"It kind of rings a bell," one said.

"Rings a fucking bell?" the desk sergeant shouted. He was quite a fan.

Eddie's immediate release was inevitable. The time spent in the police station had been very sobering. Not for the trauma – it hadn't been remotely traumatic for Eddie – but because he was unable to lay his hands on a drink for three hours. He was parched.

Arthur found him shaking hands with the police officers and wishing them a good day. If he'd thought about it, Eddie would have realised that a trip to a police station made for a perfect day off. He liked to be reminded that even on his day off, he was an edgy geezer.

"Hey Arthur, great to see you, just as I'm feeling thirsty."

As they left the police station they were greeted by the flutter of press cameras. His manager may occasionally be a cunt, but he knew what was good for ticket sales.

"Hey man, thanks," Eddie said to no one in particular, and Arthur led him off, introducing Brayman on the way.

"Great to meet you." Brayman shook Eddie's hand. It was too. Brayman was a devoted fan, and spent the first hour awe-struck, and the second hour too pissed to make much of a contribution. But Eddie, who was his own greatest fan, didn't notice.

"More, gentlemen?" Arthur said.

He'd directed them to a small pub he knew well, and the first five rounds had flowed very quickly. Brayman's eagerness had segued into a puppy dog devotion, hanging on Eddie's every word.

"Yeah, that's like, great, man." He was not deterred by the discovery that some of Eddie's words were of little consequence, and the remainder were largely superfluous.

Arthur had taken them into a tiny first floor room, which was more like a private members' drinking club. And drinking was what they were going to do. Arthur could feel in his bones that this was going to be a special session. Eventually he'd feel it in some major organs, particularly those involved in filtering, but Eddie was a master.

"Chasers. We need chasers!" Eddie shouted.

The little room was a shrine to Victoriana, complete with fireplace and wallpaper, but it was made special by its equal ratio of one table to one bar. Despite there only being three of them, the barman was not going to be standing idle.

"You okay, Brayman old boy?" Arthur asked with a new affability. This was a genius coupling. He particularly savoured the way that Brayman did not want to lose face in front of Eddie. It brought to mind thoughts of flyweights and heavyweights.

"Fine, man." On the few occasions Brayman was capable of speech, he had begun to sound more and more like Eddie.

Once the chasers, that were chasing the chasers, that might have been chasing other chasers, before which there was a principle drink, were in front of Eddie, he began to make the growling noise with his throat he thought of as singing.

"Face like a librarian, tits like a porn star."

He used his hands to illustrate the tits. Brayman picked up on the chorus, and was delighted when he was invited to contribute. He'd never tried writing songs or lyrics before, but a line appeared in his head and, in honour of Eddie, he delivered it as Eddie might.

"And you're, like, on my radar."

"Hey, way to go, man," Eddie said, slapping Brayman on the shoulder. He then reinterpreted the line with the new trademark growl.

"And you're, like, on my radar."

It was such a great moment for Brayman that he hardly noticed the chasers chasing the chasers, or the drink that they were supposed to be chasing. This was because his life, at that moment, was great. It was greater than great, but the chasing chasers may have been influencing his thoughts. He'd been asked to a small gathering of his ex-workers the following day, and he was looking forward telling them about his afternoon with Eddie. But now he was desperate for the next line, and a rhyme with 'radar.' The chasing chasers may have been an impediment at this point.

"You've got big black eyes, just like a panda."

Eddie took the usual long distance telephone call delay to process this and, even with his low standards, found it wanting.

"A fucking panda?"

Arthur looked on the pair of them fondly. It wouldn't be fair to say that he looked at them as if they were his children, more like a pair of fighting dogs. And Brayman knew he'd fucked up. A fucking panda, what had he been thinking? He had to think quickly. A moment later he had the solution.

"Tell you what," Brayman said, "Let's do the chorus standing on the table."

Eddie loved the theatre of this, and the table looked pretty sturdy. The barman had disappeared downstairs to restock, although it wasn't the sort of place that discouraged flamboyant behaviour.

"Way to go," Brayman said, although Eddie could have sworn he'd said it. The chasing chasers were weighing heavily. Arthur remained seated as his protégés climbed onto the table. The table was sturdy, but it wasn't *that* sturdy.

"Face like a librarian, tits like a porn star," they shouted loud enough for the insurance workers in the neighbouring building to hear.

The barman dragged himself, and as many bottles as he could carry, up the tight, creaky staircase. He was almost at the top, when there was the most almighty crash. It was a sturdily constructed building, but the barman wondered whether a chimney had collapsed. A moment later he discovered a body on the floor.

"Is he okay?"

Arthur looked at the convulsing figure grimly.

"I don't think he is, Brayman old boy."

Chapter Twenty-Eight

Courtney Mbabwe had been travelling. Not in the literal sense, that still remained a dream, but via the magic of Google Earth. He'd been to Venice and San Francisco, Paris and Istanbul, Athens and Oslo. He'd even been to Ibiza, although he couldn't figure out the point of the place. He'd travelled through Europe and South America, like a restless hippy. And each time he came back to the same conclusion. He didn't fit in, a square peg in a round hole, a fish on a bicycle, a not quite brown face in a very black world. It wasn't that anyone cared. They hadn't seen the world of Google, and with it the world outside that was rife with prejudice and cynicism. The sun came up and went down, and they fed themselves in between.

"What's up, Courtney?" his mum, Gloria, would say. He'd even discovered, on his journey around the Internet that didn't involve travel or naked white women, a word called introspection. It was a word that was as valid, in his community, as dishwasher, or vacuum cleaner, or epilator.

"You think too much, Courtney."

It wasn't as if his mother was incapable of introspection, she just didn't see the point of it. Why spend time trying to make yourself unhappy? It wasn't as if Courtney was particularly introspective himself. He was just certain that God had dropped him in the wrong place.

There were other differences. Unlike the others, Courtney Mbabwe couldn't see anything wrong with cheating at football. It was all a means to an end, and once you decide on the end, in this case winning, then cheating merely facilitated that end. It was a philosophy he operated with chess and draughts and pretty much everything else. This was not to suggest that there was malice intended, just a desire to get somewhere. And that was aim. He needed to find where he was supposed to be.

Chapter Twenty-Nine

The triage nurse was finding the day most stressful. Firstly, there had been no clean underwear. It was one of the pitfalls of same sex relationships, and it irritated her. She had long decided that, on the knicker front, the division should be the same as heterosexuals. She had explained where she kept her clothes, and where her partner should keep hers. And that line had been breached, which was why there was no clean underwear to be found. Worse, her partner was a size smaller than her. It did unseemly things to her breasts.

Then there was the death of that lovely man Barry Clivert. She had decided he was lovely on the flimsiest of evidence, but it didn't matter now. She was just ruminating on the unfortunate life of Barry Clivert when a familiar, square-shouldered form appeared. She couldn't stop herself.

"You bastard!"

It was an unfortunate coincidence that Eddie should be taken to the same hospital that Clivert had spent his last few hours. It was also unfortunate that he was sent to the same ward, and that the same nurse was working her shift. But the restaurant and the pub weren't far apart, and the symptoms were strikingly similar.

"I beg your pardon?" Arthur slurred. He had successfully put the Clivert business out of his mind. The file was closed. But the nurse had very definitely not forgotten him.

"Barry was devoted to you!" the nurse shouted, grateful that he'd returned, so that she could share her opinion of him. She wasn't the sort of woman who liked to keep her views a secret, but today she was feeling particularly vocal.

"He loved you and you walked out!"

It took a moment for Arthur to link the name Barry with that of the late Clivert, as he'd never used his first name. Brayman was a little surprised. His level of intoxication was such that he was only capable of processing small chunks of information. But this was strange nonetheless.

"You don't understand," Arthur began, but it didn't help that he didn't understand either. His confusion coincided with a call from Eddie's manager.

"Cholmondely-Godstone?"

"Yes." Arthur only answered to avoid confronting the nurse, as distant memories were beginning to resurface.

"What's happened to Eddie?"

Ordinarily Arthur would have been perplexed as to how Eddie's manager had discovered so rapidly that Eddie had been admitted to hospital, but his mind was not at its sharpest. He turned to the nurse.

"Would you be kind enough to let us know how Eddie B is doing. If you don't mind. Please."

The nurse eyed him suspiciously for a moment, and then got up and disappeared into the bowels of the hospital, where the more serious cases were being handled.

"Have you fucking killed him?" the manager shouted.

"I wouldn't say that," Arthur said deploying the tone of voice he generally used when he was being accused of murder.

"Well, what would you say? Is he fucking dead? Because if he's fucking dead, how the hell is he going to finish his fucking gigs? And if he doesn't finish his fucking gigs, how are any of us, including fucking you, going to fucking well get fucking paid? Do you fucking understand me?"

Arthur was beginning to understand Eddie's name for the manager. He was saved from an immediate reply by the nurse. Confronting her now seemed like a more palatable option.

"He will survive."

The nurse said it with some regret, as she'd found Eddie more obnoxious than Arthur. Also she did not have a face like a librarian.

"Did you hear that?" Arthur shouted into his mobile phone. He heard some word muttered in response, and then the phone went dead.

Chapter Thirty

Arnold Clivert was a runt of a man, from his undersized feet to his balding pate. A weasely man with a weasely voice.

"Five foot six is average," he would insist. But five foot six wasn't average height for a man, and Andy Clivert was not five foot six. He had hoped to work for the Inland Revenue – it was the sort of work that would have suited his unpleasant temperament – but he had failed almost every exam he'd taken. Instead he ran a small department ordering materials for a builder's merchant. It was a job no one else wanted, but Clivert felt it conferred some status on him. A small, tiny, low-energy light of status he revelled in. Something, he thought, that put him above the line he thought of as average. But average was as attainable as five foot six for Arnold Clivert. Except his world was going to change today.

He had lived his life in the shadow of his younger brother, Barry. Barry had not been sporty or tall either, and in many ways was as average as Arnold wasn't. That was aside, however, for his facility for numbers, which had launched him far from the average. And now he was dead.

It had prompted Barry's lesser-achieving brother to become quite emotional. But he was not the kind of person to reflect on childhood times with his easygoing, kind-hearted brother. He'd always hated him and now, through his weasely nose, he could smell an inheritance that was going to keep him very comfortable indeed. And that prospect made him very emotional.

"Tracey," he droned.

"Yes Mr Clivert?"

Tracey was a bright girl. She intended to stay another six months working in the office, and then she would be off travelling. She had got the measure of Clivert the first few moments after she'd met him, and found that a deferential approach made him easy to deal with. Although today he was in particularly excitable form.

"What would you do if you won the lottery?"

As Clivert was short on friends, he used those employed in his office, who had no choice, for his social interaction. Tracey knew that the question was not going to be related to the office, and while she didn't want to encourage him, she didn't mind winding him up either. She looked into the distance dreamy-eyed, and gave the question some thought. What would she do if she won the lottery? Of course she would never lay eyes on Arnold Clivert again, that was given. Beyond that she would travel and eventually she'd like a beach house, and she wouldn't mind a Mercedes convertible.

"Well," she began.

"Because I've just won the lottery." Clivert just couldn't wait for her reply. There was to be a reading of the will that afternoon, and Barry only had one next of kin. Him. Arnold Clivert was the only person who shared the same bloodline. And his brother had been very wealthy indeed.

"You have?" she said with some surprise.

Andy Clivert beamed at her. Aside from his MGB, his Star Wars figures, his pornographic DVD collection, his shoes with the lifts in them and his early Sinclair computers, she was the most precious thing in his life. Maybe the richer him might tempt her. He beamed at the thought introducing, for the first time for Tracey, the actual physical sensation of her skin crawling. It was quite strange.

"I've got an appointment this afternoon with a solicitor."

He hoped she would ask more, but she hadn't recovered from the skin problem. He couldn't wait.

"My brother had all the luck," he began. He had decided long ago that the difference between himself and his brother was all down to luck. It wasn't just that Arnold Clivert was a glass-half-full kind of person. For him the glass was practically empty and someone was about to piss into it, and toss it into his face. Naturally none of this was his fault.

"He made big money in the city. Very big, seriously large. Kind of massive."

He had established that in order for Tracey to find him just a teensy-wee bit attractive, he would have to stress the extent of the wealth. For a second he worried he hadn't. In his vision of lottery-winning life, he'd ideally like to wake up with Tracey lying by his side. If she could look lovingly into his eyes that would be a great bonus.

"Lucky him," Tracey said.

"No, you don't understand. He's dead." Arnold Clivert couldn't contain his smile. It gave Tracey further skin issues.

"I'm sorry," Tracey said, a little confused.

"Well yes of course, it's terrible," Clivert said. But he was still smiling.

After lunch Arnold Clivert bounded cheerfully into the solicitor's office, and saw a very tall man who shook his hand dolefully.

"I'm so terribly sorry for your loss."

For a moment Clivert wondered if something had happened to his MGB, then he understood.

"Thank you."

The lawyer then talked for a very long time, in a very hot and airless room. The temptation to prompt him forward was almost overwhelming. Finally the solicitor arrived at the list of assets.

"The house in Islington, valued at two and a half million pounds."

Clivert's heart was fluttering like an epileptic.

"A portfolio of shares, worth in the region of four point two million."

Clivert's hands were shaking as if he were on his fourteenth coffee.

"A further cash account of just over two million pounds."

Clivert knew his brother was successful, but he had no idea just how much money he had accumulated.

"There is a further portfolio of art, held in the vault of the bank…"

Clivert was shaking so much he didn't notice someone enter the room.

"Sorry I'm late."

Clivert flashed a look at the large man who had entered, and then brought his attention back to the lawyer.

"…and valued at around six million pounds."

It was overload for Clivert. He could actually picture Tracey's breasts as if they were dangling in front of him. With breasts like that, Clivert thought, who needed adoring looks?

"Then there is the property portfolio."

Clivert couldn't hear the value of the property portfolio. His mind couldn't process it. He'd actually shifted, in his mind, from the Tracey in the office in Neasden to a beach house somewhere.

"And lastly the caravan in Skegness."

Clivert, in his head, was now a love-god. Tracey was squealing with pleasure. He was a master of the universe.

"All of which I leave to Arthur Cholmondley-Godstone, except the last item, which I leave to my brother Arnold."

The words came as such a surprise, Arthur couldn't process them. He knew they were up to over fifteen million and felt disappointed that he'd taken so little off Barry. But he was here to offer his services to the younger brother. And he very much liked the look of the pallid-faced wreck in front of him.

"What?" Arthur asked. Arnold was too involved with Tracey to notice. And the dream was so dreamlike that Tracey was actually enjoying it. The lawyer repeated the most important line in the will.

"All of which I leave to Arthur Cholmondley-Godstone, except the last item, which I leave to my brother Arnold."

"The last item?"

"The caravan in Skegness."

"You're kidding," Arthur said.

Arnold, incapable of speech, made spluttering noises.

"There are a few conditions," the lawyer said.

Chapter Thirty-one

"I'm worried about Arthur," Charles Cholmondely-Godstone said to his father Henry.

"Screaming queer, if you ask me." Henry had celebrated his hundredth birthday two years earlier. His hearing was less than perfect, but mostly selective. Henry said what he wanted to say, regardless of where the conversation was going, or the question being asked. It had proved very effective when he had been faced with radio interviews. It was quite innovative at the time.

"Yes, well, that may be the case," Charles said a little uncertainly, and then added, "Actually, I don't think he is."

"Screaming queer, mark my words," Henry repeated.

"I'm not sure that is the case, but anyway, he believes he may have fathered a child or two." Charles thought he had got his case across, but waited for the reaction.

"Arthur? Don't you believe it. Screaming queer, that one."

Henry had some facility for remaining on point. But just in case he carried on.

"Probably got a little black chap, bugger-boy, tucked away at home."

Charles' eyes widened. Henry had managed to capture the two family loathings in one sentiment. Charles and Henry were waiting in Arthur's office ready to pounce. It had even alarmed Jean, who'd phoned Arthur to warn him. It wasn't likely to upset Arthur's impossibly good mood. He swept into the office as if entering a stage and expecting applause.

"Morning, chaps," Arthur said.

Even though Arthur was Henry's grandson, Henry felt a little uncomfortable. He always had with queers.

"Have you heard the news?"

Arthur looked at his father and grandfather, and wondered what was wrong with them. It might have been asking for too much to hope for applause, but this was a distinctly muted response.

"Clivert?" Arthur continued.

"Yes, of course, well done Arthur," his father said with less enthusiasm than he thought was appropriate.

Arthur sensed that they had yet to hear about the will. It was going to be further fuel thrown on the flames of his suspect sexuality. But hell, it is twenty million. Arthur went for it.

"And have you heard about the reading of the will? Clivert's will? The twenty million? Turns out Clivert was…" Arthur hesitated, unsure whether he should say homosexual or gay, then realising that the best way was to frame it as his grandfather might.

"…a screaming queer. Apparently he was in love with me."

Henry was about to make his feelings felt, but the use of the words 'screaming queer' put him off his stride. He kept quiet for a second.

"Hold on," Charles said, "Are you saying that this Clivert man has left you twenty million pounds?"

"Yes," Arthur said.

"Well, bugger me," Charles said absentmindedly.

"Precisely my point," Henry said.

"A screaming queer, you say?" Charles picked up the thought, "And you had no idea?"

"Not the slightest. Why would I? Who cares?"

Henry began to have his doubts again. Was he protesting too much? He couldn't tell.

"And all twenty million to you?" Charles asked again.

"Yes."

"Wow."

"Anyway, the thing is," Arthur began cautiously, "I don't want anyone to contest the will."

"Of course you don't, old boy. It's twenty million quid," his father reassured him. But Arthur was getting to the tricky bit.

"The thing is, I think I'm going to have to pretend."

"Pretend what?" Charles asked, but Henry was already there.

"That won't be difficult," he muttered, then he whispered loudly to Charles, "Screaming."

"You're absolutely right, you'll have to pretend, Arthur," his father told him.

Arthur had read the emotional letter that had been left to him in the event of Barry Clivert's passing. Arthur had very little recollection of anything that Clivert had said, so it came as quite a surprise. And once Clivert had admitted to himself that he was gay, and that Arthur was the object of his affections, it was just a matter of putting the two together. The letter made certain requests that weren't quite a condition of the inheritance, but it would be thought of as bad form should he not comply. There were conditions, but he'd get to them later.

"Who else is likely to have a claim on his money?" Henry asked.

Arthur shrugged, although he guessed it wouldn't be easy with the brother. He didn't know that much about Clivert. In fact, the more he read the letter the more he realised that he knew nothing at all. Charles was getting into the spirit.

"It's a very small price to pay. Frankly, for twenty million quid, you should have let him bugger you,"

Arthur winced at the fatherly advise.

"Or suck you off," Henry added, getting into the spirit of things. He was going to say more, but sensed he might incriminate himself if he appeared too knowledgeable on the subject.

The letter had been quite detailed, and Clivert had decided to take him through the steps that had led him to such a generous final gesture. Clivert had begun to frequent clubs, and had gathered some like-minded friends who were helping to guide him through this period. Clivert asked that they be present at his funeral, and that a suitable party should be held as a celebration of his life and their partnership. It was a partnership he hadn't yet made Arthur aware of, and clearly Clivert had imagined his death as rather further off, by which time the relationship would be cemented. It was strange, given how successfully Clivert had traded in futures.

"So, who are they?" Arthur's father asked.

"Darren Gilks, an accountant from Hastings, and John Brewster, also known as the Rooster, a drag queen from Bow. Or it might be the other way round."

"Really?" his father said, and added, "And the family?"

"He specifically asked that his 'bullying moron of a brother' should not be invited."

"Excellent. I don't think you have much to worry about. I suggest you work a little at the walk and the hand gestures."

Arthur's father's perception of homosexuality was routed in the fifties, but the advice still stood. It wasn't worth messing with twenty million quid. Henry raised his eyes.

Chapter Thirty-Two

Eddie left the hospital the following day. He was almost as delighted as his manager to find that his departure from the hospital was met with a clatter of cameras and friendly paparazzi cheers.

"Hey Eddie, are you going to be okay for the gig on Saturday?"

Eddie had no idea his next gig was only a few days away. His armoury of tools did not include a calendar, that was what his Cunt was for. But he didn't let on.

"Hey sure. It's rock and roll."

The paparazzi cheered again. They knew this, or a version of this, was what he was going to say. Eddie had used roughly the same phrase in answer to every question over the last thirty years. But he did believe that the show should go on.

"Do you know what they're saying in the papers, Eddie?"

Eddie had no idea, but it didn't matter. He was in the papers, and that was always good. He was still cutting it in the rock business. And they'd yet to hear his latest insightful and tuneful ballad, the conflation of librarian and sex worker.

"Hey sure. It's rock and roll."

His manager had been delighted when he'd read the papers. There was nothing an audience liked better, and therefore nothing better for ticket sales, than a massive car crash. And Eddie, the papers were predicting, was exactly that. His manager had organised more tickets, and upped the price to a hundred and fifty quid. But that was cheap to have the privilege of being there when Eddie gasped his last *I'm Wasted* gasp. It would be legend.

"Hey, sure. It's rock and roll."

Even Eddie could tell that the paparazzi had sensed that he hadn't quite grasped what was being said of him. He might have to buy a newspaper. Someone saved him the hassle.

"They say it's going to kill you."

Eddie's mind took the usual handful of beats to register this. He wasn't ordinarily sensitive, but it struck him as a little unkind. But the papers were always unkind. The doctor had been pretty blunt too. He'd begun in a gently coercing manner, and found that it had flown high over Eddie's head. He'd moved onto the blunt.

"Richard Burton, Lee Marvin, George Best," he'd begun.

"All great men," Eddie had contributed.

"All dead."

The doctor then delivered a speech about alcoholism, which Eddie half listened to. It involved much talk of the future, and the future had never interested Eddie. Even next Saturday seemed along way ahead. But as most of the alcohol had drained from his system and led to a condition known as sobriety, he'd decided to take it easy for what remained of the day. He was even considering sleeping most of the rest of the week.

Chapter Thirty-Three

Tracey had bought a lottery ticket that morning. It was the first time she'd bought one in years, as she didn't really believe in them. But if Mr Clivert's ticket had come up, perhaps hers might too. It was only possible, she reassured herself, to win the lottery if she actually took part. The other reason she didn't like the lottery was it tended to make her dream, and she liked her life to be rooted in reality. She was working and saving money. She'd moved out of her flat and was staying at her mum's, and she then was going to travel. First a little bit of Europe, the most eastern part and, if she could afford it, maybe China and India. But with a lottery win she could go anywhere.

Tracey was going out after work that evening. Normally she'd go home and change, but her mum's was a bit far, and she wasn't sure if she'd have the energy to go out once she'd landed on the sofa. She was wearing her going-out clothes, which were very different from her going to work clothes. The neckline plunged like an Olympic diver.

The office was situated to the rear of an industrial unit and crammed into the roof area, which was generally stuffy and ill-suited for the purpose. A small window had been fitted into the gable as compensation, and from there Tracey could see the car park. A moment later the gruff noise of Clivert's old banger broke the peace. She watched as Clivert fitted the long lock that ran between the brake and the steering wheel, and then painstakingly locked the doors. She wondered why he bothered. She heard him clanking on the steel staircase until he threw the door open.

"Morning Mr Clivert."

She got up to make him a coffee, at the same time as tugging up her blouse. She'd imagined that within a week Clivert would be driving a Ferrari and he'd be gone. That filled her with a sudden horror. If Clivert left, they would almost certainly offer her his job, since she did it anyway, and the salary would be higher. And more money would make it harder to leave and realise her dreams.

"How did it go at the solicitors?" Tracey asked.

She hadn't taken a very close look at Clivert. It wasn't an activity she found pleasing. If she had, she might have noticed that his skin was stretched more tightly around his balding pate and face, like an over-inflated balloon. And Clivert was fit to burst. He could hardly contain his emotions.

"Beach house," he suddenly said. Tracey looked at him anxiously, drifting towards panic, as it occurred to her that there may be some dovetailing in their dreams. Clivert's mind had been turning with thoughts of what could have been, and a beach house and Tracey's breasts had featured at some length. And now nothing.

"The bastard," Clivert rasped. It was enough information for Tracey to grasp what had happened. She didn't want to point out that there was some justice in it, given his obvious delight at his brother's death. Tracey was torn between running out of the building and grabbing the next bus signposted to 'somewhere more interesting,' and helping him. Foolishly she chose the latter.

"Sit down, Mr Clivert, let me get you a coffee and we can talk it through." And then she added, with Olympic gold medal winning-foolishness, "Can I call you Arnold?"

Clivert sat down and ran his eyes over Tracey. Dear God, he thought. Dear God. She was a metaphor for everything. For his loss. Continuing her recent policy of foolishness, Tracey made an extra effort fluffing up the milk to sit on his coffee. She came back and placed it on his desk.

"What happened, Arnold?" she asked, entering a marathon of foolishness. And Clivert told her every detail, including a very unflattering description of Arthur. But Tracey was ever the optimist.

"I had a great holiday in Skegness," she said, as her face lit up. She'd had a great time, although her memories of Skegness itself were hazy. She'd met Mikey. It was the first time she'd had sex with a black man, and she discovered that everything that had ever been said was true. Although perhaps it hadn't been Skegness. It hadn't mattered at the time.

"Bastard," Clivert muttered again. All his hopes and dreams crushed in one moment. And then he was further reminded of those hopes and dreams when he caught sight of Tracey's breasts. She'd never exposed quite so much before. And she'd called him Arnold. It must be on purpose. Clivert couldn't help concluding that it was in anticipation of the richer him. Beach house and Tracey's breasts. He'd lost them all. Bastard.

Chapter Thirty-Four

All the family had been alerted, and the ballroom had been decorated for the occasion. Arthur had been busy.

"I found the photos on his computer," Arthur said proudly. He had visited the Islington house and had a look around. There were lots of images on Clivert's computer, but many were merely inappropriate, and some were positively pornographic. But with a little Photoshop, there were now quite a few that featured Clivert in Arthur's arms. The photographs lined the walls, with a very large photograph of Clivert above the fireplace. It was quite moving. This was to be the great wake that Barry Clivert had asked for. If it was a deal, Arthur had no intention of reneging on it. People filed in. The first to arrive were Charles and Henry, his father and grandfather.

"Arthur," Charles shook his hand. Henry was too busy looking at the photographs.

"I told you," he hissed to Charles, "Screaming."

Henry turned to Arthur and drew himself up to his full height, and then gave up trying. He was, after all, over a hundred. He liked to think that very little got past him.

"So, Arthur, how do you explain the pictures?"

"Photoshop," Arthur said quietly. It was a grapple between maintaining a pretence of heterosexuality or giving up.

"You had a shop do it, did you?" Henry said loudly. "Did they send a photographer out?"

The twenty million quid won.

"Yes, grandfather."

Henry recoiled slightly from Arthur, and went off in search of a drink, muttering to himself. Arthur knew he had to get back into character. A small queue of people had formed.

"I'm so sorry."

Arthur shook a hand, his eyes moist, but it was uncle Ralph, so it was just practice. A moment later a tall man with pink hair and long fingernails entered the room with a voluptuous woman in a flowing dress. They looked up at the pictures of Barry and let out a gasp. The couple queued behind a number of Arthur's relatives. They looked further at the pictures of Barry and Arthur, and the gasps turned to sobs. Finally they arrived at Arthur.

"I'm so glad you finally found each other," the tall man said through further sobs.

"It was brief, but," Arthur stuttered, "he was everything." For a second he was tempted to give away too much from his forthcoming speech.

"Are you John Brewster?" Arthur asked.

"No, I'm Darren Gilks."

"The accountant?" Arthur asked, a little surprised.

"Yes, that's right."

"Barry talked so much about you," Arthur said.

"And you are?" Arthur asked the beautiful woman, hoping she wasn't a relative they'd missed.

"Sophie" the woman said.

"Sophie? Anyway, I'm *soo* pleased you could be here," Arthur said, lending great emphasis on the *so* and holding a hand gently in the air for no apparent reason. It took him a moment to recover from the appearance of another Sophie. He carried on, "You were *sooo* important to him." He looked at them both. She really was a beautiful woman. He rather liked them curvy. Arthur realised that he might be falling for a trap. He patted his hand on Darren's shoulder in an intimate and hopefully camp manner. He tried terribly hard to gush.

"You were the glue in his life. The thing that held him together. The…" Arthur pressed his fists together, having exhausted his metaphors. The queue was pressing behind them.

"Perhaps we can talk some more after the memorial service," Arthur said, with the intention of doing his best to avoid them. They responded with more collective sobs.

Arthur shook more hands. There were a few people that Clivert had worked with, but the rest were his family, who weren't being supportive, but hated to miss a good bash. Champagne was served before the service, which was unusual, but no one seemed to notice. When they were ready the lights went down. It had required some research, but Arthur was keen to put on a good show. A spotlight fell on the large picture of Barry Clivert above the fireplace.

"He was born in Potters Bar," Arthur began. He chose not to mention the family medical history, but focused on the detail. Way too much detail.

"It was a pink house," he continued, "with silver birches in the drive." Arthur spoke for nearly an hour. It was, and there is no other way of putting this, very boring. There were details no one else would know, including the deceased. It would have been useful if he'd actually listened to the man. Arthur came to a halt, his voice breaking. Few things made him more emotional than the prospect of twenty million pounds.

"He was my east, my west, my Sunday best," Arthur concluded, borrowing the occasional line from W H Auden, but filling in the rest. The waiters had been busy charging glasses, although most of Arthur's relatives had drifted off into deep sleep.

"Raise your glasses to the exceptional man that was Clivert, I mean Barry Clivert," he corrected, and raised his glass.

The drink and fine food then flowed, and Arthur relaxed. All this sensitive talk of Barry Clivert had made him quite keen to get laid, with a woman, possibly even a number of them. He planned to wrap it up by about ten, and then move onto a club he knew. It was going to be expensive, but hell, he'd just inherited twenty million quid. It was his day. He knocked back some more champagne. It was such an extravagant event that it made the papers the next day.

"Arthur, that was lovely," Sophie said, tears just gently brushing her discreet mascara.

"Thank you, well, Barry was very special."

"And yet you hadn't known him for that long."

"It was just a short year, it could have been so much more," Arthur said, and turned away.

"His health was never good," Sophie pointed out. "You weren't to know."

"No, no, no. Indeed not," Arthur said, as if he had every idea.

"Forgive me for asking, but you don't seem to me to be the gay type."

"I've often been told that," Arthur said, falling into a researched and practised response. "You see it's not the gender, it's the person. And Barry was a very special person."

"Do you know," Sophie said, touching Arthur's arm, "I'm so glad you said that. We're all so trapped in stereotypes, and yet we're all different, and yet the same."

Arthur smiled at her, not having the faintest clue what she had just said. He was just getting over his brief obsession with one Sophie, and he wasn't quite ready to start another. But she was rather nice.

Chapter Thirty-Five

Arnold Clivert was slumped in another airless room in front of a different, but equally tall, lawyer. This one was costing him five hundred pounds an hour. The sweat patches under Clivert's arms had reached his belt.

"The thing is, Mr Clivert, it is going to cost you a very great deal indeed to sue this man, this Mr Arthur Cholmondely-Godstone. What assets do you have?"

Arnold Clivert's slump got lower. He had a small one bedroom flat, which was located above a betting shop. On Saturday mornings he could hear the horses rumbling below him and the excited commentary. It was in negative equity.

"I have a flat."

The lawyer looked at him over his glasses and nodded. He ran his eyes through the will again and said, "And the caravan in Skegness?"

Arnold's eyes flared with anger. He'd visited the caravan the previous day. He was astonished to find that it was very decrepit. The camp site owner provided the next shock.

"Ah, Mr Clivert, we were hoping you would come down. I'll just get the key."

He'd watched the man disappear as a sense of gloom descended on him. He tried to recall the good times he'd shared with his brother, but couldn't remember any. The boy had been an obnoxious squirt and he'd enjoyed hitting him.

"Here we are Mr Clivert, and also if you could sort this out." He handed him an envelope. Clivert fingered the envelope for a moment as the campsite owner looked cheerfully at him.

"It's just that there's six months rent owing. It's just twelve hundred pounds."

Clivert nodded. He was stunned, but stirring within was a sensation which was heralding new depth of anger. A stomach-turning fury. And that was before he entered the caravan. The door wasn't easy to open. There seemed to be toys in the way, and they were scattered everywhere. It didn't make sense to him. They were stacked quite high. He still didn't get it. Until he found a note on the table, which read: 'Arnold, these are all my toys, all of which you broke. Your brother, Barry.'

"Mr Clivert?" The lawyer prompted him, although he was in no hurry. Clivert's little five minute reverie was worth at least forty quid to him.

"The caravan in Skegness has no value," he said flatly.

"Well in that case, unless you can be certain of raising around five hundred thousand pounds, I think you will have to accept the will. I'm afraid your brother was perfectly at liberty to leave his money to whomsoever he pleases."

Clivert left the office in a trance. He stood next to the lawyer's secretary, unable to process the stinking bad luck he'd been blessed with. The intercom beeped and the lawyer's voice filled the room.

"Has that vile little man left yet?"

Clivert didn't notice. He clenched and unclenched his fists. He left the office, walked into the cool air and found an off licence. He bought a bottle of Scotch. He had decided. He was going to kill himself.

"It's what you want, isn't it?" He shouted to the sky. It was obviously what God wanted, and he wasn't going to disappoint him. He was passionately hoping that God existed. Not so he could stand by His side and do His work. Or that he could step into a higher place, a paradise. No, Arnold Clivert was hoping that a God and an afterlife existed, so that he could kill himself and then wring his brother's neck every day for eternity. Or even longer. He put his hands together as if they were wrapped round his brother's neck. He took a swig from the bottle. God he hated whisky. Why hadn't God let him like whisky?

"Bastard," he hissed.

The only question was how he was going to kill himself. Arnold Clivert had not been gifted with much of an imagination, and for a second his mind went blank. He thought he might have to Google it. Then he remembered that he had his father's old shot gun under the bed. He tried to imagine himself holding it. The logistics of directing a long barrelled weapon at yourself were not straightforward. Then he realised that God had not gifted him with long enough arms.

"Bastard," he shouted at the sky.

And then it hit him. Why kill himself? His life couldn't get any worse, so what did it matter? He pictured the shotgun again, but this time it was pointing at Arthur Chum-Fuck's head.

"I know what you're thinking," he said. But Arnold Clivert's voice had a nasal quality to it. Occasionally Tracey liked to impersonate him.

"Have I shot four or have I shot five?" Clint Eastwood, it wasn't. It didn't help that the shotgun only held two.

"Well, in all the confusion, I clean forgot."

Maybe he'd buy himself a gun that shot five or six, or more, much more. Clivert started to laugh maniacally. There was a solution that was just and reasonable, and it was staring him in the face. He was ready for a change. No longer the victim, but the orchestrator. The governor, the man in charge. Clivert had made a decision. He was going to kill Arthur Cholmondely-Godstone.

Chapter Thirty-Six

"You're going to have to tell him," Rachel said.

Sophie shook her head. Rachel had coerced her into the pub, the nearer one, as Sophie had no intention of ever waking to the other side of the village again. This pub had a nice garden and lots of free newspapers. And the booze was cheaper.

"Why?"

"I can think of millions of reasons."

Although some of Sophie's problems had rotated round money, or the lack of it, occasionally the tragic lack of it, it wasn't her greatest motivation in life. They read the paper carefully.

"Look at this. Arthur Cholmondely-Godstone delivered a moving speech with tears in his eyes. Barry Clivert was, he explained, my east, my west, my Sunday best."

Sophie's mouth hung open, having temporarily lost the facility to park itself. It was as if all the things she was certain of, were no longer certain.

"I can't believe it"

"There's nothing wrong with having a gay dad, Soph."

"But Arthur. You met Arthur. I mean, Arthur."

They read on. It was a small piece, but it had captured most of the salient details.

"My God," Rachel said.

"Oh my God," Sophie agreed.

"That does say twenty million, doesn't it?"

"It really does."

It left the two of them in a new place, a place they had never encountered before. Quite speechless.

"Wow," Rachel eventually managed.

"Wow," Sophie agreed.

They remained silent a little longer, rereading the article, but finding no missing nuance. Rachel got herself in order first.

"Anyway, I say you're going to have to tell him."

"Why?"

"I can think of twenty million reasons."

Sophie could see the sense of this argument, but there was something undignified about it. She rather thought a loving and caring dad would be good too.

"In fact," Rachel continued, "It's a win-win situation."

"It is?"

"Of course. You don't have to marry him, or pretend to be in a relationship with him. You just have to suggest a bit of support is required."

"Support? Emotional?"

"Oh for fuck's sake Sophie, sod the emotional, we're talking financial. Money, moolah, wonga."

Sophie had grasped the point early on, and knew she had. So why the pause? Why the reluctance? It was a dawning realisation, and it was telling her something she didn't want to hear. She wanted more, and worse still, much worse. She wanted a lot more. Not the money, but the other stuff. Sophie wanted more and she was happy for Arthur to provide the 'more,' and she didn't mean of the financial kind. The knight in shining armour, the friend, the lover. The everything.

Chapter Thirty-Seven

Arthur left the party, claiming to the few that might care that he was too emotional to stay. His head was filled with Sophies past and present, and his stomach was filled with game pie and lubricated with St Emilion (or, as he liked to think of it, St-Twenty-Emillion). All in all, it was very nearly a perfect day. But Arthur was a man of extravagant tastes, and the day needed further garnishing. It was so absorbing that Arthur didn't notice a furiously-pedalled bicycle, with a lance-like contraption at the front, headed his way.

Neither did Rogerman, who launched the Rolls at full throttle to arrive at the kerb in front of Arthur. The melancholy riff that sets Def Leppard's *Love Bites* into frantic motion was hammering through Rogerman's ears. A mean vocalist himself, he was screaming, "No! Love bites, love bleeds, it's bringing me to my knees!" In his brief service with Arthur, he'd come to realise that beyond a destination, there was very little communication required, which suited him fine.

Arthur slumped happily into the back of the Rolls, wondering whether he might splash out on a new one, just for him. An honorary one, dedicated to the life and times of Barry Clivert. It was going to take him a moment to get out of character. He grabbed the decanter and poured himself a brandy. The old beast still looked all right, and he understood it had some classic value, but it had acquired a strange smell. Arthur couldn't quite place it. He had barely finished the glass when Rogerman got him to the club. Arthur was beginning to get used to the greater turn of speed of the second Rogerman. Maybe it was more appropriate for the fast-living times he found himself in. But he was thankful they had arrived quickly because, after the day's proceedings, he was keen to immerse himself in some heterosexuality.

Arthur got himself out of the car, remembering that this Rogerman was a bit slower on his feet, which was a little strange for someone so young. He stood outside the club, and looked fondly at the discreet pair of double mahogany doors. This was a very exclusive club, particularly favoured by French and Italian politicians. It was run by Geraldine. And once he stepped through the doors, Geraldine appeared from nowhere. She was dressed in stockings, suspenders and a basque, and little less. Although never actually on the menu herself, she offered an appetiser which Arthur particularly savoured. She was probably in her late forties, possibly more – Arthur couldn't tell – but she made a striking presence and set the tone. There was no question what kind of club this was. But, Arthur thought, it was better than that.

Arthur had no interest in young girls or prostitutes, although that was not to say he was entirely averse to either, but for him nothing beat a woman of a certain age who was just plain horny. The women who entered this establishment were there for the same reason as him. A further set of doors took him to a large room, from which there were other rooms fanning out, and promising a wide variety of sexual activity. There were discreet trays scattered around the room with condoms and viagra. And Arthur, being Arthur, ordered the most expensive champagne, just to have the pleasure of being served by Geraldine. He watched her sashay towards him, salivating at the prospect of whatever the prospect was. And Geraldine was really sashaying today, as she did with all her guests who were wealthy or foolhardy enough to order the most expensive champagne.

"Arthur," she said with a husky drawl perfected over the years, and with a tone that implied so much, although in truth delivered very little. She was, Arthur thought, quite delicious. But everyone was delicious today. Geraldine leaned over, as she gave the cork a twist and let the liquid gush out in a metaphor that was too obvious, even for a sex club. The more honoured the guest, the deeper the view of her cleavage. Arthur was deeply honoured today. She topped his glass up.

"You will join me for one?"

Geraldine was only too delighted to help him get to the bottom of the fabulously expensive bottle. She sat next to him gracefully.

"You're looking well, Arthur," she purred. Despite the Mariella Frostrupian nature of her husky voice, she could purr too.

"And you too, Geraldine, as always."

Arthur couldn't resist running his hand along an exposed thigh. Despite the huskiness and purriness, Geraldine was a pretty fearsome creature, and this would normally take some courage, but they both knew that Arthur intended to spend a very great deal that evening.

"But you know me, Arthur. You must think of me as an *amuse bouche*. The starter and main course are out there."

She cast her hands around at the frolicsome couples and women. Arthur could feel her thigh getting cooler, which was quite a talent. He cast his eyes around as requested and found two familiar faces.

"Arthur!"

"Hello, ladies."

It took a beat for Arthur to recall their names, but he had the time as they were doing some beating of their own. But they paused and came over to greet him. Fortunately their names arrived in his mouth just as they got to his table, which was also a circumstance that echoed their activities so far.

"Trish, Sal, how good to see you."

Arthur got up and kissed them. He nodded for more glasses, and passed them some champagne. Geraldine smiled and slipped away, having dispensed with the sashaying.

"Arthur, where have you been?"

"Oh, you know me. Around."

"And the best champagne as usual. You must never change, Arthur!"

It was a sentiment that Geraldine shared, at nine hundred and twenty pounds a bottle. It was why the blue pills were free.

"Do you know? You're right, I must never change. Here's to never changing!"

A second bottle appeared quicker than you can say 'Barry Clivert'. But Arthur was serious. He'd been told to cut back, and even become a family man, yet neither of these things were him. He was going to enjoy himself in the way only he knew.

"Have you been having a good time, ladies?"

Trish and Sal were women of a certain age, which was only a polite way of saying that they were getting on, but they looked after themselves and had decided, some years ago, to have a good time. And for them a good time invariably meant sex. They weren't averse to gastronomic delights, and certainly not fine wines and champagnes, but carnal sex was their main thing. It was why they'd popped into the club, and would be the only certain thing in a weekend in town.

"So far we've yet to have a great time, but the evening is young," Trish said. She leaned over and popped a little 'V' pill into his mouth. He smiled and poured a little more champagne. Trish and Sal always enjoyed an evening with Arthur, who didn't hold back on any front. They exchanged glances with each other, agreeing, with just a flutter of eyes, to stay with Arthur at least for the next hour or so.

"Let's see what we can do about that," Arthur grinned, and quicker than you can say 'twenty million quid' a third bottle of champagne arrived. Arthur was very pleased indeed to find Trish and Sal there. They never disappointed. All that talk of homosexuality had made him really very ready for fun. He caught Geraldine's eye, although it should be said, that hers were eyes begging to be caught.

"The suite?" he mouthed.

She beamed the beam of someone whose quiet, uneventful, and not particularly lucrative day was now ringing jackpot bells. The Boudoir Suite did what it said on the tin, plus a little more, with freshly laundered sex toys and sheets. It came with a hefty hire charge. Arthur didn't need the Viagra, but there was no sense in it kicking in too late. The night was, as Trish (or was it Sal) put it, young.

The pressures of the day were becoming more distant, receding in his mind with the pleasures of the moment. The champagne even tasted like it might actually be worth nearly a thousand pounds a bottle. Arthur ran his hands along the respective thighs of each girl. They were warm and inviting, and anxious for him to continue their journey. But even Arthur knew that this was the pre-foreplay foreplay.

"Do you know, ladies, anticipation, expectation and desire, they all need to be managed."

His stroking was actually quite skilled. Quicker than Arthur could have said 'caravan in Skegness' a further bottle of champagne appeared. But this one was for the rest of the evening.

"We'll take this with us, shall we ladies?"

They didn't need to answer. They threaded their way through the bar towards the suite. They had only been there once before, also with Arthur, and had savoured its lavishness, while Arthur had lavishly savoured them. Arthur wore a smile he was unaware of, as they walked at a measured pace, managing the anticipation. They had almost arrived at the stairs down into the basement, when someone accidentally bumped into Arthur.

"Arthur?"

"Sophie?"

Chapter Thirty-Eight

Arnold Clivert had a clear run. He had, by his standards, been most resourceful and imaginative, and had gaffer-taped the shotgun to the crossbar of his bicycle. Not the Eddie Merckx – that was a classic and too precious to him – but an old mountain bike he occasionally took to work. He'd worked out exit routes and a disguise.

Arnold Clivert was feeling quite the master assassin. After Arthur, he was thinking of taking on further commissions. He'd even worked out a marketing strategy, possibly with an interactive website. He'd made a further cunning modification, and strapped a homemade silencer to the end of the shotgun. But the plan had a flaw that even Clivert could see. The contraption he had created looked just like a bicycle with a shotgun attached to it. It might, he thought, be a little difficult to smuggle it into central London.

"But I'm too cunning for that," Clivert had muttered. He had started muttering a lot to himself. He had disguised the barrel of the shotgun as a flagpole and cut up a sheet to hang from it. The slogan took a little longer to come up with, but he finally decided on 'Save the World.' The disguise was so cunning. People would just think he was a madman. It was genius. There was irony in it somewhere, but Clivert had difficulty finding it, as he continued to mutter to himself.

All he had to do was wait. But he was a little conspicuous parked across the road from the office. He found some shadows, but that looked even worse. And there were police everywhere. It was just his luck that Arthur had chosen a place so densely populated by police. There was no avoiding it, he thought. Clivert began to pedal up and down the road. He was not a fit man, and Arthur was clearly not in a hurry to leave the building. Within half an hour he was wheezing. And then he was struck by another genius idea. He'd read somewhere that the best place to hide something was in plain view. He would draw attention to himself in a way that would ensure that every self-respecting Londoner would look the other way.

"Save the world!" he screamed.

He trundled up and down the street, not losing sight of the building. People looked away, even the police. It occurred to him then, as an assassin, that he would need a nickname, the sort the tabloids would adopt. It would have to be mysterious, but threatening, something with dark undertones. The word 'black' would be good, perhaps paired with a predatory bird. There was excitement growing in Clivert, as he realised, for the first time, and while riding shakily on his bicycle, that this could be his opportunity for worldwide fame. But he'd have to Google a few names. Black Eagle didn't seem right, Black Hawk too obvious and Black Kite was clearly wrong. Maybe birds were not the way to go. He interrupted his thinking to shout.

"Save the world!"

Of course he'd have to leave a mark, that was how tabloid nicknames were created. The thought coincided with a white splatter across his dark clothing and the flag as a pigeon crapped on him. For a second he thought about crapping on his victims, but couldn't imagine a cool nickname arising from that.

"Save the world!"

And then it struck him, although not quite as forcibly as the pigeon crap. Arnold thought he was a man with a big heart, such was the distance between his view of himself and reality. It was a very long way. But, he assured himself, his big heart had been abused by bad luck. Clivert decided he would place a pig's heart on his victim. He thought about it for a time and realised that it presented a few difficulties, not least locating a pig's heart and carrying it around with him. The heart part was good thinking, but what else had a heart? Ideally it would be easy to locate and carry. But what?

"Save the world!"

Artichokes have hearts, he thought. He could leave an artichoke on his victim. But it would be better if it were black. He could be the Black Artichoke. He'd have to get some business cards printed. He could throw a few at his victim's feet as well. Clivert was beginning to feel quite good about himself.

"Save the world!"

"What from?" someone shouted. The Black Artichoke would have a very strict policy when it came to hecklers. And he'd need a speech, like Samuel L Jackson in Pulp Fiction. He'd utter the same words just before he dispatched his victims, because no one messes with the Black Artichoke.

Arthur's sudden appearance was quite a distraction from the most comprehensive business plan Clivert had ever devised. But, he reminded himself, the Artichoke wasn't necessarily quick off the mark, that wasn't his thing. Arthur slid into the car, and he wasn't far away. Clivert pedalled furiously as the car jumped from one set of traffic lights to another. Just as Clivert reeled him in, the lights changed and he disappeared. And then he saw the Rolls come to a halt.

"Save the world," he wheezed, multitasking his cover with his assassin's mission. The door of the car opened. And Clivert swooped. He swooped so effectively he wondered, mid-swoop, whether he should reconsider the bird name. Arthur was in his sights.

There were, he discovered, a number of unresolved issues regarding this, his pilot attempt, at becoming an assassin. For a start it was harder to pull the trigger than he thought, and then there was a question of aim. Strapped, as the shotgun was, to the crossbar of his bike, aiming and firing required two hands, which didn't leave any further hands for the handle bars. One of the many things that Clivert had not been gifted with was good balance. So he did well to pull the trigger. It prompted other issues. The most significant was the silencer which, he discovered, didn't really suit shotgun use. The second was a recoil, the full force of which was applied directly to Clivert's crotch.

Chapter Thirty-Nine

"You have got to be kidding," Sophie said, knowing that Rachel was not kidding. She was rather alarmingly serious.

"You saw him! There he is! All we need to do is get a table, preferably near the door, and he won't be able to avoid you."

Sophie was wondering if a trend was forming. Rachel would suggest something absolutely outrageous and then ply her with drinks, after which it wouldn't seem quite so outrageous. The key was the Rolls.

"It's simple. Wherever the Rolls is, Arthur is. How difficult can it be to follow an old Rolls?"

This had been the first, and rather tricky, part of the plan. Rachel had always been quite the biker chick, and although she had plans to buy a big raunchy motorbike, she had settled on a scooter. It was easy to ride and to park. At least it would be easy to ride, had she not got Sophie so pissed, but if she hadn't done that she'd never have got her to get on the back. She had a habit of shifting her weight about, which provided them with a few scary moments. The other problem was the Rolls, which had been pouncing from the traffic lights like a scalded cat. Then they nearly collided with a lunatic waving a flag on a push-bike. Rachel had practically wet herself. Sophie hadn't noticed.

"You okay Soph?"

"Way to go girl," Sophie said, adopting a new vocabulary. The alcohol hadn't been quite enough, or it might have been too much.

"Like too much," Sophie muttered.

Rachel felt very sober.

"Onwards," Sophie said and threw herself through the doors.

"Quite," Rachel muttered.

This was all about Arthur's sexuality. Despite recent evidence to suggest that he'd switched batting order, Sophie was convinced. So that was leap number one. Next was to discover whether he wanted to enjoy the pleasures of parenting, mostly the financial ones. And then there was the possibility he might just want to save her from the drudgery of her life, and give her the whole package. It was a simple three leap plan.These were the kind of leaps that could only be made with some form of chemical assistance.

"A table for two," Sophie announced, completely unaware that the person she was addressing was barely dressed. Rachel spotted it rather quickly.

"Hold on, Soph, I don't think this is a restaurant."

Geraldine was a woman with a very wide armoury of smiles. Arthur had received the ones she favoured most, the sort that could prompt further decisions, such as the purchase of a new little convertible. This smile wasn't exactly hostile, but a very minor adjustment of her facial muscles would take it there. Firstly, these were two good-looking girls, and that was very good, as God knows her club had been frequented by more than its fair share of mingers. And mingers weren't good for business. But one of the girls looked like she was swaying.

"Perhaps we can have a quick drink, see if it suits us," Rachel improvised. She'd seen Arthur and he was laughing and joking with women. And this was a sex club. Leap one was sounding very doable. Geraldine's smile remained planted on her face, but it was only one twitch away. She led them to a table.

"Champagne?"

"Brilliant idea," Sophie said. It coincided with the realisation that most of the people in this establishment were partly clothed. That was until a couple entered one end of the room. She wasn't clothed at all, and a moment later nor was he.

"What the fuck?" Sophie asked in the most lucid fashion she'd managed in the last few hours.

"Thank you," Rachel said, and Geraldine rewarded her with a smile which verged on warmth. As Geraldine swayed towards the bar, Sophie leaned to Rachel.

"Don't you see? It's a sex place, thingy."

"I'd kind of got that," Rachel said stiffly.

"But," she continued, "not of the gay variety. This is a hetero club and Arthur is there with those two women." Rachel pointed. Sophie's pupils narrowed, which was quite a journey from their dilation.

"Bitches," she muttered, arriving too quickly at leap three. Leap three was going to take a lot of work.

"I think he's going to take them off to the back room, or something."

"Back room?" Sophie asked, still confused and assuming that this was an allusion to a sexual activity.

"This is the kind of place with rooms for sex."

"Oh, I see," Sophie said. Sex for her was beginning to seem a little historic. There was a television screen by the bar with flickering pornographic images. It was making her feel, dare she think it, just a little bit horny.

"Hey Rach, maybe I could show him a trick or two."

Rachel looked at her friend with doubt carved so deeply across her face that even her inebriated friend understood.

"Oh God," Sophie wailed, "if only I knew a trick or two. If only I was the kind of a girl who knew a trick. Come to think of it, what is a trick?"

Rachel, ordinarily a wild kind of girl, was feeling just a little tired. But they were going to have to sustain some sort of conversation, so she gave the question some thought.

"Have you ever put your finger up his bum?"

"No, seriously," Sophie began to laugh.

"I was being serious."

"Were you? Ugh."

They fell silent and then discovered the consequence of falling silent. They looked around the room. Sophie hadn't quite dispelled the image from her mind of poking a finger where she felt it really shouldn't go. The champagne bottle landed in front of them, interrupting any further trick-related thinking. It was wrapped in a sea of ice cubes, nestling in a silver bucket. Two glasses were poured. Sophie grabbed the glass nearest her and downed most of the fizzing drink, agonising over why she had never learned a sexual trick.

"What the fuck?" Rachel said with painful sobriety. She had just read the price list.

Chapter Forty

Rogerman was finding employment far more boring than he had anticipated. Although he had done very little anticipating, as employment hadn't been waiting in the wings ready to pounce. But compared to unemployment it was quite boring. At least with unemployment, he didn't have the opportunity to be bored before midday, as he'd always spent that sleeping. Then there was his virtual life on the computer, which passed by at great pace. There was so much to do.

"I mean," he muttered out loud, "like, all I've got to do, like, is like drive the car." The principal duties of a chauffeur were just beginning to dawn on him. And their limitations. There was one thing that was chief among them.

"This is, like, so unbe-fucking-lievably-like boring."

It wasn't a job that required driving, it was a job that featured hanging around and doing precisely fuck all, which should have made him ideal for the job. But the hours were grinding by. It was as if he were unwillingly transported back into a time when the world moved very slowly. Rogerman had to fill those long yawning moments that were sandwiched between the brief time he was actually required to drive the car.

This morning his mother had packed a lunch for him, which he had eaten around breakfast time, when he was bored. But that wasn't the problem, he wasn't really hungry. Rogerman was very rarely hungry, apart from when he had the munchies. Then he was ravenous. No, the problem was the rucksack she'd used. It was the small one with the hemp symbol on it, something to do with natural fibres. But that wasn't the issue.

"I mean, like, I've been straight, like, for, like, ages," Rogerman reassured himself and the empty car. He had done very well indeed. Five days was quite the longest he could remember going unaided, at least since he started saying 'like' a lot. There were no noticeable improvements to his health, which if he'd thought about it, might have been disappointing.

"Like, ages. Fucking ages."

And that was another thing. The old Rolls was painfully quiet, as if it were incapable of reflecting sound. It was just absorbed into the ancientness of the car. Rogerman was comfortable when the amps were turned to eleven, but was ill at ease in libraries.

"Fucking whispering," he said quite loudly. It was the way everybody whispered in libraries. He eyed the rucksack. The rucksack had a few secret pockets, which made even Rogerman wonder whether the hemp symbols were actually to do with natural fibres.

"I mean, he's not going to be back for, like, ages," Rogerman continued to reassure himself, and the fifty-year-old leather that lined the car. This, he knew, was going to be a long wait. Arthur did nothing quickly. He fiddled with the rucksack.

"Not for ages, like."

Rogerman wasn't normally very good at the business of time keeping. That had been another shock, and he'd never really been aware of the passing of time. And the clock in the car actually ticked.

"Tick, fucking, tock," he addressed the clock. It was as if it were taunting him with the painful and endless passage of time. He looked at the rucksack again. Buried somewhere in the intestines of the bag was quite the most powerful skunk he had ever tried. And he'd tried a lot. It was so powerful that it was wrapped in cling film, and then foil, and then more cling film. Then it was zipped into the bottom of the bag. And he could still smell it. And it smelled good. Rogerman hadn't noticed the aroma fill the car, he'd just assumed it was a withdrawal symptom. But it was calling him.

"Psst, over here," it was saying.

"Roger, Roger, Roger, Rogerman."

Despite the intimate terms on which he had been with the skunk, it was addressing him by his surname. It might have been in deference to the Rolls. Rogerman was only equipped with gossimer-thin resolve at the best of times.

"I mean, like, just a little. What harm could that do?"

The rich red leather seemed to agree. And that was before Rogerman had inhaled the skunk. His mind was set. The only question was whether he should get out of the car. He looked around, and paranoia set in. And that was before he'd taken a puff. There was a policeman in every shadow. Rogerman opted for a compromise and opened the windows. He dug around in the bag, and a moment later gave the package a toothy grin.

"Here's Johnny," he declared, and a moment later he set fire to it. Rogerman was not big on metaphors, but he was hit by a series of waves. It set him on a dialogue.

"Like, fantastic shit," he muttered.

"Real great shit, like."

It should have been a monologue, but in his head there were responses. It gave him a sense of well being.

"What a great job this is."

That was the first revelation, or it might have been a gift from the skunk. Now he loved his job. He wasn't aware of the changes that came over him, and a moment later Rogerman was now sprawled out in the back of the car. He'd made a further decision about the windows, and closed them. He didn't want the smoke winding its way towards the drug squad-filled shadows. Not when it could be in his lungs.

"Rogerman, is there enough brandy in the car?"

Rogerman had been perfecting his impersonation of Arthur. It was getting close. He tried again.

"Rogerman, old boy, a touch of brandy."

"Brandy, Rogerman, my man."

"Old man, Brandyman, roger."

Rogerman's accent was improving, but his capacity for uttering the words was declining. He changed tack.

"Yes master," he said obsequiously. He repeated it a few more times.

"Brandy, my lord and master. O superior being."

It wasn't quite slavish enough.

"Yes master. Yes my master. Yeth mastarrrr."

"Yeth my mastarrrrr."

Rogerman found himself with a cut glass tumbler in his hand. It was full of brandy. Rogerman had never tried brandy, but he had strict rules regarding drinking and driving.

"You're a chauffeur, old boy," he reminded himself in a combination of accents.

"It's, like, your lively-thingy," he was back on familiar territory. But when he thought about it, Rogerman realised that he didn't have strict rules about anything.

A sip wouldn't hurt.

Chapter Forty-One

Brayman was being led astray. It had been the principle feature of his life ever since he'd found himself with money. Every encounter seemed to involve astray, but astray, he was discovering, was a nice place to be.

"Mandy won't mind."

He'd discovered a few things about Mandy.

"I'm not in the right space for commitment," she'd told him.

She had delivered the line with the same skill that she'd suggested that they shouldn't be 'exclusive,' and in a moment that was sandwiched between unhurried and frantic sex.

And then a desperate need to leave the house. It was quite a skill. Brayman couldn't decide whether this was a good thing, or a bad thing. He liked her and he liked the sex a lot, and she looked great. She really looked fantastic, with or without clothes. But, he discovered, he had reservations about the use of the word 'space.' There were some words he just wasn't comfortable with. Mandy worked for an airline and was away a lot, which had left him at a loose end at a time when his ends were far from loose. All the sex had left him thinking about little else. To such an extent, he'd hardly followed any of Arthur's 'living well' regime. He'd prepared a salad for lunch and had eaten it with a Perrier water. Then he'd gone to the gym. Then he'd phoned Mandy again.

"I would, baby," she said, "But I'm in LA."

Brayman pined a little.

"I'll tell you what, you can meet up with the girls."

Brayman had no idea what meeting up with the girls might entail, but he was at a loose end. He'd met the girls that Mandy worked with briefly, and they'd been relaxed and friendly. Of course there was more to it than that. Since Mandy did not work for a budget airline, all the women were quite routinely gorgeous. And there were all those loose ends dangling from him, so why not?

"Groovy," Mandy said, which raised more doubts for Brayman, but she gave him the address where they were staying, and sent them a text.

Brayman wasn't sure if he was imposing, but he checked his calendar for the evening and found it wantonly blank. He got on the train. He didn't really expect them to be there – he was not that kind of a guy – but he reminded himself again, he had nothing else to do that evening. When he arrived at Paddington, he clicked his fingers for a taxi as if he had been doing it all his life and, like addressing a dog with the right masterly tone, one jumped to his side. Brayman didn't even notice it.

He'd never heard of the hotel, but it didn't take long for the taxi to thread its way there. The outside was lit up like a beacon. If light blazed, it was certainly doing it here. There was a large bar inside and propping it up were a group of gorgeous girls, who cheered on his arrival.

"Hey," he eventually managed, but bizarrely it actually sounded cool.

They were talking at a fast speed that took a moment, and a few drinks, to adjust to, and they weren't holding back. If he were required to summarise, it would be a fair assessment to say that as a consequence of working a long and intense two week shift they had not had the time to party. And they were ready to party. There was talk of some sort of sex club. Brayman couldn't figure out whether they were serious.

Chapter Forty-Two

Arnold Clivert dropped his trousers. While his genitals had hung in front of him mostly for decoration, he still felt fond of them. And he preferred them when they were pink and not the black, bruised colour he now found them. After the butt of the rifle had crushed them, the bike careered into some railings, where it lodged itself. His spirited pedalling had lent the bike some momentum and, when it hit the railings, he parted company with it. He flew over the handlebars. It was, he discovered, quite a deep basement. Luckily part of his face broke the fall. It made him even madder.

"You are a bastard," he said to the sky, shaking his fist.

It took him a while to settle down, and after twenty minutes he had reverted to being the master assassin. But, as ever, he was finding a few impediments. The first was the gaffer tape. He climbed up the slippery steps which would have provided more conventional access to the basement, and grappled with the bike. It was wedged. It had taken him five minutes to attach the shotgun, but it was going to take him a lot longer to get it off. It was as if the gaffer tape was being deliberately malicious. He'd also checked the building and found that the restaurant that Arthur had entered did not have windows.

"What kind of restaurant doesn't have windows?" he screamed at the sky. Then he wrestled a little more with the gaffer tape.

"Motherfucker," he muttered partly to the gaffer tape, and partly to Arthur, and a little bit to God. Eventually he heaved the gun in anger and the gaffer tape released its grip, and sent him and the gun tumbling back down into the basement. This time he hit the wall. It was less painful than the ground because, he realised, it wasn't a wall. At least, it wasn't unforgiving brick. It was plywood. His impact had taken a small chip off a corner. There was a little bead of light shining through. He could hear voices.

"Oh yes, oh yes indeed. Yes, yes, very much."

Even Clivert, with his limited experience of such things, realised that he was listening to someone having sex. One part of him thought it inappropriate to continue listening, but it was a small part and the very much greater part of him was enjoying it. So he carried on. He pressed his eye to the little hole. The warm air stabbed it slightly, but it was a pain worth enduring, particularly if he could see a bit more. He used the barrel of the shotgun to lever the ply, and a further little splinter pinged off. He was rewarded with a greater flash of light, which he pressed his eye to. Now he could see a lot more. But bizarrely the light was flashing on and off, which was strange. It took a moment longer to realise that the light was focused through the open legs of a real live woman, who was moving up and down.

"Bloody hell," he muttered.

"Splendid," an oddly familiar voice bellowed.

Clivert didn't care which part of him didn't want to look, this was the show of his life. It was better than the internet. He levered off more ply. It was reluctant to shift. He applied the barrel of the gun and gave it a heave. Now he had a really good view. It was as if he were was there. He pressed his face to the gap, having lost the facility to blink. There were a couple of women and a man, and then something else. A man poised to do the unthinkable. It was something he'd not seen before, and one of the many things that Clivert hated. It was an unusually long list, but the thing he really loathed and despised, was queers. Clivert was quite inordinately homophobic. He'd taunted his brother and now he was about to witness it. He gave the shotgun another heave.

Chapter Forty-Three

"Arthur?"

"Sophie?"

Arthur was surprised to find the woman he'd met at the wake standing in front of him. She was even more beautiful than he remembered. He smiled broadly, and introduced the girls.

"This is Trish and Sal."

Trish and Sal smiled at Sophie and shook her hand. While their predominant interest was in the penis, they weren't averse to the occasional vaginal foray. And this looked like a very attractive one. Arthur wasn't quite sure how to proceed, as they were bound for the boudoir suite. And he was aching to get on. Trish resolved the issue.

"Would you care to join us?" she asked. Arthur beamed approval at the idea. The viagra, at least the effects of it, were helping him to forget his earlier reservations.

"Hey, why not?" Sophie said casually.

Arthur's rampant desire to see her naked eclipsed his earlier need to impress upon her his apparent homosexuality. He was stumbling over himself at the thought. He led them down the steps into the largest basement suite. One of the great things about a sex club, Arthur always thought, is the lack of preamble. Where else would the question of sex be replied with 'Hey, why not?' There was no longer any need to cast surreptitious glances at Sophie, so he cast a lascivious one instead. This was going to be quite easily one of the best nights of his life.

He opened the door. The room was lined with dark red wallpaper and dominated by an enormous bed. The lighting was the only thing that was subtle.

"Wow," one of them muttered. And to Arthur's further delight, the three women started on each other. He was going to have to pace himself, he realised, as he gently helped the girls remove their clothes. Trish and Sal were curvy women with large pendulous breasts, where as Sophie was very firm indeed. He ran his hands everywhere.

Arthur lay back and pondered, just for a second, how wonderful it was being him. It really was bloody marvellous. The girls were now almost naked and not holding back. Arthur was not a voyeur by nature, but this was a very pleasant show. He watched them move up and down on each other. The rhythm of life. The reciprocating need to pleasure each other. Wasn't life great? They helped him shed some of his clothing with a seamless elegance. It wasn't just about sex, it was about having sex with women who knew how to have sex. This was not the confused fumblings of the young, but a real understanding of how to give and receive pleasure. The girls were nearly naked, bar expensive underwear in Trish and Sal's case, and Sophie's knickers. Arthur admired the skilful props and supports that framed the bountiful womanhood of Trish and Sal. And then Sophie removed her knickers.

And it all changed in a flash.

"Suck it like you did Barry!"

"I beg your pardon?" Arthur inquired.

It was quite a shock and, as in a car accident, everything slowed down. While Sophie had very fine breasts she also, Arthur discovered, had a penis. And quite a large one at that. She was waving it in his face, and the words of his father, or it could have been his grandfather, came back to him. What would he do for twenty million quid?

"Whoa, didn't expect that," Sal said cheerfully and grabbed it first. But Sophie was very clear on the subject.

"It's for Arthur."

Arthur tried very hard to smile. He deployed all the normal facial muscles, but what emerged looked closer to pain. But this was the moment. The will could be contested. And it was twenty million quid. A brief moment, for a lifetime's worth of dosh. What was the problem? Arthur opened his mouth. It was twenty million quid after all. How bad could it be? There was just the issue of whether he should keep his eyes open. Most women tended to have them closed, and closed removed one sense from the equation. He closed his eyes and held his mouth open.

It was followed by the most almighty deafening explosion. The wall seemed to collapse. Shots were firing everywhere, spraying the room. Trish and Sal dived down. Sophie looked in amazement. It wasn't the explosion she'd hoped for, but Arthur knew what to do. He had once been involved in a terrorist attack in a whore house in Africa and, like then, he got the hell out of there as quickly as possible. He had not been hit, but the wall, the smoke and the expectant erection hanging in the air, were enough. He opened his eyes, closed his mouth and got to his feet. And got the hell out of there.

Perhaps because he was still moving in slow motion, the moment took a surreal turn. He couldn't say for certain but, as he tore through the club, he thought he saw Sophie, the one with a vagina. And she said something. Something so shocking, it was far safer for him to continue thinking in surreal slow motion. And then there was Brayman. Arthur assumed he was hallucinating. He bashed through the doors as Geraldine looked on, her face fixed in the highest level of horror she reserves for expensive unpaid bills. He threw himself into the back of the Rolls, landing face-first onto Rogerman's crotch.

"What the – ?" they both said, but this was a getaway. Arthur recovered first.

"Drive!"

Rogerman hopped over the seat and behind the wheel. This was the moment he was waiting for. He fired up the Rolls and pressed the accelerator, and Rogerman drove. In his mind he was a grand prix god, but the Rolls didn't make the right noise. So Rogerman provided it.

"Neaoww," he began.

The gap between what was going on inside Rogerman's mind and the outside world had grown quite wide.

"Neaoww," he continued, knuckles white on the wheel.

"Drive!" Arthur yelled.

"Neaoww."

"Drive faster!"

"NEAOWWW!!" Rogerman stepped up the screaming, but they were still escaping at just over three and a half miles and hour.

Chapter Forty-Four

It was not a good first outing for the Black Artichoke, the bringer of doom and justice. The righter of wrongs, the terminator, the master assassin. Clivert had been thrown back onto his backside. The basement light-well was a small space and he was winded from the collision with the wall. But he knew he had further problems.

Clivert had forgotten that the shotgun was still loaded, and using the barrel to lever open the plywood had not been a great idea. The shot had flown everywhere, ripping up jagged strips of plywood as it went. One such jagged strip was holding him down. He knew roughly what the problem was, but was hesitant to find out more. The distant wail of police sirens was the galvanising force. He looked down. It was as bad as he thought. A long spike emerged from his trousers, the other end of which had buried itself in the wall. It was the bit in the middle of the spike that concerned him which, he was fairly certain, was occupying a space where his testicles used to be. He turned to the sky.

"You bastard," he hissed.

This moment was a perfect summary of everything in his life. It just wasn't fair. But he was the Black Artichoke, and soon he was going to be discovered with a shotgun. And Arthur Chum-thing was still alive. But he was trapped, pinned down. The wail of police cars became louder. He was going to have to summon up something. He eyed the offending thin triangle of spiked plywood, at least the section he could see that rose from his trousers.

But Clivert knew his testicles were still functioning – no one recently castrated felt this much anger. He grabbed the spike. And he screamed. There was no question that it had taken a journey through what were once his reproductive organs. He had no choice. He held the spike firmly and looked up at the sky and yanked.

"You bastards!"

The bloodied spike came out. He'd worn gloves and made sure that the bicycle and the shotgun were free from his fingerprints, but the spike held his DNA. He thought about stabbing Arthur to death with the splinter. It felt so fitting. And he couldn't leave it behind. It had concerned him so much that he hadn't noticed himself stand. The anger and adrenaline were holding him together, even if his underpants weren't. He climbed out of the basement accompanied by white pain, and flashes of black anger. He was more convinced than ever that stabbing Arthur to death with the spike of plywood was precisely what he intended to do.

When Clivert made it to the pavement he was astonished to see Arthur's Rolls meandering slowly down the road. The evening was not over yet.

Chapter Forty-Five

"Arthur has just gone downstairs to a sex room with three women. What other evidence do you require?" Rachel asked.

"I never doubted it," Sophie said with new confidence.

"And you," Rachel began, "are an exciting, vibrant, desirable woman. The kind of woman that any man would be proud to have on his arm."

"Do you think so?" Sophie asked. Rachel tried very hard not to sigh. She knew she would have to give the whole rousing self-esteem speech. She topped up Sophie's glass with the world's most expensive cheap champagne.

"Of course I think so. And so does every man who's ever met you. Haven't you seen the way the men in this bar have been looking at you?"

Sophie hadn't, and she also hadn't factored in the thought that this was the sort of bar where seduction was not required. But it suited Rachel's argument.

"So we have achieved goal number one. Arthur is straight. Excellent progress, don't you think?" Rachel was wondering whether they could finish the evening on goal number one achieved.

"I suppose," Sophie said, refilling her glass.

"We also know that, as well as the Chum-wotsit wealth, he has just acquired twenty million pounds."

"True."

Rachel frowned, she'd hoped that Sophie would be a little more enthusiastic at this stage of the proceedings.

"Do you think I should follow them into the sex room?" Sophie suddenly asked.

"Whoa, hold on girl." That, Rachel thought, was too much enthusiasm. "Keep an eye on the final prize."

"What?"

"In order to get the full shining knight you can't give it away too easily. Start with the father part, don't push for money. Never mention money." Rachel looked uncertainly at her friend. This was important.

"What did I say?"

"Never mention money," Sophie recited.

"Exactly. This is about spearing his heart, not his cock or his wallet."

Sophie couldn't take it all in.

"You see if you have his heart, and you will once he bonds with his child, then you have the rest."

"What, his cock?"

"No, I meant his wallet."

Sophie looked down in a daze. It all seemed too prosaic for her, although she'd gathered that his cock was the least important thing she needed to spear. Was spearing some kind of sexual trick she wasn't familiar with? She was reluctant to ask.

"So what am I supposed to say?"

"That he is the father."

Sophie turned this thought around in her head, but each time, with the champagne and everything else in her, she arrived at a Darth Vader voice.

"You are the father, hiss, pah," she declared.

Rachel raised her eyes. Her sobriety was making it a little harder to access her sense of humour, and Rachel was not, by nature, the nursing type. This trip was asking too much of her.

"You are the father, hiss, pah, hiss," Sophie added.

Rachel had her doubts that this was the best approach, but the club was beginning to make her nervous.

"You girls up for fun?"

Rachel looked at the short, overweight, slobbering businessman who had appeared in front of them and gave him a sneer so complete, and delivered with such clarity, that he wilted on the spot. Sophie hadn't noticed him.

"It is not good for men not to have to make the effort to seduce," Rachel declared, her views on the matter galvanising. A large explosion and noisy commotion made it hard for Sophie to respond. It was followed by the sight of Arthur in full flight, dragging some clothes with him, and clearly making an escape.

"It's Arthur," Sophie said, and rose to greet him. But as with Rocky Deep, her timing was flawed. She said something critical and important as he ran past.

Chapter Forty-Six

"Get a fucking move on!" Arthur screamed. Rogerman's racing car engine-note screams had become so loud it was difficult for Arthur to penetrate them. Rogerman shifted gear. They were now travelling at four and a half miles an hour.

Arthur looked around frantically. What had happened? What was he running from? Was someone trying to kill him, or was it the suspended penis? The penis of Damocles, taunting him with his heterosexuality. The twenty million quid question.

"Move!" Arthur screamed at Rogerman.

The Damoclesean penis had hung in front of him like a twenty million pound test. He'd had no choice. And then, with the explosion, he did have a choice. Up until that moment it was one of the best days of his life. Why had it changed so fast? Arthur relaxed. His paranoia was getting the better of him. It was all in the mind. There was just some electrical fault, or something, maybe an air conditioning unit, and he had panicked. His nerves weren't rock steady like they used to be. It was the child thing, and Sophie, that had changed things. It would explain the hallucinating. There was no chance Sophie, vagina Sophie, would be in a sex club. No chance at all. But she'd said something.

Was he the father? Of course if he were, that would be a good thing, he reassured himself. That was probably why he'd imagined her, from the shock of another Sophie with unusual physiognomy. And Brayman, what the hell was he doing there? Arthur pressed the button to raise the screen between him and Rogerman. It drowned out the noise. He was going to have to have a word with his chauffeur. There was clearly something wrong. Arthur began to enjoy the funereal pace. They had turned a couple of corners. He opened the divide again and shouted at Rogerman.

"Stop!"

There was no reaction, so he prodded him aggressively. Rogerman was coming down, and was moving into a more sentient phase. He became aware that the car was filled with loud noises. It was beginning to occur to him that they might be originating from him. A stab in the back confirmed it. He stopped making the noise, but was still convinced that everyone was out to get him. The shadows were filled with demons.

"Stop the car," Arthur asked very reasonably, and Rogerman complied. For a moment neither said anything. Arthur wasn't very well practised at suggesting someone sobers up. It would be the kind of fatherly speech he may have to give. He composed the words in his mind. It seemed best for them to leave the car, and for Rogerman to pick it up first thing in the morning. It might even be better to let the authorities tow the car, so that Rogerman could pick it up later in the day. Much later.

"The thing is Rogerman, old boy -" But Arthur was interrupted.

"Bastard!"

There was a manic bloodstained face at his window.

"Bloody hell!" Arthur said, and jumped back.

The man waved a blood-stained dagger.

"Bloody hell," Arthur said again, but this time from the other side of the car.

"Drive!" Arthur yelled.

Rogerman was confused. He'd always had issues with authority. They were never consistent. Did he want him to drive or stop?

"Drive!"

Fortunately Arthur had locked the doors, as the strange ghostly figure was tugging at the door handles. This time he wasn't hallucinating. If he were, the figure would be brandishing a penis. He wouldn't want to be stabbed by one of those. Rogerman very gently pulled the car out of its parking place. The madman moved to the front of the car. And Rogerman saw his demon. Was it his father? An old school teacher? Or the judge that said he was a menace to society? Or it might have been the 'hallucino' part of hallucinogenic, which made an uneasy coupling with paranoia. It didn't matter. Rogerman floored the throttle.

The long bonnet of the Rolls rose with a roar as the old engine marshalled as many horses as it could muster at short notice. Rogerman held onto the steering wheel and closed one eye, and used the flying lady as a sight. She wasn't contemporary with the car, as there had been a period when a number had been stolen. This one had been welded in place and, Clivert discovered, was as solid as the two and a half tonnes of car behind it. Rogerman hardly noticed the impact, which didn't interfere with the forward progress of the car.

"I'm, like, out of here," he muttered with certainty. He hadn't ruled out the possibility that the image in front of him had just been a friend that the skunk had brought along to the party. It was, he reminded himself, great shit.

It was also, coincidentally, where Clivert found himself as he landed in a pile of horse shit, which a police horse had freshly deposited on its way to a canter in Hyde park. But it cushioned his inevitable collision with the pavement. He was winded from the impact with the Rolls, which had caught him in the middle of his body. More precisely, it had left a flying lady impression on what remained of his genitals.

Chapter Forty-Seven

Sergeant Hurley had trained at some length and had passed every test with commendations. He really could shoot. He also looked great in the flack jacket with the pistol in its holster and the rifle slung round his neck, held firmly, but just a tad menacingly, down. Unfortunately, outside a firing range, he'd yet to let off a round.

"There's been an altercation, Sarge," someone said, but he was only half listening. The sentence did not contain the magic words. The words that meant that he could go down to the armoury and gear up like a soldier. Hurley came from a long line of coppers, and some had even made it to the States. For Hurley that was the holy grail, the mecca of policing. Everyone was armed, which sounded like much more fun. He'd applied to work there, and opened every letter with bated breath and, so far, disappointment.

"He's armed, Sarge."

Also policemen got to roll over the bonnets of cars, while holding and aiming a firearm. Hurley thought for a moment and amended the thought in his head to the 'hoods' of cars. He was going to have to learn the lingo.

"Sarge?"

"Yes?" said Hurley, although his mind was still on the streets of New York. There was a strong Catholic Irishness to the family, which they'd carried over to America. It had influenced the accent.

"He's armed."

"Armed? Fucking great."

Hurley sprung into life. He was down the basement quicker than you could say NYPD, and strapping the equipment on with rising excitement. He was so caught up in the excitement, he began to practise his American-Irish accent.

"Freeze, motherfucker," he muttered to himself. The two words didn't give him much to play with on the accent front, and he'd forgotten to identify himself first. He called his partner.

"Anderson? Gunman!"

Anderson did not share the same passion for firearms as Hurley, and it was his hope never to fire a shot. He spoke with a slow, deliberate West Country accent, and had only retrained with firearms because it appeared to require a lot less work. There was no tedious detection required, no door to door enquiries, no plodding the beat, just the occasional madman. And God forbid he should actually let off a round. Then the paperwork was endless. He had two years to go before his early retirement option. He'd yet to decide what to do, but knew it would be better not to have to do it on his own. Anderson needed a woman.

"Quicker!"

Anderson strapped the necessary paraphernalia to him as if he had all the time in the world, and just a little bit more to irritate Hurley.

"Faster!"

Irritating Hurley was his prime activity, and was one that he found very easy to do. It gave him undiminished satisfaction.

"Shall I drive?" he suggested with a casual drawl.

"No fucking way," Hurley said with slight embarrassment, as he'd let slip a little bit of that American accent.

"Aren't you from Leighton Buzzard?" Anderson asked.

Hurley didn't respond. Instead he cocked and uncocked some of his firearms. It was a habit he'd developed, a little like a nervous tick. He knew they were laughing at him down at the station. In response, he'd devised some un-American swearing in an effort to lead him away from the temptation of the word 'motherfucker.'

"Let's go."

Moments later they were racing through the streets of London in Hurley's unmarked car with a flashing light slapped to the roof and the siren blaring. Other road users always provided a problem for him.

"Motherfucker." Damn, Hurley thought. He'd let one out.

Anderson chuckled, braced himself and wondered what he was going to cook that night. His recent dating history had been less than successful, and he was currently occupying what he thought of as a fallow patch. Although fallow tended to suggest that there was intermittent growth. This was more of a drought. He'd never had difficulty attracting women when he was younger, which was the prime reason his wife left him, but now in his late forties it was proving a little tougher. The internet had helped, but he wasn't making it past the second date. On the third date he might reasonably expect to see some flesh, but his life had drifted into a flesh-free zone. This evening he was cooking for a nurse, and he was worried about the menu. He might have mentioned it was a passion of his. If it could get him laid, it could become a passion. He needed to raise his culinary game, but he wasn't sure how. What was he going to cook?

"Bovine moron!" Hurley screamed at a road user, deploying his un-American swearing.

Beef, Anderson thought, was way too obvious.

"Fucking pigs," the road user replied, correctly guessing that they were in too much of a hurry to stop.

Pork was definitely a better option, Anderson thought. It was much cheaper, but also a more consistent meat. The only question was what cut?

Hurley weaved past a stationary bus and two cars by taking the opposite carriageway. A car driving towards them seemed to object.

"Mush for brains."

Anderson wasn't keen on the idea of pig brains, but mushrooms were a must. He liked mushrooms, and had them with everything. Perhaps he could get hold of those expensive little ones, what the hell were they called?

"Shift!" Hurley shouted, so very nearly following it with the 'm' word.

Shallot, Anderson thought. That's a great idea.

"I'll chop you into little pieces!" Hurley screamed.

But Anderson had pretty much decided on chops, and there was a good butcher they could stop at after this call. The only question was what he should cook it in.

"Sweet mother of God," Hurley said, reverting to the Irish. In America he'd have a partner who would quip with him, maybe a black guy from the streets. He'd play the Catholic Irish cop, and their banter would be pithy and dark. Hurley yanked the wheel and, as they screamed round the corner, something clattered across the dashboard and landed at Anderson's feet.

"Grab the rosary beads, would ya?" Hurley said as if he'd addressed his from-the-streets-black-guy colleague.

Perfect, Anderson thought, Rosemary went well with pork, and now he thought about it, the nurse's name was Rosemary. She'd sent him an email message that rivalled the Old Testament in length, and he hoped he'd get around to reading it all. He'd scanned through it to get the flavour, which wasn't far off what he hoped to achieve with Rosemary.

"It's here," Hurley said. But the scene of the crime turned out to be something of a disappointment for him. He drew the car to a halt with just a soupçon of a squeal. They snaked their way out of the vehicle, Hurley surveying the roof tops for villains, and Anderson concentrating on looking cool. There wasn't much between them, and they both looked the part.

"Gunman?" Geraldine said casually. She wasn't keen on having the police, the tax office or the local council anywhere near her premises. That wasn't to say it was unheard of to have the Chief Constable, the Head of the Inland Revenue or councillors in her establishment. But discretion went both ways.

"No, I don't think so. There was a bit of noise, but I think it was an electrical fault. Something to do with the air conditioning."

Hurley's excitement evaporated quicker than an Alaskan presidential candidate, while Anderson's interest perked up. Geraldine was age-appropriate, clearly solvent and absolutely stunning. The day might have prospects after all.

"Gentlemen," she said as she launched into shameless charming, "you both look quite magnificent."

Anderson beamed, while Hurley fiddled with his guns.

Chapter Forty-Eight

Courtney Mbabwe discovered that without a birth certificate, or much in the way of public records, it was difficult to research his heritage. He drew a blank. He knew he was different from his siblings. He couldn't sing or dance, for one thing. But it wasn't enough. So he asked his mother.

"Mum, who's my dad?"

Gloria smiled, which was her face's natural default position, and her response to almost everything.

"God is your father," she said.

Courtney's time on Google had taught him not just that not everyone believed in God, but that there appeared to be rather more that didn't. The highlights from the bible he'd read evidently suggested a sound code of morals, but hardly evidence of a higher being. Courtney didn't think much like his siblings either.

"Yes, of course. But who is my biological father?"

He was hoping that his mother wouldn't force him to spell it out.

"God is everyone's father."

Gloria lived the way she lived, without the confines of western morality. She had lovers and she had children. She loved, and looked after, those children, and they were all hers. Why was it so important? They were her children, wasn't that enough?

"With whom," Courtney began, "Did you engage in sexual intercourse and were consequently impregnated by, thereby giving birth to me?"

Gloria just laughed. Courtney might have just left it there, but he was persistent. He had fixed his mind on having something, and he wasn't going to be put off. He was either going to charm her into telling him, or trick her, or fight a war of attrition. But he was going to find out. Gloria's easy-going spirit wasn't used to the attack, but she had always felt that it didn't matter.

"It's not where you're from, it's who you are that matters."

"Yes Mum, and you're right, absolutely right."

Courtney would often agree with her, and then rephrase the question.

"And I'm so pleased that you are my mother, and Eze and…" Courtney would list all the names.

"What made you choose Courtney?" he asked suddenly.

As Gloria had always been left alone to choose names, there had often been something that had prompted her. She couldn't, for the life of her, remember.

"Gosh, I can't remember."

Courtney looked at her quizzically, unsure whether she was telling the truth. He changed tack.

"Why did you call Peter, Peter?"

She thought for a bit.

"He was an apostle," Gloria said merrily.

Courtney paused for a second.

"Wasn't he a fisherman?"

"Yes," Gloria said slowly, feeling she might have been caught out.

Courtney knew which direction he was travelling. There was very little local history, just a few stories that were passed down, mostly by a local story teller. But there was one that had captured his imagination.

"Many years ago, before we had cars and electricity, didn't a man come here?"

"I don't know, dear."

"Wasn't he an explorer?"

"Was he? I don't know, it was before I was born."

"What was before you were born?"

Gloria blushed, she knew where this was going.

"Didn't he help divert the water?"

Gloria mumbled something which sounded like defeat.

"And plant new crops?"

There was a further mumbling.

"Wasn't his name Courtney?"

Gloria smiled for want of anything else to do.

"Wasn't he an English chap?

While Gloria loved all her children, she did find that Courtney could be a pompous ass at times. But Gloria knew every father just by looking into the face of her child, she didn't need clues. There was the hunter, the farmer, the roofer, the fisherman, another farmer – the tall one, the carpenter. And there was the Englishman.

Chapter Forty-Nine

Jean, Arthur's secretary, had now completed all three of the *Fifty Shades of Grey* series, and it had made her very sensitive. Not sensitive to the emotions of others, but sensitive downstairs. She slid around her typist chair, but it just made things worse. Or better. But Jean didn't want to go back to prison. She was not going to go to a hardware stall to buy ropes and cable ties and shackles and gaffer tape, like Christian Grey. She was not going to do that.

Instead Jean set about opening the post. It wasn't an office that generated much post, and Arthur had a facility for ignoring it. Arthur preferred to deal with the spoken word. Jean thumbed through a few bills and a couple of charitable requests, which she filed in the dustbin. They were not a family noted for their charitable work. Eventually, Jean had found a reason to throw every letter in the bin, except one. She took an inordinately long time doing it, as she knew the day was going to move at glacial pace. She crossed her legs and tried not to think of Christian Grey's shopping list of implements for tying someone down. Crossing her legs was a mistake. She uncrossed them. Then she opened them wide. That was a mistake too.

Prior to Jean's unfortunate foray into the world of rape she'd gone through life with almost no sexual contact, and it had suited her fine. Someone had changed her, a young man, and thereafter she had become a synaptic mass of sexual longing. The doors, as it were, had been opened, and like old, porous wooden doors, they were too swollen to ever close. She knew it might be a mistake reading erotic novels, but she couldn't help herself. The empty office was filled with just her, and her rampant sexual desires.

She looked at the remaining letter. It was marked *Personal and Private*, which made it all the more necessary that she should savour it at her leisure. She went to make a coffee. Arthur was very particular about his coffee and there was an enormous stainless steel machine with which she could hiss and fluff the specially imported beans into a frothy drink. It took some time, and she'd already had a coffee earlier. But creating another would take her closer to the end of the day. She was getting rather good at it, and eventually settled down at her desk with the coffee. She remembered she had a couple of letters to do, and decided to attack them first. It didn't take long, and took her to the end of her coffee. She sat back and relaxed letting her hands fall in her lap.

"Whoa," she muttered. Arthur, being Arthur, had selected coffee beans which were as densely packed with caffeine as nature allowed. Her hands were shaking. This on its own would not present a problem, but they were resting in her lap. She removed them quickly and opened the letter.

"Interesting."

It was from the lawyer handling the last will and testament of Barry Clivert. It included a letter from the late Mr Clivert himself, and made interesting reading. She'd had a couple of chats with Clivert when he'd been waiting for Arthur. He seemed pleasant, if a little timid. She read on. Barry Clivert did not have a devious mind. It was certainly sharp, very sharp, but he had little guile, and all the beating delivered by his misogynistic brother had slowed progress in other parts of his life. His brother had also been grotesquely homophobic, just as Barry's proclivities were emerging. It was one of the factors that had given him the determination to make as much money as he had. After that he had found the confidence to live as he chose. And having arrived so painfully at that point, he liked the idea of a managed legacy.

"Oh dear," Jean muttered. It wasn't going to be a straight transfer of the twenty million. It took her a long time to read through the document, and then even longer to reread it. It hadn't changed on the second reading.

"Oh dear, dear," Jean repeated.

She was going to have to tell Arthur, but Arthur was hell bent on getting out of the country. And she couldn't help noticing that Arthur had spent the last few days living like he was about to have twenty million quid descend into his bank account, which wasn't quite the case. There were a lot of conditions, chief among them being that Arthur would have to set up a charitable trust for battered gay men. Not on its own onerous, but the money would be available in a series of drawdowns. The first would be after that charitable trust had run for a year. And the last would be after it had run for ten years.

"Oh dear," Jean muttered. She was going to have to tell Arthur.

Chapter Fifty

Brayman was rather surprised to hear from Arthur, but welcomed the call nonetheless.

"Another jaunt to Africa, old boy?"

Arthur's tone had changed slightly, but Brayman couldn't quite place why. Maybe there was a little less authority, even a whisper of desperation. But going to Africa again was very much on his to-do list. It was growing into quite a long list, but he was also ticking off stuff.

"Of course, why not?" Brayman said, with an ease that ordinarily would have irritated Arthur, but he didn't notice it. He'd slept fitfully that night. There were all sorts of things coming at him, which hadn't been very relaxing. He hadn't quite rid himself of the image of the Damoclesean penis. It was a very persistent image. He assured himself that it wasn't the threat to his sexuality, although his grandfather might think differently. He couldn't care less. Or he didn't think so.

But there was one thing he was sure about. Someone was trying to kill him. He hadn't recognised the shadowy figure with the strange, dagger-like spike, but he wasn't hanging around to find out. He thought about Gloria. He'd spent some time with her many years ago and occasionally, when he went to Africa, he liked to drop by. She was always cheerful and never seemed to age and, if she was without a man, or between them, he'd spend the evening with her. It was very comforting. If he thought about it, and usually he wasn't introspective enough to bother, he'd have realised that she was the woman he was most comfortable with. Arthur decided that his trip should definitely include a visit to Gloria. She would help ease the pressure.

"Splendid. Well, pack your things."

"When are we going?"

"Now."

Arthur had managed to acquire two first class seats, and their visas were still valid. 'Now' was just a thought in the morning, but after nagging Jean and a few airlines it had become a reality pretty quickly.

"Now?"

"Now."

Even for the recently relaxed and laid back Brayman, now seemed very soon, but Sophie was still away, so why not? He hadn't really enjoyed the sex club. He'd had sex, he wasn't completely mad, but it wasn't really his thing. As a one off it was great. He was learning that he was the kind of guy who needed a connection and, rightly or wrongly, he had begun to think he'd like that with Mandy. Although he was aware that Mandy had been very clear about the subject of connection, or it might have been exclusivity. He couldn't help himself.

"Where are you?"

Despite the connection thing, Brayman had stayed in town and had a bit more of the sex he was uncertain about. Mandy had said that not exclusive thing. He gave Arthur the address.

"We'll set off soon, be at yours in an hour, old boy."

That gave Arthur about an half an hour to do one further task.

"Look Rogerman, old boy," he began.

Rogerman had feared this speech ever since he had finally sobered up, which had taken a day or so. In the cold light of sobriety, substance and alcohol, Rogerman preferred his new status, adorned as it was, for the first time, with a job. His prospects were like the skunk, cremated.

"Yes, I'm really very sorry, Mr Cholmondely-Godstone."

Rogerman looked as contrite as he was able. He'd had his suit dry-cleaned and polished his shoes. This was the most respectable he'd ever managed.

"Yes, the thing is that you really can't smoke that stuff and drive. And then there's the brandy."

Arthur had never delivered an admonishing speech in his life, and clearly had no talent for it. But with Eddie and Rogerman and the possibility of parenthood, things were changing.

"It won't happen again, I promise," Rogerman said with real conviction.

Arthur looked at him and nodded.

"Everyone deserves a second chance," Arthur muttered and then, "We need to go and get Brayman and then get to the airport."

"Yes sir!" Rogerman positively saluted.

Chapter Fifty-One

Arnold Clivert lay in the bath with an icepack wrapped round his crotch.

"I'm going to get the bastard!"

He hadn't noticed that the occasional word muttered out loud had extended to an ongoing dialogue.

"Everything he's done to me."

A plan was emerging. That morning he'd received a letter from the owner of the Skegness camp site. He was suing him. His brother had registered the caravan in his name and his address.

"Bastard!"

Once the Black Artichoke had completed his first contract, he was going to go to Skegness. First he was going to break the toys into even smaller pieces and then the campsite owner was going to get it. The thought prompted an involuntary laugh.

"Hah! Bastard."

But first, he was going to smash the butt of a rifle in Arthur's groin, then stab his crotch with the splinter of plywood he had preserved. And then he was going to brand him with a flying lady. He was going to heat it up with a blowtorch.

"Tissh," he said, making the sort of cooling noise he imagined a red hot flying lady would make when pressed against cool testicles.

But there were a couple of problems he needed to resolve. The first was locating a flying lady. He'd checked eBay but found his account had been suspended over a Star Wars figure altercation.

He was going to have to remove it from Arthur's Rolls, which seemed far more fitting. The second was Arthur himself. He was a big man and Clivert, even as the Black Artichoke, doubted whether he could overpower him. He'd have to hit him hard with something and then tie him down. He'd bought ropes, shackles, cable ties and gaffer tape from a hardware store that morning.

"Bam!" He imagined the butt of a rifle coming down with great force.

A baseball bat was a bit big to carry. So, in the spirit of the sawn-off shotgun, he created the sawn-off baseball bat. He had to admire his creativity. And there was more. The Black Artichoke would need a calling card. Clivert had printed a few out from his computer, but was having problems with the message. After a while he settled on "You have been judged and found wanting. You have no heart. The Black Artichoke." The design involved a lot of black ink. He'd bought a number of artichokes from the fruit and veg shop, but it wasn't enough. He'd painted them black. The next requirement was a uniform. The grim reaper seemed the best option, but presented problems navigating around London, so he compromised and arrived at a Ku Klux Klan hat in black. There were further issues with this, mostly that it was difficult to see out of, but that, he decided, was just a matter of getting used to it.

His thoughts were interrupted by the telephone. It mostly rang when people in far-flung parts of the planet felt the need to sell him something he didn't need, and which wouldn't work anyway. Social calls did not feature and the office, as far as he was aware, didn't have his number. He answered it anyway.

"Mr Clivert?"

"Tracey?"

Tracey had wondered whether she should call Clivert for a few days. It was becoming increasingly clear that the office could function without him, so his absence wasn't actually a problem.

"Yes, it's me, Tracey."

As social calls were so infrequent for Clivert, he wasn't immediately sure how to proceed. Tracey went first.

"How are you?"

Clivert being a pedantic sort of man, wasn't sure whether he should list his ailments, but as most of them featured his genitals he decided not to.

"I'm fine."

"The thing is, Mr Clivert, it's not like you not to be here, so I wondered if everything was okay."

Clivert was quite taken aback. He hadn't thought about either Tracey or her breasts for sometime, not since the reading of the will. Not since he'd become the Black Artichoke.

"I thought I'd take a holiday."

"Holiday? Are you sure?"

Clivert was not the sort of man to take a holiday, as most Star Wars conventions tended to be at the weekend.

"Yes," Clivert said firmly.

He desperately wanted to tell her about his new life as an assassin, but could see the weakness of this as a plan. He imagined himself back at the office and Tracey reading the paper. It was a comforting image.

"Who do you think the Black Artichoke is?" she would purr.

Clivert would deliver a knowing smile. He was going to re-emerge from this a new person, a person Tracey would be interested in. He'd seen what she was wearing the day he should have walked into the office a rich man. It was possible, he reassured himself. And he'd had a breakthrough as well. The Black Artichoke, as well as being a master of disguise, was also a master detective. It had helped that Google had provided two hits, one of which was Arthur's office. And once his testicles had returned to a more human colour, that was where he was going to go. And then he was going to smash, stab and brand him. Justice would be done.

But in the meantime the Black Artichoke had other issues to deal with, of a physical kind. He decided to take the day off.

Chapter Fifty-Two

Arthur felt much happier once the aeroplane had left the tarmac and the stewardess had pressed a large drink in his hand. It was still disturbing him that someone was out to kill him, but he thought it unlikely that whoever it was would follow him to Africa. The only question was, who was it? It wasn't the first time someone had taken exception to him – it was a professional hazard – but it would be useful to know who.

"Everything okay, Arthur?" Brayman asked cheerfully. He could see that Arthur was distracted.

"Of course, everything is fine."

Arthur wondered for a moment whether Brayman wasn't quite as he seemed. But as Brayman beamed back at him, he saw that he was exactly as he seemed. It wasn't him. It was most likely to relate to Barry Clivert, which left two suspects. The wimpy brother, which he doubted, or Sophie with a penis. He wished he hadn't thought of her as a possibility, as it prompted the image of the Damoclesean penis. It made him quite faint.

"Are you sure?"

"Another brandy, perhaps."

Brayman had wondered whether he should mention his trip to the sex club, but decided against it. Instead he sipped on his large brandy, and relaxed in the first class seating. For a moment he'd hoped that Mandy would be working on the plane, but it was the wrong airline and the wrong direction. He'd see her once they returned. He took a moment to imagine her naked.

Arthur's mind was in a different place. There were two things he had to deal with. The first was to get to the bottom of the Sophie and the child business. That is, of course, Sophie with a vagina. The second was to be one step ahead of the man trying to kill him. He decided to call Jean when they landed and get her to sort out surveillance equipment in the office and in his flat. If he could see the killer coming that would be a step in the right direction. He drifted into a pleasant sleep, which was interrupted by a pleasant lunch, followed by a further sleep, more food and another sleep. By the time they were in the African sunshine, the robust Arthur was back in place. He quickly called Jean and then declared, "I think a little gentle safari is in order."

Arthur's first plan was to encourage Brayman to view a few animals at close quarters. Very close quarters. After the Eddie debacle he was coming to the conclusion that Brayman was gifted with a pretty strong constitution. He hoped he wasn't losing his touch, but he feared that Brayman might be the death of him. After the business at the Pig Farm as well. He couldn't understand what the doctor, or was it a psychiatrist, had said about a psychosomatic reason. It was most strange. Arthur hadn't collapsed in a long time, although it wasn't unusual in the Cholmondely-Godstone family. But they always got up again.

"Safari? Great, I only got to see a crocodile last time."

Brayman said cheerfully. As the crocodile was only one bite away from eating him, Brayman's cheerfulness disturbed Arthur.

"There are plenty more to see."

The animals Arthur had in mind were all aggressive predators, apart from the hippo, which was just aggressive. Brayman, he noticed, had slept rather less than him and was looking distinctly tired. There was no wasting the moment. The smallness of the airport, and their first-class status, ensured that they were off the plane and into a battered Land Rover in a brief moment.

Arthur liked the air in Africa. He liked the simplicity and the unspoilt nature, and the light which altered so it never quite looked the same. It was the same thing that always brought him back to Victoria Falls. Each morning the sun, the spray in the air, the wind, and the water itself looked different. He could never tire of it. If he had to escape, this is where he would go.

"Nice, isn't it," Arthur said, without thinking.

Brayman agreed with a nod. The old Land Rover was bucking and weaving like a rodeo horse, and he was becoming quite reticent. He'd not talked for a while. He'd even abandoned conjuring naked images of Mandy.

"You okay, old boy?"

Brayman confirmed that he was fine with a further nod, giving Arthur the sneaking suspicion that he wasn't fine at all. Arthur had used the same guide on a number of occasions, as his reckless driving and fearlessness appealed to him.

"Everything okay, Winston?" Unusually for Arthur, he remembered the guide's name.

"Sure, man," Winston said. He had difficulty telling white men apart and saw no point in remembering names, but he knew this one. Lion maulings tended to stick in his mind, but not quite as effectively as big payers. It was rare to find someone who relished both.

"Got that rifle, Winston?"

"Sure, man."

Winston patted the rifle beside him. It had been through a number of wars, and done so with the minimum maintenance. Just to make sure Arthur leant over discreetly and adjusted the sights. It didn't matter. Winston was a terrible shot. Arthur knew this because Winston was known as 'Winston the terrible shot.' It had helped Arthur remember his name.

"Sure, man," Winston repeated for no particular reason.

It didn't take long for them to find themselves deep in the park, and the wildlife starting to emerge. The only thing that broke the stillness was the rattling noise of the engine. Winston found some cover by a tree and cut the engine. They savoured the silence for a moment. Brayman was grateful for it, as his head was reeling.

"What now?" Brayman asked with an impatient tone that was slightly out of character.

"We wait."

It was a good time to bring out the hip flask. Brayman accepted it without comment. It took a moment for Arthur to realise that the rattling of the engine had been replaced with another rattling. The weather was changing, gathering a hostility as black clouds rolled in. Winston tightened the makeshift hood, which would just about keep them dry. There was a crackle of lightning in the distance.

"A storm, man," Winston observed, accessing his insightful powers of stating the obvious.

Brayman felt better with the brandy and the absence of movement, but the rolling storm was creating a tension in the air. It was likely to crash near them, and it was hard to tell how brutal it was likely to be.

"Look, man," Winston said, pointing at the lion that Arthur had been following for nearly ten minutes. It too was becoming anxious with the distant thunder shaking the ground. It was also a very hungry lion. But it was always a hungry lion, which was why it had been banished from the pride, as it tended to eat everything. This wasn't balanced by hunting prowess, as it was far too overweight for that. It was a lion that favoured slower-moving prey.

"Wow," Brayman muttered, the experience sharpening his senses. He'd certainly recovered from the stinging nettle fiasco, although Arthur hadn't forgotten about the allergy. He'd even done some research. His hope was that if a big cat didn't get him, that might.

The lion sloped along describing ever-decreasing circles. He knew he was being watched, but feigned nonchalance. He passed in and out of sight.

"Where's he gone?"

"He's there, man."

"Let's get a better look," Arthur suggested. As if mesmerised, Brayman got out of the Land Rover. Winston tried to remember how to load the rifle, or was it a shot gun? Guns were not his thing.

"Look, look," Arthur said, with just a touch of contrived excitement. Brayman looked.

The lion's last circle had taken him out of the open and into the dense bush. This time he was circling lunch and dinner. As he couldn't move fast, he had mastered slow and patient. He placed one paw in front of the other with a slow and deliberate action. For a fat guy, he was very quiet. There had definitely been a fat prejudice in the pride. It was just that he was a lion that liked to savour everything.

"Can you see him?" Arthur very nearly shouted. He was one step behind Brayman and hopefully just a few leaps away from the Land Rover.

"Not, yet," Brayman said with less caution than was wise, even after a further nip from the hip flask.

"We're too far away," Arthur advised. Winston raised his eyes. They got closer.

The lion had now made his way through the densest part of the bush and was beginning to get a view, although he hadn't needed a view as they had been making quite a bit of noise. The lion stood still. He could make out two men with their backs to him. It prompted a mouthful of saliva.

"Be patient," Arthur advised.

The lion watched the two men and decided which to go for. It wasn't a difficult decision as the one with the wide back had more meat on him, and didn't look like much of a runner. He'd never tasted human before, but wasn't averse to new culinary opportunities. He was very hungry. But he was the kind of lion that was very hungry after he'd dined on an entire gazelle.

"He'll show himself soon," Arthur said, surprising Winston with his apparent expertise.

The lion gathered up his hind legs and pawed the ground to ensure a firm footing. They were getting closer to him. It was too good to waste. There was a sudden strong wind that blew the lion's ears back and filled his nose with the scent of a very good meal. He twitched from side to side preparing himself for the leap. And then he went for it. As the lion leapt the thunder cracked, and the earth shook.

Chapter Fifty-Three

Jean had not been left alone with her thoughts for long, and they had begun to spiral alarmingly. She had just reread the most-thumbed sections of her *Fifty Shades* trilogy, and she was arriving at a conclusion. The thing was that she had kidnapped and held someone down because it was the only way she could have sex. But now she was realising that there was a further element, and that further element was the tying down part. Jean had a bit of a thing for bondage.

The phone rang.

"Arthur Cholmondely-Godstone's office," she said.

"Jean, it's Arthur."

"Hello, Arthur."

There seemed to be a pause the other end of the phone. It wasn't the distance, just Arthur trying to find a way to phrase what he wanted to say.

"It is possible that someone is trying to kill me," he began.

"Oh dear," Jean said. It was further confirmation that she was the right woman for the job, as her tone barely changed. He wondered for a moment what he would have to say to shock her. You don't find that facility listed on a CV, Arthur thought.

"Yes, he attacked me in the Rolls."

Jean had heard Rogerman's account of the evening, which was very lengthy, but mostly because it was punctuated by pauses and 'likes.' Rogerman had been less forthcoming about his own part in the adventure.

"Oh dear," Jean added, still with the same unruffled tone.

Jean had also read the newspaper that morning. It hadn't taken her long to link Rogerman's account with the papers, although neither were clear on the facts. But neither were concerned about the truth either, it was a bizarre tale of shotguns and painted vegetables. Had it not been for the vegetable, the paper wouldn't have covered it, but the nature of the venue was not mentioned as the editor knew Geraldine. Gunfire was unusual enough to rank a mention, but there were no casualties, and it took place at a venue whose prime concern was discretion.

"I read about in the paper," Jean said deploying the bored tone.

"You did?" Arthur said with a concerned tone.

"It's not a problem," Jean confirmed.

"Good, but we need to make some alterations."

Arthur explained the kind of surveillance he thought would be a good idea and Jean was given a job. She was fairly sure he hadn't mentioned a budget, so Jean proceeded without one. It was the only place she'd ever worked that never seemed constrained by a budget.

"Oh and another thing, Arthur," Jean began, also unsure how best to phrase the realities of the twenty million inheritance. She knew he needed to know. But the phone was dead. Jean tried to call him again, but Arthur was too caught up in the possibility of wild animals. She sighed and set about focusing all her attention on organising surveillance and alarms.

Chapter Fifty-Four

Clivert was coming to the conclusion that either Arthur was hiding in his house, or he was hiding in his office, or he was staying somewhere else. He didn't know that the his office was his house as well, but chose to start there. Reasoning that Cholmondely-Bastard might choose to stay somewhere else, but he would still have to go to work. Clivert watched the old hag enter in the morning and that was it. Nothing. No Arthur, no movement, nothing. It was the same at nine o'clock, and then ten, twelve and four o'clock. Surveillance was not the Black Artichoke's thing, he was concluding. This job was holding up the rest of his career, but worse still, it was unbelievably boring.

He was dressed in black from head to toe, with the mask in his pocket. He had a small rucksack with equipment, including ropes, ties, a hack saw and a blow torch. He broke up the boredom by picturing Arthur tied and ready to be tortured. Then the Rolls appeared. A spotty youth dragged himself out and entered the building. Eventually he came out and got back into the car. Clivert hesitated for a moment, and then decided to take a management decision and diverted from the plan. He followed the Rolls. There had been nowhere to park the MGB, and he'd had to abandon the bike. It required a further company expense. Clivert took a taxi.

"Follow that Rolls!"

The cabby looked at him.

"You've got to be fucking kidding, mate."

Clivert rocked backwards and forwards, but it didn't encourage the cabby to drive. He riffled through his pockets until he found thirty quid. He waved the money.

"Okay, mate, but I'm not breaking any fucking speed limits."

It was the first time Clivert had been in a cab for many years, and he found watching the mounting figures on the meter almost as alarming as having a shard of weathered plywood thrust through his testicles. Rogerman, he discovered, did not live nearby. Thirty minutes later Clivert was beginning to suspect he'd made a bad management decision.

"Do you know where this fucker's going?" the cab driver enquired with the deferential tone he adopted with all his clients. Clivert did not know where he was going. Neither did Rogerman, but he turned into a yard a moment later. It boasted a particularly thorough valeting service.

Clivert looked at the meter in horror. He also discovered that the large neck of the cab driver was coupled to a large back, legs and arms and an aggressive demeanour. But when Clivert returned from the cashpoint, the Rolls was still there. He sat in a café sipping a tea, which was cheaper than a coffee. There wasn't a great deal of activity, until Clivert realised that it was close to six o'clock, and the establishment was closing for the evening. He watched as they closed the gates. The chauffeur didn't appear to be there, and the Rolls was tucked away in the corner unattended. It was empty.

Clivert had now reverted to the Black Artichoke. He walked round the building looking for a weak link from which he could gain entry. He wasn't entirely sure where he was, but guessed it was somewhere in East London on the way to Essex. It didn't matter.

The fence was pretty high. One boundary of the property butted onto a railway line, and just at the junction of that boundary was a large oak tree with a branch that soared over the fence. The Black Artichoke waited until it was dark, and reached into his bag of tools. It took him much longer than he'd expected to lasso the tree, and a hell of a lot longer to climb the fence.

Batman and Robin made it look so easy. But this time he was successful. Landing on the broken concrete surface felt like an achievement, and his life was moving in the right direction at last. He moved with stealth.

The Rolls stood in a convenient pool of light. The Black Artichoke reached into his bag and took out the hacksaw. The removal of the flying lady was not just about branding Arthur, it was a symbolic gesture of castration. At least, that was how Clivert chose to interpret it. He applied the hack saw.

Ten minutes later, he was unsure whether he'd even made a mark and his arm was aching. He carried on for another ten minutes. The occasional train and the traffic on the busy road the other side of the property helped mask the small amount of noise he was making. He hacked for another ten minutes, but was beginning to doubt whether his arm was going to make it. He was concluding that it would be easier hacking off his own arm. Why was the bloody thing so difficult to remove?

Clivert collapsed onto the floor, landing in the only pool of oily water. This exercise had began as a symbolic gesture of castrating his enemy, and had become a tragic metaphor for his life. He tried not to weep. Then he saw a lump hammer. That would teach the damn flying lady, he thought. Until his eyes fell on a sledge hammer.

"You bitch," he muttered to the flying lady.

Hitting the flying lady with the sledge hammer was a much noisier activity than dragging a hack saw along her feet. And a moment later, Clivert discovered, establishments of this sort, particularly those that are located in East London on the way to Essex, tend to favour Alsatian dogs over expensive alarm contracts.

Chapter Fifty-Five

The stillness and silence was broken with a series of explosions. The first was the elemental sound of thunder cracking directly overhead, the second quieter noise was the crack of twigs as a lion propelled itself through the air. The third was the sound of gunshot.

"What the -" Brayman managed, and turned to Winston.

"Got him," Winston said with a rare sharpness of mind, capitalising on the situation. He had not intended to fire the rifle, and its accidental discharge had been an even bigger surprise for him. He was still fiddling with it when it went off, and he quickly realised that he was lucky not to blow the heads off his clients.

"Seems I've bagged a lion, man."

Winston leaned against the Land Rover in a gesture of sublime cool.

"Hey, are you okay, man?"

It had been so close. The talon-extended paw had sliced through the air and cut through Arthur's shirt, and then the animal had just flopped to the floor.

"I think so," Arthur muttered.

They looked at the lion. It was very still.

"Dead?" Brayman asked.

If it wasn't dead, it was doing a fantastic impersonation of dead.

"He's not breathing," Winston observed.

"That's a shotgun, isn't it?" Brayman asked.

Winston was fairly certain it was. He waved a cartridge.

"There are no entry wounds." Brayman said.

"Must have hit him the other side, man."

"But the lion isn't bleeding."

They took a closer look. Brayman prodded the lion with his foot. Winston approached, this time with the shotgun loaded, cocked and aimed. He wasn't mad. He prodded the lion with the barrel.

"He's dead, man."

"What happened?"

It appeared that a lifetime of eating excessively had taken its toll. The lion was not big on vegetables, and enjoyed a diet with a particular emphasis on fresh, rich, red meat. He carried more weight than was customary, due to a particular character trait the rest of the pride thought of as greed. He was also a lion that did not favour exercise. The sudden pounce, coupled with the shock of the thunder, had asked his heart to deliver more than it was capable of.

"I think the old bastard had a heart attack, man."

Arthur had retreated to the relative safety of the Land Rover. Fortunately for Arthur he only received a sergeant stripe on his upper arm. It was very close. But it had prompted Arthur to think about his own mortality. This was not something he was inclined to do, as over the years he had engineered many similar moments, and each time it was the client that got it. The time at the restaurant was a further reminder. Was Arthur losing it? Had the psychiatrist been right?

"Are you okay, Arthur?"

"Fine, absolutely fine," Arthur said, just managing to inject a languid tone. He had a millisecond to rediscover his form. Alarming though the lion business may have been, it was the lion that had got it. It was then that Arthur realised that there was something about that lion that reminded him of someone. He tried to put it to the back of his mind, and moved back onto familiar, excessive territory.

"Have you ever fucked a black woman?"

"No," Brayman lied. He didn't want to disappoint Arthur.

Winston raised his eyes, but didn't mind. The storm that had threatened had passed by as if it were a figment of their imagination, or it might have been God's way of teaching the lion a lesson. Not that the lion had believed in a higher being. They climbed back into the Land Rover and Winston drove with greater care, until the rough ground met a tarmac strip, which would take them to the most outrageous whore house Arthur knew.

"The Chicken Shed, man?"

"Certainly, old boy," Arthur muttered with his drawl intact. But there was one further thing that was disturbing him. For a man never disposed to introspection, it was proving to be quite a day. He couldn't quite place it, but if he wasn't mistaken he was beginning to warm to Brayman, actually like him. There was something about his kindness and candour. That bloody psychiatrist had planted thoughts in his head. He needed to get back to the agenda, and more specifically some unfinished business. He just hoped that the Damoclesean penis wouldn't intrude and put him off his stride. He watched the welcome sight of the Chicken Shed hove into view. It helped the pain in his arm subside.

"Welcome, Arthur."

The whore house looked like a beach bar and, contrary to Brayman's doubts, was the friendliest and most relaxed establishment he'd ever entered. If money changed hands he didn't notice it. Two gorgeous girls fetched him a fruit juice and draped themselves around him.

"And what is your name?"

They spoke English and, Brayman discovered, both had university degrees. Arthur watched with satisfaction. Brayman grappled with thoughts of Mandy for just a few seconds. She had been very clear about the non exclusivity. He'd just have to make sure he didn't bring her back an unwelcome present.

Chapter Fifty-Six

It is a very boring life being a guard dog, particularly if the premises are located in East London on the way to Essex, as no one in their right mind would break in. Gracie was large, far more muscular than she should be for the minimal exercise she took, and her coat was a deep shiny black. She had been chosen for her menacing appearance. The intruder made her day, and she went bounding up to greet him.

Clivert was concentrating. The sledge hammer was heavy, and the process of lifting and then aiming it was proving troublesome. It was the bubbling anger that came to his rescue, the concentration had made him deaf to the padding presence approaching him.

"Bastards," Clivert hissed. The hate and anger had become his turbocharger. He raised the sledge hammer and swung it in a wide arc and, with minimal skill, and even less strength, he sideswiped the flying lady. She took her first unaided flight without the throne of a Rolls Royce to propel her, and she sailed gracefully through the air. Despite Gracie's intimidating appearance, she was a gentle and friendly creature who would have made an affectionate house pet. She was hoping to slobber all over the intruder, but was taken out by something hard, pointy and metal, which flew through the air and hit her on the head.

It took a moment for Clivert to digest what had happened. It was a double victory. He grabbed the flying lady, stepped over the big back dog, and tried to make his escape.

He soon realised that when he had entered the premises he hadn't given much thought to exiting it. It was relatively easy to fall into the yard but, he discovered, damn difficult to fall out. He had to step back over the big black dog, which was alive, but unconscious and involved in a fitful sleep in which she was dreaming of the impossible and actually receiving affection.

Clivert looked around for tools. His own collection had been meagre, but this place seemed to be full of them. There were cupboards everywhere. At the back of one cupboard, almost as if it had been hidden, was a large bag not dissimilar to the one that he'd been carrying. He dragged it out. Clivert's expertise and the low light made it difficult for him to identify everything, but the bag clearly contained many metal implements, some with handgrips. Eventually he located some bolt croppers. They were three feet long and fitted tightly in the bag. They were forged from the densest iron known to man, as far as he could gather. Either they were very heavy, or he'd been weakened by the exertion. He dragged them along the floor until the presence of the dog required him to lift them. It was a big dog, and the distance required to lift them was such that they broke free from his grip.

Gracie, the affectionate dog, had entered a new fantasy. It involved a house with thick white carpets and the constant cooing of a young couple who treated her like their child. But there were children too. They dressed her up in amusing clothing and uploaded pictures onto the internet. They often called her nanny. Gracie's emotional journey was interrupted by the bolt croppers, which landed on her head.

Clivert dragged the bloodied bolt croppers to the fence, and found that they excelled as a cutting implement as well as a bludgeoning one. He went back and grabbed the bag. Moments later he was on the high street. The bag was heavy, heavier than he remembered, but then he hoped it contained everything he needed. A moment later, once he was on the bus, he realised there was something else he should have packed.

"Can I see your ticket, please?"

"Ticket?"

Clivert looked at a polyester-suited man with a sinking feeling. If only he'd packed a travel card in his tool bag. He got off the bus and discovered it was a long walk home, but Clivert made it even longer by walking in the wrong direction. The tool bag needed an A to Z, if not a sat nav. He arrived home at a little after four in the morning.

Clivert slept fitfully that night. His dreams were the polar opposite of those that Gracie, the affectionate dog, had once enjoyed. He woke fully turbocharged and ready to attack the day. It was clear that the success of the mission may be predicated by the tools that he packed. Clivert gave it some more thought. He threw some rope and cable ties, and gaffer tape into the bag. Gaffer tape was becoming a staple for him.

Clivert tried to reassure himself that this was just an apprenticeship, and therefore it was reasonable to expect errors. He packed the flying lady with some pride. Then a blow torch to heat her up. He packed some binoculars to help with the surveillance. Then he remembered his signature and included a black, hand-painted artichoke. The triangular chard of bloodied plywood was a must-have too. Of course there was his personal innovation, the sawn-off baseball bat. And then there was the black Ku Klux Klan-style mask and, of course, gloves.

The bag was heavier than he had anticipated, but hoped it held everything he'd need. He did wonder why Batman always had precisely the tools he needed, just when he needed them. Clivert was having issues reconciling the fictional with the real. There was still a niggling thought that he had overlooked something. He left his flat with the same resolve as the winning horse he could hear from the betting shop below. Apparently, from the cheers, there were a few punters counting on the horse to fuel the afternoon in the pub.

The bus was busier than he'd hoped and he was forced to stand, which was becoming an issue with the bag. He prepared himself for a day of surveillance, just one of the facilities in the armoury of the Black Artichoke.

"Can I see your ticket, please?"

"Ticket?"

It was then that Clivert remembered what he had forgotten. Half an hour later, and now with a twenty pound fine, he bought a travel card. He waited for the next bus.

When Clivert finally arrived at Arthur's office, he discovered that it wasn't a place with cafés helpfully located across the road. There were also no convenient benches to sit innocently on. He walked up and down the road, but he recognised there was only so long he could loiter. He knew now that what he needed to do was sell the MGB, which would break his heart, and buy a van. It would look like a plumber's van, but have black windows and would be fully equipped. That's what he'd have for the next job. But for the time being, he decided that he was going to push the Black Artichoke business plan. He was going to have to be more proactive. He was going in. He took one step at a time, until he finally arrived at the front door. It was the kind that was opened by a switch, the sort that made a big clunking noise, except the door had not quite caught on the latch. It was open.

It was a grand old building of high ceilings and, he discovered, creaky floors. For such a large building it appeared strangely free of people. Most of the ground floor was made up of grand function rooms, but Clivert had seen Jean through a first floor window. He headed upstairs. He checked the utility belt: the various pieces of equipment, including the sawn-off baseball bat, were making jangling noises. That, and the bag, made so much noise it was hard for him to hear the creaking of the staircase. And then there was the question of the mask. He couldn't decide at what point it was most appropriate to don it. As far as he was aware, most superheroes went into character the moment they left home.

But Clivert knew he wasn't a superhero. He had not been gifted with super powers, or even mediocre powers. He was the Black Artichoke and his tool was justice. He put the mask on. There were no holes for his ears, which made the clattering of his kit more bearable. He hadn't quite cut the eyes level either, and the mask made it difficult to see his feet. The oak floors and banisters were stained black with age and there was a slight fall on the floor. There were alcoves cut in the wall in which hung oil paintings of Arthur's ancestors. They all looked uncannily like each other. It fuelled his rage. He got to the top of the steps and looked along the landing.

He moved through the building and looked through open doors at ordinary-looking offices. It was a long corridor, and it took a while to arrive at the last door, which wasn't open. He placed a gloved hand on the knob and turned slowly. The Black Artichoke was like a ghost, he thought.

He opened the door. It led to a further corridor. He crept slowly along it. The door swung closed behind him. And then he had just a moment to discover that the baseball bat that Jean was wielding was not of the sawn-off variety. He went down like a sack of potatoes.

Chapter Fifty-Seven

"Oh, bugger," Arthur muttered. It had been a great evening. He had put to bed, literally, many issues. He had cast off the Damoclesean penis and moved on. It had lent him new levels of stamina. He'd lost count of the number of women. So it was not surprising his old man was a bit sore.

Arthur liked the simplicity of pleasures. There was no hidden meaning, no guile, nothing inferred or implied, just pleasure. And he'd taken a lot of it. He'd lost sight of Brayman, but he wasn't going to mollycoddle him. The man could get on with it on his own.

"Oh, bugger," Arthur muttered again. It really did itch. Despite the famous Cholmondely-Godstone immunity to sexually transmitted diseases, he was going to have to take a look. Of course the plan was that Brayman would be waking up with the itching, but it was possible that Arthur was suffering for his art.

"Okay," he said, as he grabbed the sheets and pulled them down. But he couldn't bring himself to look. He drew the sheets up for a moment and then dropped them. He still hadn't taken a look. Eventually he did.

"Oh my good God." His penis, his testicles, his thighs, his stomach, his buttocks and pretty much everywhere else he could see were immersed in the biggest and most vicious rash he had ever seen. He covered it with the sheet. But it wasn't going to go away. Arthur was going to need a doctor for the first time in his life.

His plan had been to hide in Africa for as long as he was able. He'd figured that Brayman would want to go back first, unless he was able to get him to tumble from a bridge, be attacked by a lion, hippo, crocodile or anything else with a short temper, aggressive nature and a taste for human flesh. A few nasty sexually transmitted diseases would be fine too. That thought brought him back to the itchy present. He needed a doctor.

Eventually he got out of bed. It took a while to find his clothes, but much longer to wrap them round his body. The clothes elevated the itch to new levels. There was no word for what Arthur now felt, at least no adequate word. Arthur walked very slowly out of his room and into the lift; the stairs seemed like challenge too far. He found Brayman having breakfast in the restaurant.

"Morning, Arthur."

Brayman looked well rested, well-fucked and generally in appallingly good order. His skin was clear, he was smiling and happy.

"Morning, old boy."

Arthur said through clenched teeth. He tried not to cast his eyes on the glowing form of Brayman.

"Are you okay?"

Brayman had enjoyed the evening, but not for the obvious reasons. He'd chatted to the girls until four in the morning and laughed all evening. The girls had surprised him with the speed of their wit and their kindness and good spirits. It made him wonder whether he might look further at the charitable work he was involved in. Occasionally the human spirit seemed indefatigable to him.

"I'm fine. How about you?"

Arthur couldn't remember the last time he felt this uncomfortable. Even the five star facilities were beginning to get him down.

"Couldn't be better. You look slightly the worse for wear, if I may say so," Brayman said. He'd pondered for a moment whether he should mention something, but Arthur had gone through a lot. Before the lion there had been the incident at the club.

Arthur came clean. There was no avoiding the need for a doctor.

"Slight rash, old boy. You okay?"

"Perfect," Brayman beamed. "Condoms, old boy."

Arthur bristled at Brayman's use of 'old boy'.

Chapter Fifty-Eight

It was perfect. Jean had a week on her own and she'd trapped a potential murderer. She had watched him enter the building with interest on the bank of monitors that were now installed in her office. She'd made sure the door was unlocked. Watching him creep through the corridors had given her shivers. It hadn't been difficult to lead him to the unused offices. They would normally be locked. The rest was easy, as she had some practice at it.

But this time Jean was going to make sure that he couldn't identify her. What, she reasoned, could go wrong? She dragged him into the office. There was a large leather-topped partner's desk, which sat in the middle of the room. Since the twins, Arthur's great uncles, had died in 1936 in a fire in a brothel, the room had been unused as a mark of respect.

Getting him on the desk had not been easy. Eventually she got his top half on and then grabbed his arms and tugged. Something was catching. Jean found it was Clivert's crotch against the sharp corner of the desk. He seemed to grunt, and Jean panicked that he might wake up. She didn't have much time. She repositioned his bottom half and then tugged again. He slid onto the freshly polished leather, and Jean didn't waste any time. There were four convenient legs to which to tie his arms and legs, but she had nothing to tie him with. She looked around in panic until her eyes alighted on a bag the intruder had been carrying. To her surprise it contained everything she needed, plus a bit more.

Jean was not a big woman, but she had a wiry strength she was finding now. She wrapped the rope round his ankles and fastened it to the broad legs of the desk. Then she hesitated. He was no good tied down, but fully clothed. She thought a bit more and decided that scissors would be the best solution, once she had him firmly strapped down. It didn't take long, and she went back to her office and rummaged through her desk drawers until she found a long pair of scissors. They were new and unused and, she hoped, sharp. She took a moment to slow herself down and control her breathing. Then she realised that slowing down was an even bigger mistake and would expose her to the madness of her plan.

She returned to the abandoned office and took a look at her prize. He was short, that was clear. He was also slightly tubby, there was no doubt. That just left his head, which was swathed in a strange black mask. She decided to come to that later. She started on one trouser leg. The scissors cut through the cheap material with ease, but her hands were shaking with excitement. It was hard to avoid the odd nick. When she arrived at the thicker material around the crotch, the shaking had become quite bad. She began on the other leg. That journey was just as shaky. She followed the rise and fall of his chest. Whoever he was, he was alive and reasonably well. At least for the time being.

Clivert grunted. She stopped. He moved slightly, but not enough to test how securely he'd been tethered. She carried on until she arrived at the crotch. She wondered whether she should unveil the head or the crotch first. She was plainly more interested in the latter, so decided to leave that to the end. She cut from the right arm to the waist and then from the left. There was now very little material securing his clothing. A few more snips and the shirt was off. She hadn't expected the torso of a Greek god, or of Daniel Craig, or Sean Connery, or even Roger Moore. In fact, from the general shape of him she hadn't expected very much at all, but she couldn't help being disappointed. His skin was a pale colour and he had small shapeless breasts garnished with a sporadic sprinkling of ginger hair. Now that she had cut up most of his clothing, calling the police did not seem an option. She had no choice but to proceed.

She moved round to his head. The mask would have been frightening to someone of a less sturdy disposition, but Jean was beginning to feel she might have the measure of him already. She removed the weird mask.

"Ohhh," Jean said.

Jean's expectations had not been high. She knew that this weird little man was no Brad Pitt, but still. It was just as well that her plan featured a lot of gaffer tape. She had no intention of being identified. She taped his eyes, which were beginning to flicker with returning consciousness. The gaffer tape improved his appearance. She added a bit more tape. And then a little more. He began to make a strange huffing noise like a distant steam train. He got louder. And then she realised she'd taped both his nose and his mouth. She may be a rapist, but she was not a murderer, not deliberately anyway. She whipped off the tape, which brought Clivert into a suddenly alert conscious state.

Jean wasted no time and began to remove the remainder of his clothing. Clivert's rude awakening was then accompanied with a stab in his foot, then his ankle, then his calf, then his knee and then his thigh. Jean couldn't control the scissors, her hands were shaking so much. Clivert, although not a man of great intellect, was capable of predicting where the series of stabs were heading. Had he been blessed with more imagination, he might have pictured Sean Connery in Goldfinger, tied down and with a laser on course to frazzle his genitals. But Clivert hadn't quite grasped his function in proceedings.

Jean's imagination, on the other hand, was running wild. She was finding the process interesting, but a little silent. If she removed the tape from his mouth he might scream, but the building was solid and the sound wouldn't carry very far. She could also try the tongue kissing thing she'd quite enjoyed. She forced herself to wait a little longer.

She just had the remains of his trousers to attend to. They didn't cut easily. Jean was aware that proceeding this way would end in something disastrous, such as accidental castration. Then she had an idea. She'd pull his trousers down to his knees and cut them there. He had a rather strange belt with things dangling from it, and there wasn't much space between it and his bulging stomach. But she persisted and was finally able to remove the belt. She undid the button on the trousers and unzipped the fly and pulled them down, and then cut them off.

That just left a sturdy pair of underpants. She curled her thumbs round the belt and pulled slowly as if she were unveiling a trophy. And that was the second disappointment.

"Oh."

Jean did not have extensive experience with the male naked body, but she was fairly certain it should be bigger than that. One of the other things that Clivert had not been gifted with was average sized genitals. If he were a fish she would have thrown him back in. But, Jean sighed, she'd have to make the best of it.

Chapter Fifty-Nine

Courtney Mbabwe had found work with a small school in the city. They'd helped him and he had a passport. He'd travelled the world on the internet and it was his dream to do it for real. But the amount he was paid, and the cost of a plane ticket, were separated by many decimal points. He needed to earn more money. Preferably big lumps of money. That was how it started. That morning he'd visited Miss Burdon, a middle aged woman who needed her garden looking after.

"Of course, I shall cut the grass and weed the beds," he reassured her.

"Thank you, boy."

There was money in the city, actual currency, from which things could be purchased. Courtney had something expensive in mind. He stayed in the city and, for a month, he cut her garden and weeded her flower beds, and he worked hard. He worked so hard she introduced him to her friends. Soon he had something he understood was called a client base. He was earning more than he would have at the school, but a plane ticket was still a long way away. He began to work harder. He employed some of his brothers, but they wouldn't work as hard as him, and he ended up doing the work himself. Then he made a proposal.

"Miss Burdon," he began, "at the moment it costs you five shillings an hour for me to do your garden. If I could find a way for it to only cost you three, would you be interested?"

Miss Burdon liked the sound of a bargain.

"How could you do that?" she asked.

"Well, if you were to pay me for the entire season, then that will give me enough money to invest in better equipment with which I could carry out the job quicker and more efficiently."

Miss Burdon had always been a sucker for a well-spoken boy, and Courtney certainly had a way with words. Hadn't he said something about training to be a doctor? She couldn't remember.

"That's going to be quite a lot of money, you know."

That thought had occurred to Courtney.

"Don't worry, it was just a thought. It's no problem."

Courtney smiled. He'd inherited his warm, honest smile from Gloria. He took off his shirt and began to remove the errant weeds. He pretended not be aware that Miss Burdon was watching him, as she always did. It was all part of the service. That day was particularly hot and Courtney worked up quite a sweat. When he finished, as was customary, Miss Burdon gave him a cold lemon juice. She really enjoyed watching him drink it. There was something about the way his throat moved and then his stomach muscles rippled.

"That's great Miss Burdon, thanks very much."

It wasn't long afterwards that Miss Burdon invited him to sit down, which turned out be only a short leap to lying down. Thankfully Courtney rather liked older women, and he would include the time spent after the gardening in the invoice. He developed some useful skills: the internet had been most helpful in this matter, particularly a piece he found entitled 'How to make a woman orgasm.' He was very diligent, and it prompted Miss Burdon to be very generous. It was fortunate that Courtney was young and gifted with great stamina, as it also prompted Miss Fortescue, Miss Smythhe-Buckhurst, Mrs Pyke, Miss Gaynor, Miss Standon and Mrs Derrington to be very generous. On his most profitable days he cut very little grass.

But Miss Burdon liked the foreplay of watching him work up a sweat in the garden first, although at first she was worried what the neighbours might think. That was before she'd had the most shattering orgasm of her life. After that she didn't care what the neighbours thought, or even what they heard. She watched him through the sitting room windows, her hands shaking in anticipation. It was the management of that anticipation that was his particular talent. She couldn't wait any longer. She invited him in and handed him a cold glass of lemon juice.

"Are you busy?" she asked sweetly.

"Yes, always busy," he said carelessly, but tactically removing the moisture from his lips, and letting gravity take little rivulets of well-tended sweat down his body. The work had firmed, toned and generally arranged his body in a fashion which made it possible for him to casually roll muscles like a lapping tide. He gave the moment the full muscle-rippling theatre as he delivered his next line.

"But I'm thinking of cutting down my gardening work. The school has asked me to do a few things. And then there are my studies."

Miss Burdon looked at him with panic in her eyes. Did she hear right? Was he suggesting that he was no longer going to work for her? Miss Burdon felt forlorn for a moment. More than forlorn, she felt the tension rising in her, and feared that it would no longer have a vent. It would build within her until she exploded. The sex had had quite an influence on her imagination.

"I might move out of the city," he said casually and then added looking outside, "but your garden looks great."

Miss Burdon gave the garden a rapid glance. That wasn't the garden she wanted tending. And then it occurred to her.

"How much money would I save if I pay a season up front?"

It wasn't just the longing and anticipation or the orgasms, Miss Burdon really did like the sound of a bargain. As did, it turned out, Miss Jones, Miss Smith, Miss Tandy, Miss Gaynor, Miss Standon and Miss Pike. He wasn't entirely unkind, he gave them each a farewell that they would remember for the rest of their lives. It was an avalanche of multipleness. It was that, and the possible embarrassment of admitting to their neighbours that they had been fleeced, and what had prompted the fleecing, that kept them all quiet and content with their memories.

Courtney took the next available plane going north, very far north, to London. A further trip through Google had directed him to the man he was sure was his father.

Chapter Sixty

Dr Peter Fitzsimmons had been tempted by a life in the clergy, and had worked with the curate at the local church while training at the hospital. It was no surprise that he should become a doctor, as his mother was a doctor and his father a surgeon.His grandparents had been doctors. What was more surprising was his interest in things of a spiritual and religious nature. In this regard he was rebelling, coming from a long line of atheists. But he had a sharp mind and found the mechanics of the body enthralling, and had a particular talent for diagnosis.

"Morning, bossman."

He smiled at Ratsy. When the African posting came up, it seemed a perfect opportunity to merge his Christian ministry and medical skills. It had been quite a challenge.

"Good morning, Ratsy, and how are you?"

It was also a place rife with characters, some of whom came to see him just to chat. There were days when it wasn't possible, there were just too many people who needed treatment. It was certainly like that when he arrived two years ago. Most were easily cured and, as he always asked where they came from, he was able locate any poor water sources. Correcting that had reduced the queues in his small surgery and given people like Ratsy the chance to come by and socialise.

"I am good, but he not good."

Ratsy put his hand in a rough leather bag and pulled out a creature. Ratsy was so called partly because his appearance resembled a rat, with large buckteeth which he'd filed into rather alarming points, and also because he always carried a collection of pet rats. Peter took the rat.

"He does look poorly."

He stroked the animal and looked into its gummy eyes. Ratsy was also known as Dr Ratsy for his rat-healing powers. He was a rat whisperer, but this rat was defeating him.

"Fix him?"

Peter had made an immediate diagnosis and knew there was no hope.

"I'm sorry Ratsy, but I can't do anything about old age."

He handed the rat back and Ratsy took him, eyes wet.

"I can make him sleep."

Ratsy nodded as Peter administered the injection which would send him to sleep and beyond. Ratsy sat down and cradled the rat and murmured quietly to him. Peter's phone rang.

"Hello."

He had grown used to interpreting the different dialects and the tendency to either speak very slow or very quickly. This person spoke quickly. A moment later he grabbed his bag.

"I'm sorry Ratsy, but I've got to go. Will you be all right?"

Ratsy nodded and looked back down at the rat as the doctor swept out of the surgery. Ten minutes later a voice distracted him.

"Hello? Doctor?"

"Yes," Ratsy said without looking up.

It took a while for Arthur to take in the scene, but it didn't auger well. The doctor's appearance was, for Arthur, less than doctorly. He could have accepted it, but then he opened his mouth. The razor-like teeth were another obstacle. And the doctor was holding a dead rat. Frozen at that moment, Arthur's itching disappeared, but he wasn't going to hang around. He needed his man in Harley Street.

Chapter Sixty-One

"Is that working, honey?"

Jean found her victim's lack of response rather off-putting. It hadn't occurred to her that the gaffer tape she'd wrapped round his eyes had also covered his ears. It was hard to tell with the weird mask wrapped around his head. She reread her favourite passages from *Fifty Shades*, and she went for it again.

"How's that?"

There was a muffled noise which she chose to interpret as a positive response. All her young life she'd had no interest in sex but, ever since a strange encounter with an attractive man, a switch had turned. It was a sort of synapse along which sexual pleasure travelled. Or perhaps it was more like a sluice gate. Whatever it was, it was flowing now.

"Is that good?"

Jean really would have preferred it if the sex were consensual, and veered somewhere towards a normal relationship. But her appearance had not made that easy. It was her intention to give pleasure.

"You like that, don't you? That feels good, doesn't it? What do you think?"

Clivert didn't know what to think. In his entire life no one had ever been inclined to molest him, sexually or otherwise. It was therefore reasonable to assume that Arthur Chum-wotsit was one step ahead of him, and he was going to be tortured. Of course, for the Black Artichoke this was something he could easily take in his stride, but Clivert on the other hand, was shit scared. He was so scared he was shaking.

The other problem was the sensory deprivation. He couldn't hear or see, but he could feel, and if he wasn't mistaken hands were being run along his legs. Apart from a hooker in Thailand, this was also a new experience, but after the repeated stabbing when his clothes were removed, it didn't bode well.

Jean's plan was to begin at a point of mere sensuality and move subtly towards the sexual. Although there was nothing subtle about holding someone down and feeling them up, she hoped to approach the enterprise in this way. She was also a little concerned about his genitals, which as well as being unusual in terms of scale, or more accurately lack of scale, were also a strange colour. She continued to massage his thighs and stomach in a pattern of ever decreasing circles. The final target was obvious even to Clivert.

"How's that?" Jean asked. Her fingers were now skirting the target area, but there was no sign of movement there. He started shaking violently.

Clivert thought about all the things and people he hated and tried to shake himself free with anger and frustration.

He wanted to shout at the sky, but the gaffer tape prevented him. It was quite exhausting. The hands continued to travel up his body. They bypassed his crotch, and settled on his chest. Why, he had to wonder, was he so unlucky? He could be living it up with his brother's money, and instead he was strapped down and about to be subjected to torture. If he got out of this he was going to kill someone. The hands were moving closer. He held his breath. Did he hear snipping noises? Was he about to be castrated? Could the Black Artichoke still function after that? He shook some more, but the shackles were secure.

"Are you ready, honey?"

Jean decided to abandon subtlety and go for the prize. She looked at the mass of ginger hair and the tiny bit of flesh that was projecting from it. It was too late to abandon the project. She went for it.

Clivert was finding his rage very easy to access. In the past it might have been a bubbling rage just below the surface, now it rested firmly on top. It gave him strength. And then something strange happened. He was fairly sure he'd heard a woman's voice. And the hands were soothing. It wasn't pain. Then something wet and soggy landed on his genitals. What was it? He couldn't identify it. Then he realised he could. If he wasn't mistaken he was being given a blow job. He relaxed. It felt good. Very good.

"Glug, glug, glug," Clivert said. It took Jean a while to recognise that this was a response to pleasure, but she wasn't certain. She was going to have to take the gaffer tape off and find out. She removed her mouth from his genitals.

"Is that good?"

Clivert couldn't hear, because if he could, he would have nodded his head rather than shake, imagining the question to be: should she stop? Jean wasn't sure, but gave it another go in the hope that there would be less of a taste of urine.

"Glug, glug, glug," Clivert affirmed.

The urine taste had disappeared and the object of her intentions had become rather firmer, if not actually much larger. She gave it quite a spirited attack.

"Glug, glug, glug," Clivert said.

His luck had turned. He was hooded and blindfolded, but he was feeling something that was nice. Clivert relaxed and it felt good. It was more than good. For a moment it suppressed his anger. And then it stopped. Just, he thought, his bloody luck.

"Okay, honey?"

Jean was having a few reservations. Some were brought about by flashbacks from her time in prison, others by her previous attempt at this. This time, she reckoned, he was enjoying it. She didn't want to waste it. If she was going to remove the gaffer tape she was going to have to be fully prepared. And she was starving. She hadn't noticed the time fly by, with the planning, concentration and, of course, execution.

"I'll just be a second."

Jean needed to keep him fit and fed. She remembered her previous experience had gone up a notch after they'd shared a pizza together. But she didn't want to order them, that would involve telephones and addresses. Jean ran her hands along his legs, smiled at the little flagpole, then grabbed her handbag and nipped out to the pizza place at the end of the road. It shouldn't take long.

Chapter Sixty-Two

Rachel had got fed up. If she didn't do something, nothing would happen. She had a particular capacity for finding a way of justifying her actions, which was a useful facility as it had ensured her a guilt-free life. This was an action that required quite a bit of justifying, but it wasn't holding her back.

"Move it," she hissed to another road user, who was only travelling at fifteen miles per hour above the speed limit.

She was still working on the notion that her cause was a selfless one, and that Sophie would thank her in the end. This was something of a leap. She had met Arthur a few times, and although he wasn't her type, he'd been agreeable enough. That old school charm wasn't really for her, she was more long hair and motorbikes. But then there was the money. The money, for her, always made a compelling argument. She knew she couldn't go on living like she did for ever. There would have to be some settling down at some point, which was not to say she was ready for it. Perhaps just not averse to the idea.

"Bastard!" she yelled as she honked the horn.

There was no getting away from it, Rachel had honked a lot of horns and gone through a lot of men. She liked men. She thought about that for a moment and realised it wasn't entirely true. More specifically, she liked sex. But, and she hated to admit it, she'd never really felt anything much stronger.

"Love," she muttered. It was one of those words everyone was familiar with, and a few had said it to her, and some men she knew said it all the time. But she'd never once said it, because she'd never once felt it. Perhaps, she wondered, there is a scale of desire, feeling or it might just be being.

"Fuck off," Rachel muttered at a road user with a limited understanding of the rights of way. For her the right of way was always hers, whether she was driving or not. She was heading into town. She didn't much care for the train, and the personal space in the car made it easier to rationalise what she intended to do. And there was a lot of rationalising to do. So what came one notch below love?

"Passion," she said. She'd felt a bit of that, she was sure. Unless what she felt was a further notch below.

"Desire." This was much more certain territory for her. This she felt fairly often. But what was one notch below desire?

She couldn't think. Rachel began to wonder whether she could function without sex. When she thought about her three notches; love, passion and desire, they all said variations of sex to her. And was there a notch above love? Something even more than love? What the bloody hell could that be? She was getting bogged down. She had decided to see Arthur.

"Lust." Was that on the scale? Was it above or below desire? Was it the same thing? It wasn't entirely a selfish trip. She had with her pictures of Sophie and child. She was going to open the doors to Arthur's child. Nothing wrong in that. The only complication was that now that she had thought through the hierarchy of feeling, she realised that she had never placed a toe on the ladder. Or on the scale she was devising in her head. She'd come to a halt at lust, and hadn't made a further step. All those higher treads that people wrote about had evaded her. She'd have to work it out, though. For a brief second she pictured herself publishing her ideas to create the world famous Rachel scale.

"Out of my way," she yelled at a bus, which had the temerity to occupy the bus lane. The point was, she thought, that it was very liberating to know that she had never felt any of the higher-scale emotions. It didn't constrain her. Or, put another way, it left her free to marry for money. Better still someone with plenty of money. And that thought dovetailed nicely with Arthur

Cholmondely-Godstone. It had taken two minutes to locate his office via the internet. She would tell him all about Sophie, while offering him tempting glances at her fabulous cleavage. She'd donned the tight trousers and an even tighter blouse, which meant that a few open buttons gave her breasts an escape route. Her only concession had been her cashmere jumper, which was beautifully soft and fantastically expensive. It wasn't rocket science, but then neither were men. If there was chemistry, then she could lead him in the right direction.

"Chemistry," she suddenly said. Was that the notch below desire? But she remembered that Arthur had eyed her up a little. That would be lust, in which case it was definitely below desire. The scale was making progress.

She steered her car into an empty bay and threw the disabled badge on the dashboard. It wasn't love, certainly not passion, probably not desire, but there was definitely chemistry.

But what Rachel was really after was more like alchemy.

Chapter Sixty-Three

Eddie was coming down. He'd smoked a couple of joints and knocked back a few whiskies, but he was coming down. And with the coming down came a dawning realisation. Why had he not seen it before? Obviously the answer to that was that he was either too stoned, or too pissed, or both. He'd never been one for analysis. His was a soul even he didn't want to look into. He was, after all, the man who had penned the platinum-selling *I'm Wasted*. So the insight was more of an accidental journey for him.

Last night's gig had been sensational, and he was coming down from the greatest high known to man. It was natural and there were variations of it. But the highest form was being a rock god performing to a huge crowd. Adrenaline. It was the best he'd felt in years. And he wanted to tell someone. He thought about using the telephone, but as his conversation was so often peppered with pauses, people tended to hang up. His hands shook too much to text, although he'd never tried. Instead he was going to nip into the West End. He took a bus.

"Isn't that -"

Eddie liked taking buses. He'd often take one when he had nothing else to do, just to amuse himself. It wasn't that he wanted to tell the world that he was a man of the people, just like everyone else. Not at all. Eddie took the bus because he liked being recognised, which reminded him that he wasn't like everyone else.

"Wasted, man," Eddie said. When he spoke to the public he tended to end most sentences with man. It was kind of expected, man. The problem with Eddie's life – at least one of the problems, there were really a great deal, which he would have discovered had he favoured analysis – was time. Eddie had way too much of it. He'd stopped writing songs years ago, and he had no interest in practising the guitar. His primary passions were alcohol and narcotics. But today he was going to change things with the adrenaline, and the glorious musical rendition that would be *Face of a Librarian but the Tits of a Porn Star*.

"Autograph, Eddie?"

Eddie always carried a pen, and had perfected an indistinguishable scrawl that said, he hoped, wasted rock god. He wasn't sure whether he should go and see his Cunt, or Arthur. He couldn't remember on what terms he had last left his manager. His lack of memory had been a great factor in sustaining their relationship. But Arthur's office was closer than his Cunt's, so that was going to be his first port of call. If Arthur wasn't there, he'd find the Cunt, or maybe hang out in a bar. People liked to buy him drinks, which, as luck would have it, fit nicely with his passion for drinking and the fact he was invariably skint. Except he was on a new mission.

"Cool, man." Eddie had also perfected the art of saying 'cool' in a way which was actually quite cool.

Eddie was going to rearrange his stimulant spread to take in more stage-induced adrenaline. Even Eddie realised that this would involve slightly less off-stage input. He wasn't going to give up. His new super-gravelly voice was, he reckoned, a bit of currency. He'd have a few whiskies before and during the performance, it was expected. But he'd smoked his last joint that morning.

"Way to go, man," Eddie said to no one in particular, as he got off the bus. That morning he'd even thought about taking a run. He'd gone as far as buying a pair of trainers, which took an incredible time, and was tiring in itself. He wondered how people with jobs found the time to buy trainers. He even put them on. He walked around the apartment smoking the last joint. It was a start. The other thing he was thinking was that he needed a woman. A bit of a Sharon, Ozzy's wife, to keep him on the straight and narrow. Just a little, mind. Not too much. Eddie wished he'd worn the trainers now, as he'd got off the bus a stop early. His old boots were heavy, but they were kind of cool. He could see in the distance the grand building that housed Arthur's office.

Chapter Sixty-Four

Sophie felt a little bad about what she'd done. Only a little, but it hadn't told her anything. But today she wasn't Sophie, she wasn't even the Rooster, she was just plain old John Brewster. She was John. There was no question she made a better woman than a man. She'd had almost as much practice at it. But chromosomally she was a man. Yet she'd always felt that there was something wrong trapped in something not quite right.

Her parents hadn't just despaired, they'd thrown her out. She was surprised to discover a subculture of existence that was just like her own. She'd done some things she didn't want to remember. And then she'd retrained and became an accountant. She was good at it too. But not all her clients appreciated their accountant shifting gender as she, or he, pleased. She certainly had the drag queen market sewn up, and strippers and hookers who liked to declare their income followed. Then a client had got her some very lucrative work with the Inland Revenue. It was very easy, and for that she was John. And today she was John. She'd made quite an effort.

She'd grown up hating her penis. It shouldn't have been there. What was its purpose? She'd hated it up until the point that a surgeon had talked about removing it, and then she began to appreciate it. The week after the threat of the knife, she'd really understood its purpose. It was sore with understanding. She realised that she was who she was, and wasn't going to change. She could be Sophie one day and, if she felt like it, John the next. The hormone injections had given her rather fine breasts, but they could be disguised or displayed as she saw fit.

But both Sophie and John had one thing in common. They wanted someone to share their lives with. And both of them had hoped that person would be Barry Clivert. His death was shocking. But Barry hadn't been ready for the two of them. She'd wanted to look after him, but he seemed to be on a suicide mission. A suicide mission prompted by Arthur Cholmondley-Godstone. Barry was frail, and Arthur had encouraged him to do everything that was bad for him. Sophie was pretty sure it was deliberate. There was money involved, aside from the monumental inheritance.

Her brief encounter with Arthur had not told her very much, although she had found it rather exciting. Having sex with women was an occasional joy, and did demonstrate the primary purpose of her penis. It was a shame they were interrupted, but it had looked like Arthur was going to go for it. Her emotions were as conflicting as her gender, but she missed Barry, and something underhand had happened.

It was why John, in his capacity as inspector for the Inland Revenue, was heading to Arthur's office.

Chapter Sixty-Five

"This stops right naaah!"

It was something of a catchphrase for the McCarthy brothers. It was one of the legacies they had inherited from their old dad, who was quite the villain in the sixties. The other was a propensity for violence.

"This stops right naaah!"

The correct pronunciation of 'now' was 'naaah." The old man, shortly before he was incarcerated for the fifth time, had invested some of the proceeds from a bank job in his sons' education. He'd hoped they'd become the true modern thieves: bankers or lawyers. But some things are too inbred.

"This stops right naaah!"

They were getting the hang of it. When their father had said it, it was the calm before the storm. Someone had crossed him and he was going to mete out a fairly serious bit of violence which would, he hoped, bring the matter to an end.

"No one kills Gracie and gets away with it."

The dog had barely concerned them for six years, but now she was symbolic of something greater. Liam looked at Noel, hoping for tears to appear in his eyes to express the depth of the loss of the dog. But he hadn't much cared for the dog either, and Liam was the contemplative one. He was the one that worked things out, while Noel was just violent.

"Poor Gracie. She never done no one no harm," Noel observed.

The rough bit of land next to the railway line had served many purposes over the years, all of them legitimate businesses masking criminal activities. The car valeting service actually turned a profit, and the authorities tended to leave it alone. It was for that reason that they'd hidden some stuff there.

"Who was the geezer with the Roller?" Liam asked.

They'd not seen Arthur's Rolls before. Rogerman had driven past the valeting place that Jean had recommended, found the McCarthy brothers' operation and assumed that was it. It was why he left the car overnight.

"Dunno, mate."

The time that the brothers had attended private school was brief as they had trouble fitting in, showing a distinct reluctance to pick up the received pronunciation of their peer group. It was that and their propensity for violence, which was only matched by their father, who was incarcerated for a sixth time shortly after his payment plan proposal was rejected by the bursar.

"Caantt," Noel said for no particular reason. When they first discovered that the Rolls had been vandalised they had put it right, with a portable angle grinder and a quick trip 'up west.' It took a while longer to realise that Gracie wasn't sleeping.

"Caantt."

Liam confirmed. A moment later the shit really hit the fan.

"Fuckin' caantt."

They were angry.

"It's fuckin' gone."

They had discovered that there was something missing. Something that was very valuable to them. Their father's biggest triumph had been the great heist of Potters Bar in 1967, in which three bullion vans were successfully plundered. The old man should have gone to Spain, or Spine as he called it, but he'd stayed on and gathered more incarcerations.

But he retained the spoils. He'd used a bag of tools, which the brothers revered like the lost Ark of the Covenant. They'd even added to it for a job they were planning. It was positively packed with incendiary devices and armaments. Now some bastard had stolen it. It prompted a series of deductions.

"The stuff for the big one. All gone," Liam said incredulously. Their father had always said that you only need to pull off one big one.

"Bastard."

"Do you know what it was?" Liam asked.

"What?"

"The Roller?"

"A Rolls Royce?"

"No bruv. It was a Trojan Roller," Liam said.

"Really? I thought it was a Silver Cloud," Noel asked, unfamiliar with the model range.

"No mate. A Trojan Roller."

Somewhere aged around eleven they had been subjected to classical studies and something had stuck.

"A fuckin' what?"

"It's a fucking Trojan Roller," Liam affirmed.

When the problem occurred they were keen to get the Roller off their land as quickly as possible, but now they were beginning to think they might have been duped.

"Hold on bruv, I get it. There was someone hiding in the Roller, who got out killed Gracie and nicked the bag."

"And we let the fucker drive straight out of here."

They fell into a contemplative silence. A plan of action needed to be formed. It was going to involve the van.

"We're gonna need the van," they both said.

They had acquired the van from a paranoid syphilitic African dictator who stepped out of it one day to discover that he wasn't paranoid after all. The dictator had modified the van to withstand land mines and rocket attack, which made the spear that killed him all the more ironic. The modifications made the van very heavy, so he also had it fitted with the biggest and most powerful engine he could locate. He wasn't the kind of dictator who would have upgraded the brakes at the same time. But it was pretty leery even for a part of East London which was on the way to Essex.

"Unusual motor, that Roller. What was the registration number?" Liam asked.

The registration number had been in Arthur's family since the dawn of the horseless carriage, and had been shifted through progressive Rolls Royces. It had landed on this one fifty years ago. Either way it was unfortunate for Arthur, as it was brief and memorable.

"Wasn't it CG 500?"

"It was, bruv."

The McCarthy brothers were proper villains. The kind that robbed banks and post offices, deploying violence where necessary, and frequently where it was entirely unnecessary. As such they were precisely the kind of people who would have a friend on the police force, who would give them an address for the car. A phone call later they had it.

"Arthur Cholmondley-Godstone."

They rolled the name round a little with distaste, and then started to collect together the equipment that would accompany them in the van. They then simultaneously deployed the catch phrase.

"This stops right naaah."

A moment later they tapped the name into a Google search. They discovered many things.

"He's a flamin' fuckin' queen."

This was a particularly sore area for the brothers, especially after their father's disappearance to Spain with a waiter called Pedro. They'd never talked about it, but if anyone so much as mentioned their old man and Pedro in the same sentence, it was going to hurt.

"No one stops us pulling off the big one," Noel hissed. It was ironic, as that was also what their old man had done to Pedro.

"Here he is," Liam said grabbing the paper from the printer. Now they had a picture of Arthur, and they knew what to say.

"This stops right naaah."

Chapter Sixty-Six

Rogerman had received his first pay cheque, and it was much larger than he'd imagined. It was enough to move from home and get a place of his own, but he couldn't see the point of that. It was enough to buy his own car, but he seemed to have use of the Rolls, so there was no point in that either. It would have been enough to take a nice holiday, but he couldn't think of anywhere to go. The problem was that it was also enough to buy some very interesting narcotics.

"Jean?" He tapped on the front door. There didn't seem to be any response from the intercom. He door was locked. He shook it a bit and then remembered a key on the Rolls keyring. He tried it and it fitted.

"Jean?"

Rogerman entered the building cautiously. He didn't notice the door swing closed and the lock click firmly. He'd spent the morning polishing and cleaning the Rolls, although there was no need. But he was conscious that he should stay out of trouble. Too much spare time prompted trouble for him.

"Jean?"

Rogerman had initially been frightened of Jean, but she had been kind to him, much kinder than his mother. He knew that Arthur wasn't due back for a while, although he hadn't said when, but he was getting a bit lonely. He'd only come into the office to have a chat with Jean.

"Jean?"

It was strange. She was always here. He had also made a decision. A decision he was proud of and wanted to share with Jean. After Arthur had spoken to him, and about the same time he received the pay cheque, he realised that he had tumbled into a pretty good number. What job involves so much leisure time? It's well paid and he gets the use of the Rolls. Rogerman had decided to go straight.

"Jean?"

Rogerman made his way up the staircase. He'd taken the Rolls to the pub a couple of nights earlier. He'd stuck to orange juice, which he'd found easier than he'd expected, and he'd chatted up a girl. She was a little spotty like him, but she was willing. Very willing, when they got in the back of the Rolls.

"Jean?"

He was surprised to find Jean's office empty. Rogerman wanted to keep his job and serve Arthur. He couldn't afford to mess with that. He wondered if Jean was somewhere else in the building. He tried a few doors and found more empty offices. Had Rogerman had more work experience he might have found this odd. But he had, via the medium of narcotics, had quite a lot of experience with the odd. So the odd was not so odd to him. He crept through the building, only mildly curious at its silence and finding nothing of interest. That was until he got to the final door in the office. What he found, when he opened it, was very odd indeed.

"Oh shit," he muttered. There was a naked man spread-eagled on a desk. He had a very little flagpole erection, absolutely nothing like Rogerman's in the back of the Rolls the other night. Indeed it was so small it wasn't immediately obvious to Rogerman that this was a man in an excited state. It seemed as if the man were being held against his will. Rogerman wondered if he should go and get Jean, but he'd been round most of the building. He'd read that some people enjoyed this sort of thing. He decided to ask.

"Excuse me," he said in the deferential tone he was developing for Arthur. There was no response. He looked at the head and realised that there was gaffer tape round the eyes and the ears. What should he do? He spoke louder.

"Excuse me, old boy." The 'old boy' was an Arthur mannerism he'd picked up.

There was still no response. He would have to remove the gaffer tape. If the man was happy, he could leave him there and mention it to Jean. Although the man was mostly bald, he had a small strip of hair to which some of the gaffer tape was not so well bonded. Rogerman ripped it off.

Clivert had never felt ecstasy quite like it. It had easily been his best sexual experience, although this just served to illustrate how few sexual experiences had come his way. The removal of the gaffer tape was quite a shock. The pain was a shock, and the sudden bright light was a further shock. But the biggest shock of all was meeting the perpetrator of the pleasure. His eyes flared like a wild thing. It was a man.

Clivert didn't hear the thumping noise, but Rogerman felt it landing on the back of his head. It took him by surprise. He saw stars, and then darkness, as he fell open-mouthed onto Clivert's crotch.

Clivert looked in shock as his rapist's mouth fell around his little flagpole. It was such a shock he closed his eyes for a second, which was just long enough to find them wrapped in more gaffer tape. He hated homosexuals, as much as he'd hated his brother. And now he'd been raped by one. It was just his luck.

Chapter Sixty-Seven

"Sophie?"

"John, actually."

"Whatever. What are you doing here?"

"I'm carrying out an investigation for the Inland Revenue."

"Shit. Inland Revenue? You've got to be kidding. I didn't know you worked for the Inland bloody Revenue." Geraldine was keen on many things, positively enthusiastic even, but paying tax wasn't one of them. Discovering that her transsexual accountant also worked for the Inland Revenue was quite a shock.

"I mean, shit," she continued, "the Inland Revenue."

"Don't worry, you're safe," Sophie reassured her.

They were standing outside Arthur's office. While Sophie, in her guise as John, had chosen to wear a conservative pinstripe suit – care of Marks and Spencer – Geraldine had pushed the boat rather further out. Arthur had only ever met her at the club, where her uniform was a tax-deductible Janet Reger. Outside she had a wider variety of clothing. When she had to take the kids to school and meet the other mothers, it was jeans – discreet, but fitted, with a nice top and a hint of mascara. But today she needed to extract four grand from a client she wished to retain. She'd given it some thought, but there was no question she'd got it all wrong.

"Anyway, what are you doing here?" Sophie asked.

"I'm trying to get the four grand that Arthur owes me."

"You're dressed like you're about to receive an Oscar."

While Geraldine had gone slightly over the top with a very elegant dinner dress with a plunging neckline, she still thought that was pretty rich coming from a drag queen. Although it had to be said, the dress *was* very red, as were her nails and lips.

"You say Arthur didn't pay?"

"Yes, he scarpered the other day when someone let off a gun. Come to think of it, weren't you there?"

"Was I?" Sophie said, her memory suddenly troubling her. Although the moment was etched on her mind. It had been quite exciting, not least because she enjoyed having sex as much with women as men. She couldn't really separate them, which was why both at the same time was rather nice. She made a mental note to try it again. Although it did look like Arthur had been ready to receive, in which case maybe he and Barry had got it on after all. But she had her doubts.

"Hold on, you *were* there. Weren't you with him and Trish and Sal? I was surprised, I didn't think that was Arthur's thing, but hey, whatever."

If Geraldine had a philosophy in life it could be defined as 'hey, whatever', although this didn't apply to being paid, or more accurately to not being paid. She was very clear on that.

"Well, I'm here now, and working on behalf of the Inland Revenue," Sophie said with authority. She pressed the door bell again and shook the door.

"That's strange. Doesn't he have a secretary?"

Geraldine shrugged. She was more than happy to know as little as possible about Arthur beyond his capacity for paying. And she'd certainly seen that. There were fewer and fewer people prepared to pay a thousand quid for a bottle of champagne. It was a shame, as the champagne alone had been enough to privately educate her kids, but the entrance fee just covered overheads. The sex business wasn't as lucrative as it used to be.

"There should be someone here," Sophie in the form of John said impatiently, and rattled the door again.

Worse still, Geraldine thought, while the number of people, even the fantastically wealthy, prepared to buy thousand quid champagne was declining, the school fees were always rising. She wondered why there was no one at Arthur's office. It prompted a thought.

"He has a chauffeur. And a Rolls Royce."

"Does he?" John said, now fully in character as a representative of the Inland Revenue.

Chapter Sixty-Eight

Rachel walked the walk of the sexually confident. There was a small sway to her hips, she held her head high and her mouth fell slightly open in a pout. And, of course, she looked the business. She was slightly dismayed to see a tall, elegant woman in a flowing red evening dress standing outside Arthur's office. As she approached, she hoped that the woman's features would dissolve into mutton, tired haggard and trying too hard. Sadly they didn't. The bloody woman was gorgeous. What the hell was she doing there? Had she arrived at an awards ceremony? She contemplated walking past, but Rachel wasn't like that. The red dress hadn't noticed her yet. She undid another button on her blouse. A second later she addressed her directly.

"Is Arthur in?" she asked cheerfully. It was also confident, slightly assertive and with just a hint of territorialism. It was almost as if she had said 'my Arthur,' which prompted her to think that she was getting ahead of herself.

"We are just trying to establish that," an accountant type with a high voice said. Rachel hadn't noticed him. She gave him a quick eye over, established that there was nothing of interest for her, and turned her attention to the red dress. And she couldn't help herself.

"Fancy dress do?"

Geraldine was many things, but she was certainly not someone you want to cross. She narrowed her eyes and looked down at Rachel's breasts, which looked like they were trying to escape.

"You on the pay roll?"

It was fairly evident that Geraldine did not mean in a secretarial capacity. They measured up to each other, although Geraldine's interest in Arthur was just financial, but she wasn't someone who liked to be defeated. They were sexual gladiators, poised for attack. It irritated Rachel that she rather liked the red dress, and wondered where it had been bought from. Of course, she could acquiesce and ask her, thereby breaking the tension. But she was Rachel. She was also Rachel on a mission, in which she hoped to trap a very rich man. She pouted some more, and inflated her chest. Geraldine caught the chest in her peripheral vision and wondered, for a moment, whether they'd been enhanced and, if so, by whom. They certainly looked real, but asking that would prompt defeat, and Geraldine was not a woman who liked to be defeated. Fortunately, they were interrupted.

"Hey, girls, great," Eddie said with real, unforced enthusiasm. He still had a great feeling about the day. It had been a great trip to buy trainers, and a great bus ride. When Eddie liked things, he really liked them. Sometimes he'd grab an adjective, and he just wouldn't leave it alone. And today everything was great. But he was bouncing on a new high. He'd caught a review of his gig that someone was reading on the bus. It wasn't difficult to miss, as it was headed *I'm Wasted*. It was a five star review. Eddie was floating on air, rather than the concoction of narcotics and alcohol he normally favoured. The two beautiful women standing outside Arthur's door were only there to make his day even more great.

"Hey," Geraldine said first, not sure whether she was going to punch the girl in front of her, or admire her breasts.

"Hello," Rachel said. She'd actually turned, looked at Eddie, thought she was looking at a tramp and turned away. Then it fell into place. She'd had a boyfriend who was a great fan, and they'd been to a few of his gigs. When she was younger, much younger, she'd also had a girlfriend who'd been a fan, and they'd also gone to a few of his gigs. It was a very vague groupie phase and it troubled her that she couldn't remember if they'd met. Or had sex.

"Hello, Eddie," Rachel continued, back in her stride, and thankful that her breasts were thinking of making that escape.

"I'm Rachel."

"That is great, Rachel, really great."

Geraldine had met Eddie a number of times, although she certainly hadn't had sex with him. She hoped she wasn't going to have to introduce herself. Not again.

Eddie smiled at the two of them. He could remember every detail of every great gig he'd ever had. He could even recall the precise taste of some skunk he'd cherished, and he knew all the dates of his guitars. Chicks' names, however, he was hopeless at.

"Hey, great, and you are?"

Geraldine smiled. If she admitted that they had met a number of times before, that would not look good, particularly in front of Miss Breasts.

"Geraldine," she offered her hand and Eddie shook it enthusiastically.

"That's great, really great. Hey, Arthur in?"

Chapter Sixty-Nine

Jean tried to calm her breathing. If it had just been the hooded man with the small penis it wouldn't have mattered, but Rogerman as well? That was a problem. Not that she had molested Rogerman, he was like a son to her. But what could she do? She hadn't hit him too hard, but his fall would have been a surprise. She wanted to protect Rogerman.

Jean had locked all the doors in a panic, and she could see a crowd of people outside. She was twitching the curtains. She had to form a plan, and quickly. She calmed herself, checked that her men were locked away safely, and made her way downstairs. If she could get rid of everyone and get to the end of the day, that would be a good start. Then she would find a way for Rogerman to release himself, and she would lock the office up and go home. But Rogerman might call the police, after all he had been hit on the head. Then the police would find a man tied up and naked, and she would be the chief suspect. That wasn't a good plan. What was she going to do?

Jean stopped on the landing. What if she told Rogerman? But, she reminded herself, he was like a son to her. That wasn't the kind of conversation she'd want to have with her son. Then a plan occurred to her. She ignored the knocking on the front door and went back up to the old twins' office. There was a small kitchen before the office and, as a precaution, she pulled an old frying pan out of the cupboard.

She walked to the end of the hall and opened it slowly. But she was interrupted by the persistent buzz of her phone. Only Arthur was that persistent. It would have to wait for a moment. She walked towards the door. Jean was operating on raised senses, but she still hadn't anticipated what she saw when she entered the room.

Chapter Seventy

The Black Artichoke was making plans. It was fortunate that Clivert had developed an alter ego, as he was floundering. He wasn't sure if he wanted to kill everyone, or cry. The Black Artichoke was clearer on the matter, and they'd been given a little help. Such was the shock of seeing another man suck his cock, and it had taken him twenty minutes to admit that to himself, that he jerked his right hand with greater force than he would normally muster. And something had moved. There was definitely more movement. The question was whether there was enough movement for his right hand to get to his left. If he could achieve that, then he might be able to remove whatever it was that was binding him.

"Aggghhh."

Clivert stopped moving. There was a groaning noise in the room, and he was fairly certain it wasn't him. He listened for a second. It wasn't him. Either he, or the Black Artichoke, had to move quickly. Clivert tried to snake one hand to the other, but they came to a halt just inches from each other. It was a metaphor for his life. Everything he ever wanted or desired was always just out of reach. He thought about Tracy. Clivert had clearly spent too long as the Black Artichoke and had convinced himself that Tracy was just out of his reach, where in truth she lay just the wrong side of winning an Olympic gold medal. Nonetheless he focused on her. Or it might have been on her breasts.

"Aghhh."

Rogerman was not a stranger to bad headaches. Hallucinogenic experiences had passed his way, but this lay somewhere between the two. In a new territory that he wasn't sure he liked. He was sort of awake, but unable to get up. It hadn't occurred to him that the awful groaning noise he was hearing was him.

"Agghhhh."

Clivert heard the groaning escalate and panicked. Whatever his rapist was doing he was, in Clivert's view, clearly arriving at a denouement. It would be better if he were able to release himself prior to the rapist releasing himself. He was struggling to come to terms with everything. He had a fixed picture in his head of Rogerman, open-mouthed. It was someone else he was going to have to kill. He tried sliding down the table and, after a further shove, something gave. This time he realised that the chains were caught on the four corners of the table, and two had come free.

"Agghhh."

Rogerman remembered vowing to himself to go straight, so he couldn't understand why he felt the way he did. The back of his head really hurt. He was looking for Jean, of that he was sure. But he hadn't found her. He hoped he wouldn't get in trouble with Mr Cholmondely-Godstone. He'd been polishing the Rolls all morning, almost as enthusiastically as he had polished the leather seats with that girl from the pub. Things were becoming clearer in his head.

"Hmmn," Rogerman said, this time recognising his own voice.

It was then that it occurred to Clivert, or it might have been the Black Artichoke, that he was going about things the wrong way. He lowered his right hand to his right foot, and this time it reached. It was easier to unite that he had expected and, once he freed one leg, the other wasn't difficult.

The Black Artichoke's spirit was returning, and he knew what he was going to do with it. He began his speech to himself. This was not his fault. He was all heart, a good man, who'd been brought down by the unjust. It wasn't fair and had never been fair.

With this firmly in mind, he leapt from the desk, ripping off the gaffer tape. Mid-air he saw his assailant floundering on the floor, and he threw himself on him. The inheritance should have been his. He deserved it. It was right and just. He'd been assaulted by a queer. He wrapped his hands around his assailant's neck and began to choke him to death. It was accompanied by random mutterings.

"Unfair! Queer! Rapist!"

Rogerman's eyes rolled to the back of his head although, again, not for the first time. As the supply to his brain lessened he began to drift, not entirely unpleasantly.

"Agghhh."

This time the noises were coming from Clivert, who had just realised the other possible connotation of the Black Artichoke. He would choke his victims to death. Rogerman was not a strongly built man, but he was wiry. And, Clivert was discovering, there appeared to be more skill involved in choking than he'd thought. He'd have to Google it when he got back. Such was his concentration, he didn't hear the door open behind him, or the frying pan swing through the air. He did feel it land, hard, on the back of his head.

Chapter Seventy-One

"Rachel?"

"Sophie? What are you doing here?"

"No, Rachel, the question is what are *you* doing here?"

Sophie eyed her friend distrustfully. Rachel wondered how she could launch into the altruistic nature of her being there at the same time as closing at least three buttons on her blouse. It would be difficult to make it convincing.

"Hey, great, I'm Eddie."

Sophie turned round and eyed the old long-haired bloke suspiciously. She returned her gaze to Rachel. Rachel did not want to admit that she had any interest in Arthur but she knew, such was the high visibility of her breasts, that denying it might be a mistake. But Rachel had nearly been expelled from school four times, and each time she'd demonstrated a great talent for thinking on her feet.

"I'm with Eddie," she said, and threw her arm over Eddie. Until recently, Eddie wouldn't have remembered who was with who. But hell, what did it matter? He'd had a good feeling about the day, and this girl had fantastic tits, which was as good a basis for a long-term relationship as any other reason he'd ever had. He wondered for a moment if Ozzy's Sharon had great tits. There must have been some foundation for their relationship. He hated to find himself on such contemplative ground, so returned to shallower pastures.

"Great, girl," Eddie said, having already forgotten her name, although not her breasts.

Sophie recast her cynical and distrustful eye, but then wondered if Eddie was someone she should know. No normal person would wear clothes like that.

"Okay, is Arthur in?"

"No," someone beside her said.

Sophie looked round and found a tall elegant woman wearing entirely inappropriate clothing for the occasion. She looked back at Eddie, and wondered if it was a fancy dress do.

"Who are you?" Sophie asked with only mild curiosity.

"Geraldine, I'm Geraldine."

It was then that both Rachel and Sophie recognised her as the woman from the sex club. That is Sophie with the vagina, and not Sophie with the penis, who was currently John from the Inland Revenue. He or she already knew who Geraldine was. Geraldine had no interest in women, and didn't recognise either of them, and didn't much care.

"Look, I have no interest in Arthur, I'm just after the four grand he owes me." She directed her lack of interest in Arthur to both of them, as she had her suspicions.

"Me too. He owes me four grand, too."

A further man had appeared. It took Sophie, who was currently John, to ask the question.

"And who are you?"

"I'm from the Pig Farm."

Derek always tended to overestimate the level of fame his restaurant enjoyed.

"You're a pig farmer?" John asked, confused.

"Cool, man," Eddie contributed, which took him away from staring at Rachel's tits for a second. Hell, the girl was supposed to be with him, whoever she was.

"Sophie?" the man who wasn't a pig farmer said.

"Derek?" Sophie had never made it back to the restaurant to sell her cheeses. This was going to be embarrassing.

Chapter Seventy-Two

Arthur was grateful to land on British soil. He'd asked for a wheelchair. He'd tried walking, but it felt like his groin was on fire. He was forced to get a taxi. Unbelievably, he'd been unable to get in touch with either Jean or Rogerman. He was going to give them both a talking to when, or even if, the pain subsided long enough for him to talk. His doctor had, however, responded immediately and the taxi was on its way to Harley Street. It appeared to have a rougher ride than the Rolls, and after a while Arthur gave up and just scratched. The walk from the pavement to the front door of the surgery seemed a long way.

"Arthur, old boy," his doctor said with the same genial tone he adopted for all occasions. Arthur didn't bother to explain. He pointed.

"No problem, Arthur. Just take off your trousers. Sit up there."

Arthur peeled his trousers off and did as he was told.

"Dear me," his doctor said, with precisely the same genial tone. He could have been unwrapping a birthday present.

"Quite."

The doctor busied himself with a detailed inspection of Arthur's genitalia, moving them around as if it were part of the conspiracy and hiding something.

"Dear, dear, dear," the doctor said.

He moved Arthur's genitalia around a little more, now as if he were a child hiding uneaten vegetables on a dinner plate.

"You have more than one infection," the doctor concluded.

"Two?"

"More, but don't worry. Antibiotics and a cream. I have a cream that is very effective."

Right at that moment Arthur would have considered trading Clivert's inheritance for that cream. He didn't have to. The stuff worked like magic. The pain went down a notch, and then another, and then it was just very uncomfortable, which was almost no pain at all.

"Oh and by the way I have, I'm afraid, some rather bad news."

"You do?" Arthur asked suddenly alarmed.

"Yes, I have the results of the sperm test you took last time you were here. I would have called, but it's a delicate matter," the doctor said still cheerfully.

"And?"

"Nothing."

Arthur was confused. He was fairly sure he had ejected a reasonably adequate sample.

"No sperm, I'm afraid. It would appear your extravagant lifestyle has rendered you infertile. But that has its benefits."

Arthur left the surgery thinking about Sophie. He was sure she had carried his child and legacy. His intention to head directly to the office was subverted by an absence of taxis and by the pub he inadvertently found himself standing outside. It looked warm and inviting.

Chapter Seventy-Three

"Bung!"

Jean was quite shocked by the noise the old frying pan made when she applied it to the mad masked man's head. It would have been reasonable to assume, given the number of heads that Jean had hit, that she would have some skill at it. She panicked for a moment that she may have hit him too hard. He certainly collapsed. Rogerman was making choking noises.

"Rogerman, what happened?" she asked in a very unconvincing way, but Rogerman had been close to death, and so was not best placed to provide a critical review of her performance.

"Ack, ack, ack," Rogerman said, delivering a perfect performance of someone who had nearly choked to death.

Jean dragged him out of the room, and closed the door behind her. Now she had a plan. She hadn't locked the door and the masked man was no longer bound. Jean's plan was less than brilliant, but it was better than no plan at all. She desperately hoped that the masked man would get away, all on his own. She led Rogerman into her office and sat him down. He was wheezing, but sound.

"What happened?" she asked again. There were problems with her intonation and delivery, but Rogerman didn't seem to notice. A police inquiry would be less convinced. The buzzer on her desk buzzed, which was the front door again, and then the phone rang, again.

"Are you okay, Rogerman?"

There was a homicidal maniac upstairs she'd tried to rape, and a crowd of people at the door. The phone seemed the least demanding option.

"Jean, where the bloody hell have you been?"

It was Arthur. Jean decided to wrap this one up quickly, and get to the front door.

"We've had an intruder," she began. This was fundamentally true, and this time she was far more convincing.

"Damn, is everything okay?"

"He attacked Rogerman, but everything is okay," Jean said.

Rogerman eyes opened further than they were used to. He had more or less recovered but, and he was fairly certain about this, the man that had tried to kill him was still in the building. Even for someone as laid back as Rogerman, that didn't seem entirely okay.

"Have you phoned the police?" Arthur asked very reasonably.

"Police?" Jean said, as if it were a creative solution she'd yet to arrive at.

Rogerman was nodding his head in agreement, despite his uneasy relationship with law enforcement representatives. This, he thought, was precisely the appropriate moment to call them.

"I was just going to call them now," Jean said, thinking fast. The man hadn't seen her. He had attacked Rogerman, and he was no longer tied up. If she could just get his clothes back on before the police arrived, then she'd be off the hook, or close to off the hook. Or something.

"Right," Arthur said, "I'll be there in five minutes."

"What?" Jean said at close to a scream. "I thought you were in Africa?"

"No, I had to come back, I'll see you in a moment."

The buzzer from the front door sounded again. This time she answered and shouted through the intercom.

"I'll be down in a minute, my apologies. The door release is not working."

Rogerman was a little surprised by the change in her tone. He also wondered why she hadn't even tried to press the door release button. And then there was the issue of the strangler.

"Shouldn't you have, like, mentioned the mad man in the building?"

"Yes of course," Jean said, "you're absolutely right." She said it as if they were discussing the fastest route to Hammersmith. And a further plan occurred to Jean.

"I'll call the police and you go down and tell them downstairs."

Jean picked up the phone, but Rogerman was still standing in front of her. She repeated the plan.

"Go downstairs and tell them."

Rogerman was rather more stunned than she'd thought. Another plan was required.

"You just stay there, I'll call the police from the other office and go downstairs. Just stay there. Don't move."

Rogerman was very good at not moving and, happy that the plan was set, Jean left the room. She needed to phone the police, but she also needed to allow time for the masked lunatic to escape. Rogerman watched her leave.

The room was suddenly very silent, and Rogerman was left with his confused thoughts. They were bouncing around his head in a way that would have been much easier had they been accompanied with a joint. He had never been physically assaulted before, and had found the experience very unsettling. His brief period of employment with Arthur had been unsettling. There was that crazed face with the dagger at the window of the Rolls. It took a while for the all the pennies to slot into place in Rogerman's mind, but it finally struck him that he might have been attacked by the same man. And last time that man had had a gun. It prompted a strong feeling of paranoia in him. He wished

Jean would come back. He felt safe with her. Then it struck him that he'd been given an instruction. At least he thought he had. He picked up the phone and stabbed the buttons.

"Police?"

It was the first time in his life he'd phoned the police. It was easier than he'd imagined. He explained the address and the nature of the assault. He remembered something his father had said. He wasn't a man who imparted much, so it had stuck. His advice had been simple. If you need an ambulance quickly, just say someone's had a stroke. If you need the police, tell them there's a man with a gun. They'll be there in no time.

"He tried to kill me."

There was suddenly much more focused activity the other end of the phone, and Rogerman ramped it up one more notch.

"Gun, yes, he had a gun."

Chapter Seventy-Four

"Sarge?"

Hurley was sulking. He'd received a letter that morning, and it didn't look like he was to fulfil his dream of working the streets of New York with his from-the-streets-black-guy buddy. There would be no 'covering' each other or witty banter. He had even taken his car into the woods, where he hoped no one could see, and practised rolling over the 'hood.' He knew he'd have his accent and intonation perfect in no time. And here he was stuck with a carrot-munching partner.

"There's been an incident, Sarge."

The boredom was getting to him. He'd been waiting for something to happen, something that would challenge his skills, and nothing. Worse still, Anderson seemed to revel in nothing happening. He couldn't understand the guy. He only ever talked about cooking.

"It's a gunman."

Hurley perked up.

"I'm on my way."

Anderson had brought some books to work, and had been studying them. He preferred Nigella, even though Delia's recipes seemed to work better for him, which was a less than subtle insight into Anderson. He put the books down and followed Hurley.

"I'm driving," Hurley said, although Anderson knew that already.

"Hey, what happened to your car?" Anderson asked. "The bonnet's got dents all over it."

Hurley shrugged like the hard-drinking, living-on-the-edge kind of copper he wasn't. He wondered if American cars had stronger hoods. He clicked the seat belt on, fired the car up, and squealed unnecessarily up the road. Today his firearm, or should that be piece, was going to see some action.

"No siren?" Anderson inquired with only passing interest. Hurley shrugged the same shrug. He was getting quite good at it. They'd been called out to a large council estate, and had arrived with sirens, and it had occurred to him that one of the reasons his piece was never out of its holster was that a noisy siren tended to warn the gunmen. And that was no good at all.

"No flashing light?"

It rankled Hurley, but he said nothing. He considered another shrug, but thought that might be overplaying it, which was unlike him. It had happened at the council estate. When they'd got back to the car, there was just a wire hanging uselessly. Some bastard had nicked his flashing light.

"Do you think we'll need a chopper?" Anderson asked with a broad smile on his face. Hurley couldn't help himself this time and shrugged. But he really hoped he could call in a helicopter. He dreamed of a siege, orders beamed down from a circling chopper armed with infra red. A rooftop chase would be good too. He wanted to cock and uncock his pistol, but it was a bit awkward while he was driving.

"High roofs," Anderson noted. They had arrived at Arthur's office and there was a crowd outside. They flung the doors open, and got out of the car. They both adopted heroic poses, although not for the same reason: the flack jacket and guns tended to make a wide stance necessary.

Hurley wished it wasn't so overcast, as he would have liked to have worn his sunglasses, the ones with the mirror lenses, but he made the most of his entry. He checked the roofs and open windows. He was doing his job. But he couldn't disguise his disappointment. If there was a wild gunman, then it hadn't registered with the crowd of people outside. They seemed very relaxed. Anderson put on his sunglasses regardless of the sun and, as soon as he saw Geraldine, adopted his heroic pose. He recognised her from an earlier callout. Then there were Sophie and Rachel. It was quite a gathering. It was hard to say who was swaggering more by the time they arrived at the crowd.

"Where is the gunman?" Anderson said, taking charge for the first time, and addressing Geraldine personally. Ever since the evening with the nurse, Rosemary, he'd been fantasising about her. He had cooked the pork to perfection, and the herb had been a great choice. The problem was that he didn't get round to reading all her message, which was rather lengthy and verbose. Had he read it, he would have discovered that she was a vegetarian. As a result of which he never got his pork into Rosemary.

"Gunman?" Geraldine said.

"There's been a call from this address," Anderson continued, but he was beginning to realise that he had underestimated the lure of her cleavage. Her dress was astonishing.

"From here? Are you sure?"

Anderson looked at Hurley and wished he hadn't taken charge.

"Hey, cool man."

Anderson turned and recognised Eddie. He felt the situation slipping away from him. Rock stars, even old and wizened ones, had all the luck.

"God dammit," Hurley muttered with more than a hint of Clint Eastwood. It was another wasted call. He ignored the approaching raw of an American V8 engine, and turned to his partner. But everything changed as something landed next to them, followed by quite the loudest explosion he'd ever heard.

Chapter Seventy-Five

Clivert was feeling tired. He was exhausted. His brief liaison with pleasure had been offset by discovering the author of that pleasure.

"Shit."

A bloody man. Wasn't that just his luck? Why did it have to be a man? It didn't even have to be a beautiful woman. Female of the species would have been enough.

"Shit."

His head hurt so badly it felt like he'd been hit with a frying pan. He tried to get up. It took a while. His clothing hang like rags, exposing him. Eventually he got to his feet.

"Shit."

Clivert now knew he was capable of killing, but he also knew he had to get out of there. If he stayed he'd get caught. If there was an upper hand, it wasn't with him. Not that he'd ever had an upper hand – that privilege had always been denied him.

"Shit."

He would have liked to have said so much more. Shit certainly didn't seem enough to adequately characterise where he found himself.

"Shit."

Clivert shook his head. Now was not the time for thinking. Now was the time for composing himself, and getting the hell out of there. His senses were coming back to him, and the pain in his head was moving to a more manageable level. If he could make that transition to the Black Artichoke, he might be able to find some strength.

"Shit."

He moved to the window and looked out. He couldn't see much. He opened the window and leaned out. The good news was that the building had a mansard roof with a parapet and a wide box gutter, which meant he could escape along the roofs of the neighbouring buildings. He looked down.

"Shit."

Clivert said 'shit' this time for two reasons. The first was that it was a bloody long way down; the second was that there was a crowd of people by the front door. And two of them looked like police.

"Shit."

He had to look away, but a closer inspection was required. They were the kind of police that wore flack jackets and carried machine guns.

"Shit."

Clivert was beginning to realise what he was really very deep in. The roof was his only escape route. He grabbed his bag. It was heavy, although it seemed to get heavier every time he picked it up. He'd just have to grab the essentials, whatever they might be. He opened the bag and looked in. His face creased as he pulled out rope he'd thrown in. It creased a little more because beyond the rope he didn't recognise the contents. He rummaged around in the bag a little more, and came to a conclusion. This was not his bag.

"Shit."

There were no black painted artichokes. But there were other things, and they were something of a surprise. Clivert pulled them out in bemused shock.

"Shit."

It was what it looked like. A gun. Clivert felt it in his hand and then plunged his hand back in the bag. He pulled something else out.

"Shit."

It was ammunition. He couldn't believe it. There was something else, something heavy. Clivert pulled it out.

"Shit."

It was a machine gun. He held it up and imagined firing it. It was quite an impressive weapon. If he couldn't escape, he could hold them all up. A smile appeared on his face. It had been a long time since that had happened. He thrust his hand back in the bag. It was incredible. He hesitated to think that his luck had changed again, but this was a gift from heaven. There was a small thread pointing at him. He pulled it curious to see what it was attached to. It made a noise.

Fffttt.

That was a strange noise. He wondered what would make a noise like 'fffttt,' and then it struck him with a further smile: fireworks. He'd always liked fireworks. Particularly big rockets. He often bought the biggest, and let them off from the small balcony at the rear of his flat. It was great watching them spiralling into the sky, and erupting into a series of colourful explosions. This foray into nostalgic Guy Fawkes nights might have been a very brief one had Clivert not suddenly linked the 'fffttt' noise with his present predicament.

"Shit."

He thrust his hands back in the bag and found a cylinder which had very recently had its fuse removed. It was what he feared.

"SHIT!!"

The door was probably locked. The room was small. He was doomed. He had no choice. He grabbed the cylinder and hurled it out of the open window.

Chapter Seventy-Six

The lure of the pub proved too much. It was that and a sense of confusion that was new to Arthur, and which he had difficulty reconciling. He'd never looked inwards – it wasn't a family trait – but something was prompting him. It was something to do with kindness. He sat at the bar.

"All right, mate?" the landlord asked him cheerfully.

"I'm not sure," Arthur asked honestly. Something was definitely gnawing at him.

"Will a drink help?" the landlord asked. He was thinking about abandoning the pub and becoming a psychotherapist, once he had sorted a few unresolved issues of his own.

"It certainly will," Arthur said brightly, "I'll have a bottle of that." He pointed.

"The Brewmeister Armageddon?"

"Yes, that's the one."

"Are you sure?"

"Quite sure."

"It's forty quid."

"No problem."

"It's very strong."

"Perfect."

"It's sixty-five percent alcohol."

"Great."

Arthur hoped that he could anaesthetise the itching in his pants with the beer and, if was really effective, it might anaesthetise the unwanted emotional feelings that were emerging in him.

"Okay," the landlord muttered. He'd missed a few of his AA meetings lately, but he was okay. He watched the golden liquid fill the glass. Most of his customers drank lager. He hated lager, which meant it was never a temptation. But Armageddon was something else. It seemed to take forever to fill the glass, as if it was deliberately tempting him.

"Thank you," Arthur said, taking the glass off the landlord, who seemed reluctant to part with it.

"So, why do you say you're not sure?" the landlord asked, getting himself onto a more stable footing. Arthur considered the question.

"Kindness," Arthur said eventually. The landlord was deeply grateful. It was exactly the kind of esoteric thought that he could debate at some length, which would take his mind away from Armageddon. He needed a more specific definition of the kindness.

"Your kindness, or somebody else's?"

"Oh definitely someone else's. I've never shown any kindness."

"Haven't you? Are you sure?"

Arthur hated to say it, but he was pretty sure. He just shrugged.

"Why does somebody else's kindness bother you?"

And there it was.

"I've never shown any kindness, yet there were people around me who are routinely kind."

Arthur knew there was a word for what he was feeling, but he had no idea what it was. It was a very new feeling.

"Guilt?" the landlord suggested.

Chapter Seventy-Seven

"This stops right naaah."

Liam was growing tired of Noel's over-deployment of the catchphrase. It was becoming almost as irritating as that stupid noise that Jimmy Saville had made when he had nothing witty to say.

"Hold on bruv."

Liam was weighing up the relative merits of suggesting that the catchphrase would have more impact if it used more sparingly, but Noel's face was creased with anger. Noel had been closer to Gracie: he was better with animals than humans. But it was quite possible that he had bashed his way out of the womb with those creases of anger already on his face. Liam left it.

"We need to find a parking place," Liam said, changing the subject very slightly. It was not an area of London that was fond of accommodating the motorist, and it involved circling Arthur's office a few times. Eventually Noel made a management decision.

"There! Put the motor there."

While it was part of the Queen's highway, it wasn't a spot that was designated appropriate for parking. But they were the McCarthy brothers, from a part of East London that was on the way to Essex, and they were in an African dictator's big trouble van. And it was equipped for trouble. It was a location that afforded them a good view of Arthur's office. They settled in for the wait. Liam slipped in a CD.

"Start spreading the news," Frank Sinatra began.

"You have got to be fucking kidding me," Noel said. Their musical differences had prompted arguments in the past. He stabbed the eject button and hurled the CD into the glove compartment. He rummaged around and reloaded the machine.

"I can't get you out of my mind," Kylie insisted.

"Oh, for fuck's sake," Liam said, "We're not going to sit here for hours listening to Kylie fucking Minogue."

Noel placed his hand close to the stereo, and turned it down slightly.

A moment later Kylie said, "Er naw, naw, naw. Can't get you out of my mind."

Noel turned the ignition off and was rewarded with silence. The tapping on the window took them by surprise.

"Caant," Noel observed, "it's a fucking traffic warden."

Noel couldn't believe it.

"I'll deal with this."

Noel got out of the van and closed the door behind him, while Liam switched the music back to Frank Sinatra. He could hear the discussion outside and turned it up. He'd heard enough of Noel's altercations.

Noel approached the traffic warden. He was further away than he thought. It was something to do with scale. In all violent altercations it was wise to assess the opponent first, and weight up potential strengths and weaknesses. Although Noel just tended to thump them. But Noel couldn't help noticing that this man was almost exactly twice his size.

"Fuck me, you're big," Noel observed.

Cyril was Jamaican, and had taken the job so that he could work the afternoon and evening shifts. This gave him the time, and the funding, to spend five hours a day in the gym. Last year he had been seventh in the Mr Universe competition. He would have fared better, but the balance between his deltoids and his pecs wasn't considered quite right. It was all about proportion these days, although at six foot seven, he had been the tallest entrant.

"You can't park here," Cyril the traffic warden repeated.

Before taking up body building, he'd won Tae Kwon Do competitions. But there wasn't much money in that, although it had helped keep him supple. Cyril had quite a wide range of emotions – he'd even shed tears when Mustafa had died in the Lion King – but fear wasn't one of them.

"I think I can," Noel said.

"No, you can't."

Cyril looked at him. More accurately, he looked down at him. It was a long way down, and it was quite a stare. Cyril was no fool. He clicked the ticket machine onto his belt and let his hands fall into a place that would prepare them for combat. He was longing for him to have a go. He uttered the words as if he were saying, 'I'm going to tear off your head and shove it up your arse.' But he actually said, "You can't park here."

"I think I can," Noel said. He knew something about big men falling hard, and also that they are rarely challenged, and therefore had no experience of the street. He was also aware that surprise was a useful weapon, although he wasn't sure if it was too late for surprise. He did think that if he had a chance of controlling the situation, he would have to do so rapidly. Or put another way:

"This stops right naaah."

Noel threw a punch. Cyril, before the body building and before the Tae Kwon Do, had quite a promising career playing cricket. But, much as he liked it, he wasn't passionate about it. Bowling and fielding were his thing, and he'd seen balls travel far faster than Noel's fist. He caught it with his left hand. Noel looked at his hand. It wasn't a particularly small hand, but rolled into a fist as it was, it was entirely enveloped by the traffic warden's vast hand.

"I think I can," Noel repeated, but this time without much conviction. He hadn't even thrown in a 'fucking' for good measure. He spread his legs in a forceful pose. But it was a hell of a lot of mountain to climb. Noel was a coiled up spring of aggression. He was nastiness garnished with an autistic emotional range, but he wasn't mad.

It was just as Frank Sinatra had decided that if he could make it in New York, then he could make it anywhere, that Noel rejoined Liam in the van. The song ended with a massive crescendo, and then silence. It was the end of the CD. Noel broke the silence.

"We can't park here."

Liam looked at him knowing he was going to have difficulty suppressing a smile.

"Problem with the traffic warden?"

Noel muttered something.

"What was that?" Liam asked, taking a deliberate stroll on very thin ice.

"Move the fucking car, naaah." Noel said. He hoped it wouldn't become a catchphrase. They moved the van and were lucky to find a legitimate place only two hundred yards away. Liam knew that Noel's silence was going to end nastily. He was surprised he hadn't shot the big fucker. Noel wasn't sure whether to break the menacing silence with more Frank Sinatra. He decided against it, and found a sports channel on the radio. He tried not to laugh.

Chapter Seventy-Eight

Rachel was many things, including fickle. She'd made the journey to see if she could seduce the not entirely fanciable, but undeniably wealthy, Arthur. But now that Sophie had turned up, this did not seem like a goer. Her plan required more on-your-feet type improvisation. And he'd arrived in the shape of Eddie. There were pros and cons.

"Yeah, like great, man," Eddie said.

His command of the language would certainly count as a con, but she didn't really use that as a measure of marriageability. He was a rock star, famous, and his gigs were packed out. Therefore he must be loaded, and that was the measure she'd most recently decided on. So on that front he was definitely a pro.

"Great, girl."

Eddie put his arm around her. Of course she would have to have sex with him. He was old, which wasn't necessarily a disaster, but he wasn't in great shape either. He would be a pretty nasty sight naked. She couldn't help herself, and cast a glance over Eddie. She wish she hadn't.

"Shall we like, go somewhere? A drink? Lunch?"

Eddie had no fixed plan for the day, but that good feeling about the day persisted. He also knew to grab opportunity when it presented itself, and Rachel's breasts had certainly done that. He could see Arthur another time, and he wasn't there anyway. And Eddie didn't really want to see his Cunt much.

"A drink? Why not?"

While Rachel didn't actually jump at the chance, she did see that it was a great escape plan. Eddie seemed like a kind bloke, too, which was another pro. And he was famous, so there's yet another pro. Fame opened doors. She tried to imagine herself on his arm at an awards ceremony. She'd even stretched her imagination far enough to picture him winning something. She struggled with the image for a moment, until she saw herself in Geraldine's dress. In her mind, it fitted as well on her body as it did on Geraldine. Now that the hostility had abated, she wondered whether it would be appropriate to ask her about the dress.

"So, shall we, like, go?"

They were about to move away, when two armed police arrived. They were fully kitted out, and the taller one presented a problem for Rachel. She pictured Eddie naked again, and wondered whether his wizenedness extended to his genitals. Would Eddie have a wizened penis? Do penises wizen? She felt something nasty appear at the back of her throat. Not a good sign. But the tall policeman, she could go for him. And he had the guns.

"Where is the gunman?" He seemed to take charge. Rachel was strong-willed and frequently belligerent, but she liked a man who could take charge.

"Drink?" Eddie croaked in a less than forceful way, as if he saw the greatness of the day draining away.

Rachel hadn't heard him. The tall in-charge-with-the-guns policeman was giving her some serious eye contact. Eddie's eyes had been too rheumy for that, and they had mostly been focused on her tits. Another con.

"Gunman?" Geraldine said. Rachel watched the gunned-up policeman's gaze shift like cloud eclipsing the sun. One thing Rachel knew for certain, she wasn't going to leave without finding out more about that dress.

"From here? Are you sure?" Geraldine seemed to be taking charge. The other policeman seemed slightly deflated at this news.

"Hey, cool man." Eddie seemed delighted at the prospect. A gunman was a very interesting twist on what still felt like a great day.

It was a thought that was followed by something landing close to them, and making quite easily the loudest explosion he'd ever heard.

Chapter Seventy-Nine

Sophie's sinking feeling was drifting from the mild to the Titanic. She had no illusions about Rachel. She was a rapacious woman, and she admired her for that. She liked the way that a prospect-free evening could turn out to be an adventure.

She shuddered at the memory of Rocky Deep. But Rachel wasn't burdened with a moral code. If she decided she wanted Arthur, then she wouldn't let a friendship stand in her way. Not that Arthur would be remotely right for her.

She looked at Rachel, which was hard to do without looking at her breasts. Which prompted a further question: why were they primed for action? Sophie couldn't help taking just a soupçon of delight at Geraldine, who had very successfully upstaged Rachel. As she had done before, Sophie considered abandoning the plan. She did not want to reveal something so personal in what was becoming a public meeting. She turned and then noticed Arthur approaching.

The others were too preoccupied to notice Sophie (that is, Sophie with the vagina) walk off. She could see Arthur walking slowly, as if in pain. She imagined that he was grappling with pain of an emotional or philosophical dilemma. She was so enraptured she didn't even consider sexually transmitted diseases, which is just as well as it would have prompted memories of herpes. The crowd behind her had become so preoccupied with each other, they didn't see the distance between herself and Arthur shorten. Arthur waved.

"Hey," Sophie muttered. It was one of those 'heys' that carried some meaning of past, present and very possibly future. She waved back and watched Arthur wave and smile. She hated to admit it, but her heart had jumped just a little bit. She knew what she was going to say, and how she was going to say it. And she really didn't care about the money. What happened, happened.

Chapter Eighty

"That's him."

The brothers compared the picture they'd printed off from the internet to Arthur. He was walking slowly and rather stiffly, and it was unmistakably him.

"That's him, all right."

Liam cringed, waiting for it to come. He was reassured by the pause, but Noel couldn't stop himself.

"This stops right naaah!"

Noel knew that this was the mantra he needed to get himself back into character. He got in the back of the van, and made lots of metal on metal noise. That traffic warden had sent him into an introspective silence. This was new territory for him, but had prompted a chain of thoughts. If there was no respect, what was there? There was a pecking order, and he pecked high up it. A fucking traffic warden was with the amoebas.

He had difficulty putting into words how belittling the experience had been for him, so he gave up. He was going to put it into violence and, if he felt like it on his day off, he would track down the traffic warden. Knowing that helped a lot. He cocked a few more guns.

Liam was discovering problems of his own. He wasn't sure if it was the dust of the African plains, or a dictator's relaxed attitude to servicing schedules, but the bloody van wouldn't start. Noel popped his head over.

"What's going on?"

"Fucking van won't start."

The engine continued to turn over, but it seemed to have no intention of firing. Liam looked up to see Arthur beginning to move away. Their plan had been to grab him and throw him in the back, and then get the bag from him.

"Start, you bastard!" Noel screamed and, miraculously, it did. It took Liam by surprise, but he didn't waste any time. He floored it. Arthur was approaching a crowd of people. A girl was walking towards him.

"Liam," Noel said, but Liam was concentrating, discovering it wasn't easy to steer.

"Liam!" Noel had noticed something quite worrying, which Liam had not seen.

"What?"

"Liam, for fuck sake. It's the police. The armed police!"

It took a moment for Liam to refocus his attention, when he did, he saw flack-jacketed, machine-gun toting police.

"Oh shit."

Liam applied the brakes. It didn't seem to prompt a corresponding reduction in speed. He slammed them to the floor. They were as effective as an African dictator's polling booth. Noel had fallen back and was scrabbling around trying to regain his balance.

"Oh shit."

They were heading for Arthur and a girl. The van, Liam was discovering, had the handling properties of an oil tanker. Worse than than that, it was behaving like a guided missile. He yanked the wheel and kicked at the brakes. The noise of the engine was drowned out by a huge clank on the roof of the van. The explosion that followed was even noisier. Fortunately for the brothers the van was built to resist exactly this moment; and fortunately for Arthur and Sophie, the bomb was powerful enough to shift the van off course.

Liam grabbed the steering wheel for comfort, as it appeared to have no facility for guiding the car, and he watched as the van suddenly veered past Arthur. At this point, and in the steering wheel's defence, the van was only rolling on two wheels. Liam adjusted his body, leaning sharply to the right to compensate. But the van continued to tilt, arriving at a point where gravity could no longer keep it on two wheels. The momentum of several tonnes of steel propelled by a large American V8 engine was such that the van continued to travel on its side until it hit something very solid.

Chapter Eight-One

Arthur had stood outside the pub for an age without once attracting the interest of a taxi. He had committed his first act of kindness. He could see that the landlord was salivating over the pint of Armageddon, and Arthur had only taken a few sips when he decided he had to go. It was to do with Brayman's friends, Harry and Sally. They'd said something about if you've decided what you want to do with the rest of your life, you want the rest of your life to start now. Brayman had wise friends. Arthur had passed the pint to the landlord and left. Of course, his first act of kindness had prompted the landlord to relapse and, after one hundred and twelve days dry, plunge into a binge in which he would wallow in deep despair.

Eventually Arthur gave up waiting for a taxi. The pain was more bearable when he moved than when he was stationary. It might have been that the movement provided enough friction to satisfy the various itches. It had been a long time since he'd taken public transport, but he was growing tired of waiting. The tube journey had been more rapid and agreeable than he'd imagined, but the station was rather further from his office than he'd remembered. He'd thought about trying again for a taxi, but they seemed to be operating a conspiracy against him. He'd walked very slowly.

Walking, he'd discovered, gave him the time to reflect on life. Life had been a little strange lately. But there was something that was itching at him that wasn't in his trousers. It wasn't Clivert or Eddie. It was Brayman. More accurately it was Brayman's kindness. This was something he had never given and rarely received, or if he had, he'd never noticed. There had been others. Gloria for one. All she had was kindness. It was this thought that was contrasting with the core of his life. While he wasn't actually a hitman, he'd profited from the deaths of others. He'd encouraged it, provoked it. And Brayman had shown him nothing but kindness.

It was an epiphany of sorts. Most bastards went through life being bastards, never stopping for a moment and realising they were bastards. He wanted to change.

Change. Such a short word, but such a lengthy endeavour. The problem was the family, and the solution was also the family. He was going to have to leave. He'd thought about the things he could do to make up, maybe even set up a charitable trust. Before that he would do what he could to right some of his wrongs. Obviously righting all of them would be too ambitious a project.

"Hey," Arthur said, and waved. There was a small group of people outside his office, but he'd seen Sophie. She was a perfect starting point. He hadn't treated her well, but then by the standards most people set, he hadn't treated anyone well. And then there were his clients. It was surprising that no one had tried to kill him earlier. The madman on the bonnet of the car had been an alarming experience. It wasn't one he wanted to repeat.

Arthur could make out other members of the crowd: Geraldine, Eddie, Derek from the Pig Farm, and that feral friend of Sophie's. He wondered why she was there. She'd never shown any interest in him in the past. He had certainly been interested in her. He even recognised that they were curiously well suited to each other. He got the impression that an unconventional lifestyle would suit her. They would have made good well-dressed, wealthy hippies. She might even give him herpes.

"Strange," Arthur muttered. He'd just noticed that there were two policeman, and they both appeared to be armed. But his eyes switched to Sophie, who was approaching him and was now quite close. She was looking good, and uncharacteristically confident. That was something he'd dented in the past. Finally they were facing each other. There was just a foot of air between them.

"Hi, Arthur," Sophie began. She was smiling. She'd made a decision about telling him, and she knew what she wanted to get out of it. She was there, but she wasn't going to work for it. If it was going to happen, Arthur would have to put in the work. She intended to keep both hands firmly clasped round her dignity. There was no letting go. It was quite an agenda.

"Sophie, how good to see you. I've wanted to see you, but you keep disappearing."

"Well, I'm here now," Sophie said, worrying that she might have put too much work into it already.

"The thing is, I want to say I'm sorry. I mean for that time," Arthur paused as he realised he was about to ruin the moment by uttering the word 'herpes'. And there was never a good moment to use that word. Sophie kept to the agenda and said nothing, prompting Arthur to fill the gap.

"And anyway, I'm sorry and it would be nice, if you would like, if we could have lunch or something."

It wasn't an outstanding apology, but it was Arthur's first. Sophie recognised it, but she found the 'something' part of the sentence distracting. And now was the time to deploy the second part of her agenda. She could have done it at the lunch or something, but she wanted it out in the open, before she committed herself to lunch. Or something.

"Look, Arthur I should have told you. It was just after that incident with the -" Sophie realised she was about to tumble into saying the word 'herpes', and that wasn't going to help. Arthur looked confused. He thought it unwise to assist her by saying 'herpes', so he kept quiet.

"Anyway, I was angry, Arthur, I was very angry."

"I know that and I'm sorry. Very sorry," Arthur added, shifting rapidly up the class for delivering apologies.

"No, you don't understand. I was very, very angry because…" Sophie was trying to find the right word, although there was only one word. Arthur, who was not gifted in the intuition or insight department, just wondered why relationships with women had to be so complicated. It was an argument for homosexuality.

"I was angry because I was pregnant."

The words rolled over Arthur. His mind worked in reverse, thinking first that it at least explained why relationships with women had to be so complicated. The business of someone growing inside you was very complicated indeed. Arthur was clearly weakened by his epiphanic moment, and found it rather moving. But there were questions. The first had to be asked, but was in danger of causing insult.

"Mine?"

Sophie knew he'd ask the question, she'd spent enough time with him. It didn't offend her too much.

"Yes."

There was a roaring noise in Arthur's ears. There was something equally vital she hadn't told him.

"Did you have the baby?"

Sophie smiled. The herpes and the time with Arthur had not always brought her joy, but her child certainly had.

"Yes."

Arthur gulped. The family had put pressure on him to father a child and maintain the legacy. It didn't seem possible. And here he was thinking about abandoning the family. That might have been awkward timing, but Arthur felt something else. He wanted to meet and get to know his son.

"What's his name?" Arthur asked. The roaring in his ears had increased, as if it were a metaphorical reaction to riding the emotional rapids of grown-up life.

"Molly."

"Molly? That's a strange name for a boy."

"That's because she's not a boy."

Arthur and Sophie turned and saw a van heading for them. It explained the roaring in Arthur's ears. It was travelling fast, and it didn't appear to have any intention of stopping. It was followed by an almighty explosion.

Chapter Eight-Two

Despite Hurley and Anderson's antipathy to each other, and their differing interests and ambitions, they reacted professionally. "Keep down, move round there!" Anderson commanded, and he shepherded Geraldine, Rachel, Sophie who was currently John, and Derek the pig farmer, round to the far side of a parked car. It involved a little bit of appropriate-for-the-moment manhandling, but brought about the discovery that Geraldine had a reassuringly firm backside. Hurley dropped to one knee and trained his rifle on the open window. Should someone appear, he was primed to shoot. He reached his hand over and clicked his radio to transmit. His eyes almost welled with emotion, as he finally got to say, "We're gonna need a chopper."

The call was picked up by dispatch, but there were issues with it. Hurley couldn't stop himself.

"What was that? Please repeat."

"We're gonna need a chopper."

Hurley had deployed the American accent. But it wasn't Clint or Bruce, and it certainly wasn't George or Brad. It was more Marlon at his most methody. The dispatcher put him on speaker.

"We're gonnaneedachopper," Hurley slurred.

Her supervisor stood beside her.

"What did he say?"

"I don't know. It sounded like he's shopping."

The supervisor grabbed the microphone.

"Please repeat."

Hurley was finding the multitasking of training a rifle on the window, from which a bomb had recently been ejected, and maintaining a conversation, a little tricky.

Anderson was preoccupied. While he had, in the course of preserving the safety of the public, brushed his hand across the firm buttocks of the striking woman in the red dress, there was the matter of the other woman. She was most notable for her breasts which had, prior to the bomb exploding, existed in a state of fine balance. There was a bra, which had been expensively innovated, primarily by men, to make the most of a small package. But Rachel did not have a small package, and the dive to find cover had upset that balance.

Anderson found himself staring at her naked left breast. It hung in the air like a faux pas. It was as if it had become sentient, and wished to make a pertinent observation. Like a department store closed circuit camera, it was watching Anderson. But it was doing more than mere observation. It was assessing, judging. Anderson was clearly having issues with the breast. It was quite possible he hadn't seen as many as he'd have liked, recently. Rachel's response, on the other hand, to an exploding incendiary device, was to attempt to preserve her life over her cleavage. She hadn't noticed.

"Er, excuse me," Anderson ventured. It was better than his first thought, which was to relocate it personally. On further reflection, he considered it unlikely that a police enquiry would find in his favour, if he suggested that popping the breast back would be part of a public service.

"Hey," Rachel said lazily. This policeman had easily the bluest eyes she'd ever seen, and they looked straight into her eyes. This was mostly to do with the fact that he was desperately trying not to look elsewhere. Anderson stood over six feet tall, he had light brown hair that turned blond in the sun, and he did indeed have very blue eyes. He was also armed and dressed in clothing that inflated his stature. His next line was something of a disappointment to both of them.

"Er."

Geraldine had all the qualities that would make her the antithesis of a nurse. If there was a purpose for patience, she hadn't gathered it.

"For God's sake, woman, your tits are hanging out."

It tripped Anderson back into professional mode. He surveyed the scene, checked on Hurley, who was having difficulty making himself understood, and decided to call the helicopter in himself.

"There is a gunman. Helicopter back up required."

Even with his west country accent dispatch understood. The chopper was scrambled quickly. Anderson looked at the ground behind them and declared, with some authority,

"We're going to have to stay here, for the time being."

Rachel, now with her breasts back in place, and most of her buttons done up, realised they were missing something. There had been something scruffy next to them. It took her a moment to remember.

"Where's Eddie?"

It coincided with Eddie's appearance, who strolled casually round the car. The bomb had prompted a memory of a gig back in the seventies. He might have pissed on some electrical equipment. He couldn't remember.

"Great gig," Eddie said, referring to the seventies, but leaving it open to saner interpretation.

"Bloody hell Eddie, your hair's on fire."

"Hey, cool, man, great," Eddie said, never averse to the odd bit of flattery.

"No," Rachel insisted, "I mean your hair is on fire."

Eddie had wondered why the strange smell was following him, although it wasn't the first time he'd thought that.

"Get down," Anderson instructed, and began to pat Eddie's head with his hands.

"Shit," Anderson muttered. For his age, Eddie's hair was remarkably thick. It was also bound together with some serious hair product, which had all the properties of lamp oil.

"We're going to need something to put it out," Anderson said. He looked around for something appropriate, and concluded that a piece of clothing would do the job. The accountant-like man was wearing a suit, and if Geraldine removed her dress – he stopped himself right there. Rachel could see where his mind was going and it was, with horror, that she saw his eyes alight on her, or more accurately her jumper. Eddie's hair product turned out not be merely flammable. This stuff was positively explosive.

Eddie was on fire. If he had considered a future with Rachel, this might have given him just a little insight into what it might be like.

"But it's pure cashmere."

Chapter Eight-Three

"Shit."

Clivert leaned out of the window. Everyone had scattered. There was a van on its side, and an old man's hair was on fire. There was no sign of his target, Arthur Cholmondely-Godstone. He leaned further.

Phutuc.

A strange noise had come from the window frame. Clivert examined it for a second before he realised that it was a bullet hole. It took an equally long time for him to grasp that someone had shot at him.

"Shit."

He ducked back in. Arnold Clivert knew that either things were getting out of hand, or they were already completely out of hand. His business plan as the Black Artichoke, the assassin, did not include being caught or shot at. He would have to abandon the plan and escape. It was going wrong, just like his previous attempt. He tried to compose himself. He had immediate issues to deal with, most notable his clothing, or lack of it. He wasn't going to get far stark bollock naked.

"Come on, be resourceful," he chided himself. He wondered what the Black Artichoke would do, then realised that he was thinking along the wrong lines. Then it came to him.

"Of course," he said in a strangely intoned drawl. It was obvious. What would Captain James T, for Tiberius, Kirk do? Of course that wouldn't necessarily be the same as Captain Jean Luc Picard. He hesitated for a moment, wondering which role model he should go for. There were pros and cons for either but Jim, in the early days, had been involved in more hand-to-hand fights. Jean Luc, on the other hand, always remained cool. And there was the hair issue. Clivert was closer to Picard than Kirk, aside from toupee issues.

Phutuc.

Clivert realised that he had to get a move on and decide. He remembered an episode when Jim had fought a monster. He'd run around and constructed a bomb. Then there was another episode with a sling. As a child, Clivert had made a sling and used it, first to hurt his younger brother, and then to hurl stones over their neighbour's greenhouse. It had taken a few broken panes, for which he blamed his brother, but eventually he became almost quite good at it.

"Affirmative," he said to himself although, if questioned, he wouldn't be able to say why. But someone had shot at him again, and it was likely to be police. He didn't have much time. The place would be swarming soon. He searched the bag and found gaffer tape. He looked at it for a moment. He'd seen Gok Wan do something with gaffer tape, but he couldn't remember what. He supposed he could gaffer tape his trousers back together. He looked through the rest of the office office. There were cupboards and wardrobes, and finally he hit gold. Or at least he thought he had. It was a suit, and quite a nice one, too. It was a Savile Row made-to-measure suit that one of the twins used to wear on formal occasions. It had survived in very good order.

"Great," he muttered with unusual enthusiasm. He pulled it off its hanger and stepped into it. At the same time, and as a demonstration of how he was raising his game, he thought about escape routes. There were only two he could think of. One was out of the back garden, and the other was along the roof. The only other option was the front door, but that would be suicidal.

"Bugger."

The multitasking had been a mistake. While the suit had been made to measure, it had been tailored around the girth and height of the twins. They were comfortably twice the size of Clivert. He abandoned the suit idea and went back to the gaffer tape plan. It was quite a delicate and skilful task, and there was something upsetting his concentration. He could hear sirens. He stepped it up. He would discover later that applying the gaffer tape direct to his genitals was a mistake. But a moment later he was ready.

Phutuc.

He looked up. If he wasn't mistaken, that was another gunshot. If he didn't do something soon, they'd enter the building. He had another look in the bag. There were five more incendiary devices. A cunning idea emerged. The office was on the corner of the building. He opened one of the windows on the far side, and peered out slowly. It was clear. He leaned round to get a view of the garden, but couldn't see it. He tried leaning out further, but was in danger of falling.

The plan was simple. Possibly too simple. At the moment the gunfire was aimed at his window and at him. If he hurled a bomb as far away as he could, it would shift the attention to the street behind. He would make a sling and twirl it far away. It was so Jim Kirk, it made him smile. And there was further cunning to the plan. He'd escape through the front door. Just for a moment he felt like Raffles, the gentlemen burglar. But his appearance was more akin to a refugee from an S & M club.

"Come on out, with your hands on your head!" A voice with a strange mid-Atlantic accent shouted.

"Shit."

There was no time to waste. He moved close to the open window, unravelled the sling, took a cylinder and removed the fuse.

Fffttt.

Clivert fumbled with the sling and began to twirl it. There was a strange rumbling noise upsetting his concentration. He extended his whole arm in a wide arc, the consequence of which was that the gaffer tape tore at his crotch. It was agony. He would have stopped, but the cylinder was eerily quiet, and then a small plume of smoke appeared. It was about to go. He twirled it faster and released it. It took a few seconds.

Remarkably, the plan was not without merit, but there were a couple of flaws. The first was that the building did not have a garden. The bomb bounced merrily off the side wall, and then off another wall, and landed on a roof. It tumbled down and landed in a neighbouring garden. This had exactly the consequence he'd hoped.

Bam!!!

It was better than Guy Fawkes' night. Clivert pulled a few more things out of the bag. There were only a couple of incendiary bombs left, but there was something solid wedged in the bottom of the bag. It took him a while to pull it out, and a while longer to identify it.

"Bloody hell," he said. It was a bazooka. That could really spread the mayhem. Clivert strapped it to himself and got out of the window. He walked along the parapet, and lobbed another of the small incendiary devices. It was then that he realised that the clattering and rumbling noise was a helicopter. It was just above him. And all hell was let loose.

Chapter Eighty-Four

"Hey man," Eddie wailed. It wasn't a very loud wail, more tinged with confusion, like a dog chasing its tail. The fire on his head raged.

"Your jumper," Anderson commanded with a level of urgency consistent with encountering someone with their hair on fire.

"It's cashmere," Rachel said. Geraldine couldn't help herself, she reached out and touched it. It was quite the most beautifully soft cashmere she had ever felt.

"Nice," Geraldine said.

"Thanks," Rachel said with a smile, and all the urgency of someone watching a goat actually grow the stuff. It was a bloody nice jumper, and had cost her three hundred and twenty quid, which was a bloody lot of money. Eddie, she reasoned, could probably grow his hair again.

"But his hair is on fire," Anderson observed.

"Is my hair on fire?" Eddie said, as if he was a dog who had just grasped that his tail was attached to him.

"It was three hundred and twenty quid," Rachel pointed out.

"Wow," Eddie muttered. That was hell of a lot for a jumper.

Anderson needed to assert his authority. It was important to manage the situation, to protect civilians and, more importantly, to make himself look good. But he could see there was no way Hanging Breast was going to give up the jumper.

"Hey, man. It's, like, hurting," Eddie observed.

Anderson removed Eddie's jacket and used it to smother the flames.

He pulled Eddie down under the cover of the car and waited. There were bangs, pops and explosions. Despatch gave him his instructions. Thankfully his job did not include shooting back, or running around the building waving his gun. Hurley was doing enough shooting for the both of them. Anderson's job was to protect the people on the ground, and that was fine with him. There was just one difficulty he was struggling to overcome.

"Everyone okay?"

"Yes, I'm fine. Now can I bloody well go?" Geraldine had endured enough, particularly as Arthur had buggered off. She was not going to see a four grand cheque today, and that was all that mattered to her. Anderson, on the other hand, had other thoughts. Most specifically he wondered how he could get the banter flowing. He wasn't required to do much and, aside from the odd explosion to the rear of the building, he was getting worried that it might become boring.

"I'm under instructions to keep you here until the gunman is apprehended. If you leave the cover of this vehicle and get shot that would be my responsibility."

Of course, Anderson had decided that Red Dress was a lost cause, and was really hoping to make some impact on Hanging Breast. If he couldn't achieve that with witty banter, then calm authority might crack it.

"You just need to remain calm, until it is made safe."

"I am calm," Geraldine said with icy calmness, "I'm just getting pissed off."

"You've ripped your dress," Rachel pointed out. She did so equipped with a conciliatory tone, verging towards the sisterly. She had decided that she wanted to get two things out of the situation she found herself in. One was the telephone number of the tall policeman with the blue eyes. The other was where that dress came from.

"I know, it's one of my favourites," Geraldine said with a rare air of defeat. She'd not had it long, which meant she was more likely to find another. The only thing was that she hated to admit where she bought it from and, worse still, how much she had paid. It flowed and clung and hung like a work of genius. It was also astonishingly cheap. In any other area of life this would be a good thing, but admitting to a younger woman she barely knew that her Oscar-winning dress was only twenty quid, was another thing. Geraldine began to get up. She didn't really intend to leave the cover of the car, she wasn't mad, but she couldn't help challenging authority. Her movement concerned both Anderson and Rachel. Rachel went first.

"Before you go," she said. Geraldine looked round at her, not unkindly.

"You can't go," Anderson said with authoritative firmness. He fixed his eyes on hers. Geraldine found it quite a compelling argument. But Rachel wasn't going to let the moment slip.

"Before you leave."

"Yes."

"She's not leaving." Anderson insisted.

"What is it?" Geraldine asked. Rachel went for it.

"Where did you get that dress?"

Geraldine was a classy woman of elegance and style. She prided herself on her appearance. She wasn't just born stunning, she maintained herself stunning, carried herself stunning and dressed stunning. It was for that reason that she decided that she'd rather be shot at than admit she was wearing a twenty quid dress, particularly to someone who had paid three hundred and twenty quid for a jumper. She got up and ran.

"Damn," Anderson muttered, disappointed that his authority hadn't been enough to anchor her. He watched her run to safety, surprised that she could run so well in such a tight dress. Anderson was not acquainted with the magic of polyester.

"No one move, please," Anderson said, aware that his authority had been eroded, and certain now that he wouldn't be able to think of anything remotely witty to say. He checked his two remaining charges.

"Yeah, man."

Eddie was sulking. He had much to sulk about. There had been a time when women threw themselves at him, although he chose to ignore all the times that divorce lawyers had also thrown themselves at him. Now he wasn't worth a jumper. He wouldn't have put it past the girls to suggest that the copper urinate on him. Maybe they wouldn't even have done that. What really got Eddie was the realisation that the day was not going to be a great one.

"Beautiful dress," Rachel said, although she was beginning to have her reservations about it. She'd wished she'd felt it, as her jumper had been felt. Rachel put that to the back of her mind, and concentrated on Blue Eyes. She'd only just noticed how large his hands were.

"Yeah, beautiful," Anderson muttered, although he was really referring to the body inside the dress.

Rachel frowned. It was no good having Blue Eyes admiring someone else but, she reasoned, no one went forwards without occasionally being a bit forward. She undid a few buttons on her blouse and introduced herself.

"My name is Rachel." She put her hand out.

Chapter Eighty-Five

Ben, Dan and Tim were playing cards. They had sat at the table and played cards the previous day, and the day before that, and the day before that. Playing cards was quite a feature in their lives.

"Two nines," Ben said.

It would be reasonable to assume, given the enormous amount of practice, that they would be good at.

"Flush," Dan said.

"That's not a flush," Ben said.

"Isn't it?"

Or even on the boundary of competent. But playing cards was not their calling in life, just something they did to pass the time. There was an awful lot of time to pass. They'd gone through the procedures, checked the locks and monitors. And that hadn't taken up much of the day. The rest of the day was spent doing nothing, or playing cards.

"That's a flush."

Once their superior had told them that they weren't allowed to play for money, their interest in cards went into sharp decline. They were, at heart, three competitive individuals.

"Darts?"

"Fuck it, why not."

Dan was in the SAS, something he didn't mind mentioning to Ben, who only worked in the police force. Tim came from MI5 and didn't tend to say much. But he was good at darts. They hammered the dartboard for half an hour, until someone rang the door bell. There was a lot of clicking and cocking, but it was just a routine paper delivery.

"All clear?" Tim asked. He was nominally in charge. There was a lot of nodding.

"Okay."

Their room was subterranean, and sat under the garden between the main house and the mews house. It gave them access to both, and provided the possibility of entering, or exiting, via either. It gave them a greater area to protect, but their surveillance cameras covered both the main road, and the mews behind. Their charge was currently upstairs in the main house, with plans to stay in London for a further week. There was going to be a lot more cards played. They preferred it when he was travelling, which was frequently, as it gave them more to do, and a look at the world.

"Poker?"

"Fuck it, why not," Dan said with a wave of his hand.

They removed their firearms, loosened their belts and sat at the table. There was a long way to go before any of their shifts ended.

The card were dealt out.

"That's the one with five cards?" Ben asked.

"Jesus H Christ," Tim muttered, never quite sure whether Ben was serious, or taking the piss. He didn't like people who took the piss. Tim was done with this detail in two weeks, and pleased to leave. It should be a retirement gig, not for someone like him, in his prime. He missed the darker world of MI5.

"I need a piss," Tim said and disappeared. He frequently disappeared, prompting the others to wonder what he was up to.

"She's quite a girl, pussy."

Also when Tim was out of the room, Ben and Tim tended to talk to each other in Sean Connery accents, at the time of James Bond, although they could have been impersonating a Russian U boat captain. Impersonations weren't their thing either.

"Of course she has, Moneypenny."

Tim returned quicker than they had anticipated, and prompted an uncomfortable silence. They tried not to look at him twitching in their peripheral vision. It didn't last long. A large bomb landed on the roof of their building. They moved into action.

"Check the exits," Tim yelled through smoke and fire, "I'm going to check on Tony."

Chapter Eighty-Six

On the ground Hurley was having the time of his life, but he was itching to do more. People were falling into place, the chopper was flying above. He was at the centre of it all – or perhaps that should have been center, as he was having difficulty keeping control of the American accent.

"Issgamanonroof."

"What? What did he say?" Despatch were having difficulty following him. They could only hazard a guess.

"Was that something about gammon?"

"You mean as in ham?"

"Is it a butcher's?"

"No, gamanchuckedabam." Hurley provided greater detail, but the helicopter above him was making so much noise, he couldn't hear.

"A bam?" Despatch asked, "What's a bam?"

"Did he mean bap?" the supervisor added helpfully.

"Why's he telling us about the ham in his bap?"

Although they were not reading Hurley's voice loud and clear, the explosion that followed came through very clearly.

"Bloody hell," the supervisor observed.

"Bam, bam, bam," Hurley confirmed.

"Oh, a bomb, of course."

"What was that about gammon?"

The hissing noise from the radio was interrupted with gunfire.

"Gunman." Despatch and her supervisor both said.

"Hold on," the supervisor asked, "What's the address?"

Despatch gave it to him.

"That sounds familiar. Is it an embassy?"

"No, I don't think so."

"Definitely sounds familiar."

"I'll just check."

A few seconds later they had the answer. Despatch got it first.

"Bloody hell, does that say what it says?"

"Bloody hell, it does," the supervisor confirmed.

"Tony bloody Blair."

"We better alert MI5."

"Isn't that MI6?"

"Better alert both of them."

"What about the army?"

"Best not, for the time being."

"Why not?"

"They're more likely to shoot Blair themselves."

"Weirgonnahaftagin," Hurley shouted in the radio, but he really meant him, as Anderson seemed preoccupied.

"What?" Despatch asked.

"No idea," the supervisor said.

Hurley rephrased it.

"Gonnahaftagooin."

"No, didn't get that either."

But Hurley hadn't heard the response. He was going in.

"Cover me," he shouted at Anderson, but Anderson wasn't listening as he was trying to cover Rachel.

"Eh?" Anderson replied. There was no question that there was interest there. There had been eye contact. The only question was how to go about it. How did he go in for the kill? He thought it likely he'd have to let off a few unnecessary rounds as a sort of peacock activity. Hell, he was cleared for it.

"Cover me!" Hurley shouted again.

"Eh? You're not going in?"

Anderson realised it was too late. Hurley was going in for the kill.

"Shit," he said, forgetting his audience. He braced himself against the car, drew the rifle up and trained it on the open window. He hated firing the damn thing, but he was losing ground. He fired off a couple of rounds.

"Go, go," he shouted, once he'd established that no one knew that Hurley had gone already.

Hurley launched himself at the front door, and gave it a karate-style kick. It was beautiful. His armography, as they say in dance competitions, was perfect. He flew through the air, and delivered the kick smack in the middle of the door. Unfortunately some fifty years earlier a great uncle of Arthur's had been involved with a not dissimilar altercation. They had briefly harboured a political fugitive, who'd followed the family advice to the letter and incensed everyone. They'd had to fit a steel door.

"Shit, shit."

The door barely shuddered and Hurley crashed to the floor. Thankfully there were no errant mobile phones following his cause. There was a strong chance he'd broken something.

Chapter Eighty-Seven

Jean stood frozen, unable to move. What had she done? How had it gone so very wrong? She was going to have to look into female castration, or whatever would rid her of her libido. She really didn't want to go to prison again. She hoped Rogerman was okay. The plan to allow enough time for the hooded man to escape may not have been genius, but it wasn't without merit. Who would have thought that in that brief period there would be gunfire and explosions?

One thing that was certain was that Jean had no idea what to do next. She was sitting on the stairs, half a landing up from the front door. Going back upstairs was unwise, and leaving the building wasn't a good idea either. She was rooted to the spot.

"Cover me."

She could hear shouting from the other side of the front door. She had to get a hold of herself. If she wasn't careful, this would look like it was her fault. Jean had to remind herself that the hooded man had entered the building with the intention of doing harm to Arthur. She was innocent, sort of.

"Cover me."

On the other hand, she had tied down and sexually assaulted the hooded man. That wasn't good. But it wasn't murder. The door shook as if something had been thrown at it. She had to get a grip. She stood up and walked down the stairs. She was going to have to be bold. She took in a sharp intake of breath and opened the door.

"Are you okay?" she asked an armed policeman, who was writhing around on the floor.

"Fine," Hurley hissed through gritted teeth. He was not going to let a broken foot stand in the way of this moment. A bravery award could really influence his prospects of making it into the NYPD. He dragged himself up, and pulled himself through the front door. Fortunately it was the kind of building that had a sturdy handrail.

"Are you sure?" Jean asked.

Hurley didn't answer. He pulled himself up the stairs. This was going to be his moment. The meek, he reminded himself, did not inherit the earth. No sir, the motherfuckers would get blown out the way. He pulled himself onto the first step. It was quite a big building, with six floors and many stairs. It was going to take sometime. For a second Hurley wondered if he could get the gunman to come to him. It was worth a try.

"Come on out, with your hands on your head!"

It wasn't a very loud shout, but it was a start.

Chapter Eighty-Eight

Heart rates were soaring. It was the problem with the protection business. The contrast between sitting around and doing nothing, and defending their charge against a terrorist attack. It was a big leap. But Ben, Dan and Tim, were professionals.

"Under the bed, Tony!" Tim enjoyed the opportunity of shouting at their charge, who had been very specific about being called 'Tony.'

"You stay here, Ben." As Ben was plod rather than the dark forces of SAS and MI5 he got the job of covering their client, who was now cowering under the bed. But it was procedure. The bed and the room were all reinforced steel. It wouldn't be easy getting through them.

Tim had hooked into the helicopter, and was attempting to locate the source of the attack. The helicopter pilot was very experienced and rather prone to be cynical, particularly when he discovered whose house he was hovering above.

"You have got be fucking kidding me."

Tim didn't have a sense of humour, and kidding was not his thing. Although the pilot had flown in the army, and was no stranger to flying under gunfire, it distracted him.

"Bring it down and confirm source."

The pilot was not entirely convinced that it was a good idea bringing the helicopter closer to the explosions, but there was something about the tone of the man issuing the commands that prompted him to follow them.

"Shit."

Clivert froze. The incendiary devices were clearly more explosive than their size would suggest. They had created mayhem. He raised his head and found that the helicopter above him was not pointing his way. It was clattering over a neighbouring garden. It hadn't seen him. He couldn't go back in, someone was coming upstairs. He'd have to make his escape along the roofs. The roofs were a mixture of slate, flat roof and box gutters, with chimneys poking out at uniform intervals. He looked up. The helicopter was turning. He only had a second. Clivert scrambled over the chimneys.

Tim had now ascertained from the helicopter, and dispatch, that the perpetrator was on the roof of a neighbouring building.

"Dan," he instructed, "you stay here, on the outside. No one enters or leaves."

Tim was going after the gunman himself. It reminded him briefly of a moment in Beirut, but he didn't like to think about that. He ran. Fortunately Tim's high quality but largely polyester suit was also mixed with Lycra, which meant that he could go about the business of running without disrupting all the firearms hidden beneath. When he arrived at the front of Arthur's building, he found it quite a mess. He assessed the situation, conferred with an armed policeman, and entered the building. He ran up the stairs taking them two at a time. And then he heard something.

Chapter Eighty-Nine

"Sonofabitch."

Hurley was sweating. Whatever he had done to his foot, it was verging on the serious. The pain was terrible, which meant he had to hop on his other leg. This was okay for the first couple of flights, but was proving to be something of a problem after five more. He addressed his foot directly.

"You son of a bitch." The accent was coming along – much less Marlon, and a lot more Bruce. It could almost be understood. He didn't have far to go. He rechecked his little machine gun. He stroked it with some pride. He couldn't stop himself. He stopped at the landing, and then realised that he should have checked the rooms as he'd risen through the building. He wasn't sure if he had the energy to do that and climb the stairs as well, but suddenly he heard something. It was coming from inside one of the rooms.

"Son of a bitch," he muttered again. He tried to hop as quietly and discreetly as he could. He needed to maintain the element of surprise. The first room was empty, but the noise came from the next room. The door was ajar. He couldn't open it slowly and raise his gun, his leg was holding him up. He had no choice. He threw the door open with his gun raised and trained.

"Freeze!" He was just one grunt away from uttering the word 'nigger,' but held himself back. It didn't matter. The room was empty. It was a grand room with tall ceilings, and three tall windows. At the end of the room was a large fireplace. He moved around the room with his gun extended. It was still empty, which didn't explain the noise. It was hard to identify. Hurley turned, was it coming from the fireplace?

Chapter Ninety

Clivert threw himself over the ridge of the roof, and discovered it was more slippery than he'd expected. One of the many things he had not been gifted with was good balance. He began to slide and was relieved to discover that there was a valley gutter at the end. He knew if the helicopter soared directly overhead he would be seen. He had to keep moving. There was a large chimney stack separating the buildings. If he could get to the other side of that, it would be a good start.

The helicopter had moved away briefly. It was his moment. He launched himself at the stack and used the gaps in the crumbling masonry for a foothold. He found various brackets that had once been used for fixing television aerials, and grabbed them to pull himself up. It even looked quite athletic.

"Way to go," he muttered to himself. Right at that moment, and despite everything, he felt alive. The adrenaline was surging, luck was on his side. He was going to get away. He was relieved to find the top of the chimney stack was flat, as if the flues had been capped. With one heave he scrambled over them. There was a further bracket that he hadn't seen. It caught a strip of gaffer tape. Clivert was temporarily paralysed with pain. It was as if his testicles had been torn off. He balanced on the top of the chimney, unable to take a breath, unable to move. Not even capable of screaming. It was then that he noticed that the helicopter was turning. It would only be a handful of seconds before he'd be seen.

"Shit."

In a condensed moment Clivert was able to think about all the bad luck he'd ever had, but the helicopter wasn't going to have the chance to see him. The brittle cap on the chimney stack gave way. There was nothing below his feet. As he fell, the bazooka cracked against the edge of the chimney and flew from his hands, but not before he'd pulled the trigger. A small rocket spiralled away from him.

"Aaaagghhhh!"

They were big chimneys designed to heat large rooms, but right now it was chute through which Clivert was falling and gaining speed. It was a fork which broke his fall, or more accurately it was his testicles which took the brunt of the fall as his legs straddled two flues. It was dark and sooty and claustrophobic. But those were the least of his problems. There was pain and he was stuck.

Clivert tried to regulate his breathing, and decide what to do. And then he had a brilliant plan. He would do nothing. It was genius. He could hide there until nightfall or the helicopter went, or something. But he would have to make himself more comfortable. This involved taking the weight off his testicles.

The inside of the chimney was more slippery than he had expected, as the build-up of soot had created a smooth surface. He drew one leg up, and then the other, until he was perched on the fork. But that wasn't comfortable either. He sat on the fork with both legs dangling down one of the flues. It was a lot more comfortable, but he wasn't certain he could remain perched there for any length of time. He couldn't. He slipped, and fell down the flue.

Chapter Ninety-One

Tim froze, his back tight to the wall, his firearm loaded, cocked and pointing in the right direction. In a flicker he concluded a number of things. The first was that the perpetrator was a flight of stairs away, the second was that he was injured, and the third was that he was American. He relaxed. If it had been the Taliban there would have been a number of them, they would have been organised and premeditated. A lone American was more likely to be the father of a soldier that had been killed. Alone, bitter, emotional, and untrained. He waited patiently. He was listening to the creak of the stairs to give him a more accurate indication of the gunman's position. There was a huge thump.

"Son of a bitch."

Definitely American. Midwest, probably. Tim had never spoken about it, but he'd once worked under secondment to the Pentagon. He knew a few things about Americans. It was strange that the perpetrator was making so much noise. Perhaps he wanted to be killed. With such a high profile client, Tim would normally shoot and ask questions later. He heard the cocking of a firearm. He listened to the foot steps. The perpetrator was leaving the staircase and entering a room. Tim slowly and carefully tested each step for creaks, and climbed a further flight. The next turn would take him onto the landing.

"Son of a bitch."

There was a strange thumping noise coming from the room. Tim eased onto the landing and positioned himself to get a view through the gap between the door and its jamb. He could see outstretched arms, at the end of which was an automatic weapon. It was now or never. He jumped in.

"Don't move!"

Hurley swung round and found a tall suited man pointing a gun at him. This was his moment.

"Freeze," Hurley said.

They were feet apart with just the fireplace separating them, guns trained on each other. They both sensed that something wasn't quite right. While they were both on the same side, they weren't quite, between the police and MI5, on the same side of the same side. Both were on edge, assessing the other. There was certainly no reason why the man lobbing bombs couldn't also wear a suit. It also made sense that if you were going to start a small war, you'd do so with the right equipment, including a flack jacket. Neither was going to drop their weapon. Someone had to say something.

It was the moment when the only truly bit of bad luck occurred in Clivert's life, as he came tumbling through the fireplace, and landed between them. It was tense, and fingers were lighting brushing triggers.

Chapter Ninety-Two

Arthur had run. This had become his default reaction when confronted with large explosions. It had proved to be a successful strategy in the past, and it wasn't without merit. The van had missed them by inches, but it was hard to say what had most commanded their attention, the van or the missile. It had made a huge noise and streaks of fire seemed to spray in all directions. Arthur couldn't be sure, but he thought he could see one of the plumes heading in Eddie's direction.

"Bloody hell."

For a second it was unclear whether the 'bloody hell' was a reaction to the van, the bomb or the bombshell news that he was a father. Fortunately the mayhem gave him a few moments to digest Sophie's words. He was a father. He couldn't at this stage describe himself as a proud father, as he'd not actually met his offspring. But she was a girl. The family, in addition to its collective racism and homophobia, had a less than positive view on women's rights. But he was leaving the family. He wasn't sure which of these factors had prompted him to grab Sophie's hand and hold onto it. For the time being, she was coming with him.

"Arthur!"

They were round the corner from the office and behind a parked van. It seemed relatively safe. But it was as if a war had been declared.

"Arthur, what's going on?"

Arthur was about to explain about his intention to leave the family and set up some sort of charitable trust, when he realised that she was probably referring to the errant van and the bomb. Although, being a woman, he couldn't rule out the possibility that she was referring to the other bombshell news.

"I think someone is trying to kill me."

This was the explanation he plumped for, as it didn't require him to comment about the other thing.

"You think?" Sophie said, unable to refrain from sarcasm. She was tempted to ask why, with even more sarcasm, but that wasn't the purpose of her trip.

"I would like to meet Molly," Arthur said, getting to the other point with uncharacteristic speed. Strangely, it was consuming his mind more than the possibility of being shot.

"Of course," Sophie said, feeling just a little guilty about her sarcasm. It left a pause. Neither quite knew what to say next. Fortunately the pause was filled with gun shots. They seemed to be getting closer to them. Arthur didn't flinch. He was too caught up in other matters.

"Crumbs," Sophie muttered. She was a country girl at heart, and never felt comfortable when she ventured into the big city. But this was becoming quite surreal. A further gunshot, followed by a small explosion, refocused Arthur's mind.

"Let's get the hell out of here," Arthur suggested, not straying from his original policy. He was still holding her hand even though convention would suggest that it no longer needed to be held. Why was he doing that? One part of him felt that one epiphany a day was enough. He didn't want to make a habit of it.

"Bloody right."

Sophie wasn't sure what to make of it, although recently she wasn't sure what to make of anything. She hoped he could learn to love Molly as much as she did, but she didn't want to set the bar too high. Not for Arthur, as she seemed to remember referring to him as emotionally stunted. The word 'herpes' had been in there as well, but now wasn't the time to think about that.

"This way," Arthur said, still with her hand in his. By 'this way' he was not suggesting any greater philosophy, merely the direction to the tube. But in the back of his mind he was asking, what way? Parenthood, living together, a future? Bloody hell. On the other hand, this wouldn't necessary preclude hefty lunches, although sex clubs would be off the agenda. And then there was leaving the family.

"Isn't it that way?"

Sophie suggested. Although she was a country girl, she wasn't entirely unfamiliar with the underground system.

"Of course."

Arthur had been too preoccupied with the metaphor. He headed for his second recent trip on public transport. They turned and a large black man appeared in their path.

"Sorry," they muttered, and tried to walk round him. But he stood transfixed, smiling at Arthur.

"Sorry," Arthur repeated, and looked closer at him. It seemed as if he knew him.

"Arthur Cholmondley-Godstone?"

Sophie's country life was such that her experience with black people had been confined to a DVD that Rachel had lent her. As an exercise in cultural enlightenment it had been less than illuminating, but boy, did he have a big weapon. This, Sophie concluded, must be Arthur's assassin. She hated to admit it, but she wanted to run. But there was nowhere to go. Also Arthur was holding her hand rather firmly. She was asking herself why, and coming up with too many conclusions that didn't conform to her experience of the emotionally stunted. Or Arthur.

"Yes," Arthur said, having not considered the assassin possibilities. The man was young, more of a boy really, but he was tall and his shoulders were wide and square, unusually square. He stood on big tree trunk legs. A good looking boy, in Arthur's view. He looked familiar.

"I am your..." the black boy said.

Bamm!!

His words were followed by a huge explosion.

"What did he say?" Sophie asked, but she guessed it was something about being an assassin. Although, it did seem a little odd to her that an assassin should announce himself. The boy tried again.

"I am your…"

Bamm!!

There was another explosion, even louder than the last.

"You're my what?" Arthur asked, intrigued. Sophie couldn't believe it. Why would he tell him he was his assassin?

"I am your…"

Bamm!!

The mixture of a further explosion and the helicopter above them took the words away. And worse, Sophie thought, why would Arthur ask him? They looked at him with differing expectations.

This time the boy filled his lungs and shouted.

"I am your son!"

Despite the dark skin, Arthur could see the family resemblance. This boy had the genes. Arthur would have liked a little more time to think about, and he was given it. They hadn't noticed that the bombs had become like an approaching thunder storm. Once again their collective minds had been in other places. Arthur had discovered, within a handful of moments, that he was a father not just once, but twice. Sophie's daughter Molly now had both a father and a half-brother. And Courtney had found the missing link in his life. The Englishman in him had been guiding him all his life. The obsessive desire to drink tea, and to adhere to unnecessary formalities and to occasionally refer to people as 'old chap'. He was home.

"Oh…" was all Arthur managed to say. They didn't hear the *pop* of the missile as it left the bazooka, nor were they aware of its flight path. But they couldn't ignore the noise as it ripped through the van. Nor the moment just after, when it hit Arthur square in the chest.

Epilogue

"Looking bloody good, old boy."

"Thank you, that's very kind of you to say so."

"Please, have another brandy."

The lunch had been the immense side of considerable. From the foie gras to the sticky toffee pudding and the four – or was it six? – bottles of wine, it had been quite a lunch. But there was still half a bottle of brandy left.

"Thank you, Mr Cholmondley-Godstone."

"It's absolutely my pleasure."

He then delivered the speech.

"There is an art to life. Life is not about going to work and paying bills. It is not about loyalty to a cause or a people. It is not about what others think or do. It is about living. And living is seeing, doing, feeling, tasting and not denying, and passion. Seeing everything the world has to offer, enjoying everything there is to taste and savour, and exploiting every sense you've been blessed with. Living is about the best, the best of everything. And now you are not just my client, but my friend, and together we must explore these things."

His client looked on, entranced.

"Thank you, Mr Cholmondely-Godstone. And how is the family?"

He smiled a broad, reassuring smile. He'd been working on that smile, and its purpose wasn't just to express mirth or happiness, but a family solidarity. Everything was okay with the Cholmondley-Godstones, and there was no need to worry.

"They're fine. Now let's just try a little more of this brandy."

"Thank you, Mr Cholmondely-Godstone."

It had taken the family a few days to accept, but there were financial demands that needed to be addressed. And the boy clearly had talent.

"Courtney, old boy, please call me Courtney."

A Further Epilogue

The McCarthy brothers made their escape. Liam thought it through. It involved abandoning the former dictator's van designed for trouble, and a dust down to remove fingerprints. The madman on the roof had kept the police distracted and, armed with the number plates, they took the bus back to a part of the East End of London that was on the way to Essex. This was no retirement plan, but keeping their heads low seemed a wise idea. Noel kept his eye out for traffic wardens.

Geraldine bought two further twenty pound dresses from the same shop and wore one at the inaugural opening of a new dungeon in the basement. It, and her dress, found favour with three Tory MPs, the chief executive of a high street bank, an Anglican vicar, a fallen French politician, the headmaster of a prestigious public school, a well known TV chef, a minor member of the royal family, a sheik, a trade union leader, a retired colonel, a serving general, an American senator and a chief constable. Business was on the up.

Sophie, the one with the penis, took a full time post with the Inland Revenue and is spending more of her time as John. She currently has a girlfriend and is discovering issues with her breasts. She remains confused.

Rachel and Anderson have bought a flat together. Anderson has attended further cookery courses and is considering opening a restaurant in two years' time when his option for early retirement comes up. Anderson is talking about children. Rachel is resisting.

Hurley, Tim and Arnold Clivert remain in hospital. Their futures are uncertain.

Yet Another Epilogue

Arthur's dreams had become quite colourful and endlessly unpredictable. His broad chest had not been missile-proof, but its width might have ensured that his major organs weren't too tightly packed. It had made a mess and he'd lost a lung, but it had passed through him and, against all odds, he'd sort of survived. It was not a full recovery, and the boundary between dreams and reality were clearly confused. He'd imagined that he was sharing a large rambling house with Sophie and Molly and fourteen battered transexuals. Friday nights were show time and Barbara Streisand, Cher and Judy Garland would make an appearance. Strange.

Someone was pushing his wheelchair. He couldn't say who. And then a smiling face emerged from the fog. It took a moment for him to identify it. The recognition didn't nauseate him as he thought it might. But the man looked in extraordinarily good health. There was a woman with him. Nice looking. He'd been introduced. He said her name was Mandy. Arthur thought it might be Brayman.

"Arthur!"

It was Brayman. Brayman leaned over and whispered in his ear.

"Looking bloody good, old boy."

If you enjoyed this book you can find more Giles Curtis comedies on Amazon -

'A Very UnChristian Retreat'

Hugo has only himself to blame. The bookings in their holiday complex in France are few and Jan, his wife, is forced to organise a yoga week. She remains in Godalming, which leaves Hugo alone with the irresistible Suzanna, who gives off signals he has difficulty interpreting. Jan is talked into hiring a private detective to lure Hugo, but his problems have only just begun. Hugo meets Lenny and Doris who claim to run art parties, which turn out to be more of the swinging sort. Hugo's friend, Gary, books in his gay friends, who have a penchant for the feral. But wild is how Lenny and Doris like it. Hugo doesn't tell Jan, and an unpaid telephone bill means she can't tell him about the Christian Retreat group who are on their way.

And then the chaos really begins.

'It's All About Danny'

"How does he manage to go away for a few weeks and come back a Nobel fucking Prize winner?"

Kathy can't believe it. Nor can Danny, who has tripped through life gliding past responsibility, commitment and anything that involved hard work. But when he is rejected by all the women in his life: his girlfriend, landlord and his boss at 'Bedding Bimonthly,' he has no choice. His better looking high-achieving brother, whose earnest phase has taken him away from the big money in the city, invites him to build a school in Africa with him.

Danny discovers that all the flatpack battles he has fought have given him a talent for it, and it lends his life new purpose. But his life changes when, during a fierce storm, he saves the only child of an African chief, who claims to have mystical powers. The chief invites him to make a wish. Danny can't decide whether he should wish for world peace, a cure for cancer or to be irresistible to women. Shallowness prevails.....

Does the Chief have strange powers or has Danny changed? He misses Kathy his girlfriend, who realises she's made a mistake. And then the wish turns into a nightmare...

'The Badger and Blondie's Beaver'

Madeleine misses her old life in Paris. Her work as a forensic scientist is going great, but now she's marooned in the country and her social life, or more accurately her sex life, is a disaster. When she's called upon to extract a severed head from a weir, she meets Sam. Sam is her perfect man, but murder, mannequins, cocaine, the drug squad, Customs and Excise, multiple arrests and the Mafia get in the way.

Sam, Oliver and William are three young graduates desperate to make a fast buck. The plan seems so simple, it just involves the not entirely legal business of transporting silver which, by way of a cunning disguise, has been fashioned into dildos. But the journey refuses to go to plan.

'The Wildest Week of Daisy Wyler'

Daisy had lived her life as if on a merry-go-round, and she'd never stepped on a roller-coaster. There had been a husband, children and even grandchildren, but things had changed. A change dictated by her fickle ex-husband, and which prompts a new life in London.

But Daisy wants more. A bigger life, a wilder life. An exciting life. She finds an unlikely friend in Sophie, her neighbour, and there is an imminent party planned for Sophie's 'sort of' boyfriend, the dissolute Lord Crispin. Crispin's parties are legendary and favour the excessive. And so begins the wildest week of Daisy Wyler.

Find out more on gilescurtis.com

Acknowledgments

I'd like to say there are a million people to thank, but it isn't true. I would therefore like to thank Steve Caplin who has patiently taught me to spell, adjusted my grammar and added a profusion of commas, in addition to designing my front covers and making it all Kindle friendly.

I also would like to thank my wife, Sarah, for her patience and tolerance, even though she believes it all to be "a waste of fucking time."